SOULLESS PRINCE

FIRST LIFE

SOULLESS PRINCE: FIRST LIFE

ISBN   978-1-7778357-0-5 (e-book)
ISBN   978-1-7778357-3-6 (paperback)

This novel is a fiction and the characters and events are fictitious. Any similarity to any real persons, living or dead, is coincidental and not intended by the author.

Permission to use material from other works
Credits goes to Aries W.R.C for the map
Credits for cover design goes to NightCafe.
Edited by Naomi D. Nakashima

Printed in Canada

Visit alexsknyghts.ca

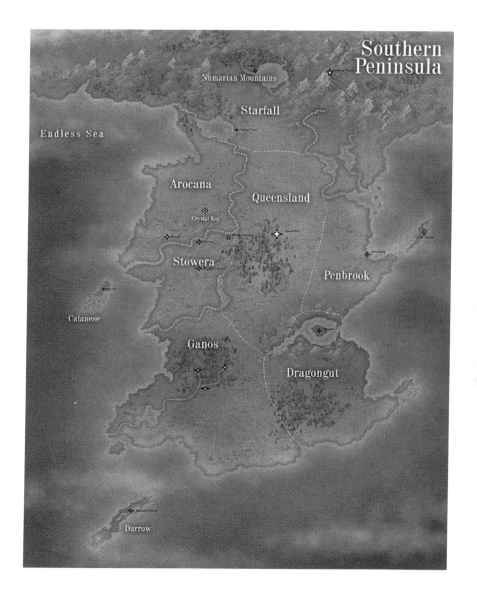

Dedication

To my rents- Ha! Got it done.
I'm an author now and forever.
And to my Hubby and Teri, who actually gave a damn
All my guinea pigs.

Acknowledgements

TikTok made me do it.
But no, seriously, without my friends on that app, this book would
not be here right now.
And thank you to my editor, who must think I'm batshit crazy by

now.

Damn you, WriterTok, and Who Wants To Write A Book

community for being so damn supportive.

ALEX'S NOTES TO READERS:

I'm letting you know that this is adult content. Nasty shit happens. Forced intoxication. Rape. Attempted murder. Kidnapping. Incarceration. Physical and mental abuse. Forced manslaughter. Harm to children. You have been warned.

PLANETS

The years are different.

Earth is the third planet from the sun. Our seasons are basically four months, each leading to a 364-day year.

Arowan 3 is the fourth planet from its sun. So its year is longer and the seasons are broken up differently. Winter and summer are six months, while Spring and Fall are three months. That leads to an eighteen-month calendar of 546 days.

When Humans crash landed on this planet, they were still using the Gregorian Calendar. It took them a while to get the new calendar adopted.

BONDING

There are two ways to be Bonded.

By sex - Normally when two people are married. This is considered the purest form. People fall in love, then learn they are Bonded as divine soul mates.

By blood - Happens when couples exchange blood either through battle or ritual. This is the darker of the two, as it requires some sort of violence.

Life Loves *are the people who are married but not Bonded. These unions are childless.*

SOULLESS PRINCE
FIRST LIFE

Alex O. Knyght

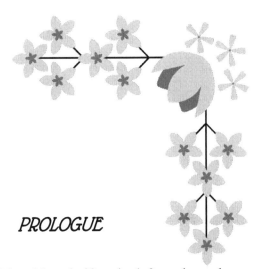

PROLOGUE

That red-haired girl, with a half-melted face, leaned over him, bleeding. Her literal dark-haired prince had defended her from her villains, be it street thugs or a demon father, but not from the torturous aunt. I didn't think he would remember the girl. Hell, I barely remembered her, and I was there. Now, she trounced his royal ass in the last tournament. He always had issues keeping up with her.

After last night, he had an ice cube's chance in hell of beating her. She had been so angry with him for helping her when she was just the child against the bullies. She is still so angry fourteen years later. This time was even more furious with herself. That red-haired girl, destined to marry the prince, found him having sex with her Aunt Roseden.

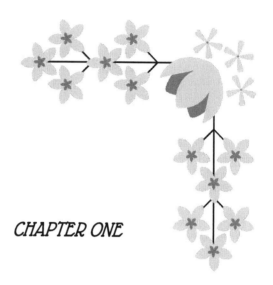

CHAPTER ONE

"You betrayed us!"

I'm back to being shorter than him. With my hair down, it created a red-orange waterfall around his head. Rain falling from my eyes. No doubt my scars were a brighter red. I'm monstrous when I'm crying. One hand touching his face, the other on the hilt of my sword, pointing into the blood-soaked ground. I didn't feel safe kneeling over him without my crystal sword to hold me up. Despite wanting his death, I still cast one of my aunt's spells to take all the damage I had dealt to him. He was to be king in a few days.

He was the future.

Liquid rubies soaked into the would-be fatal slash I had given him. I, too, had received it. If it wasn't for the *Bond* we shared, he never would have known my broken heart.

"Why?" My whisper cracked as it left my lips.

"Lys." His voice.

My weakness. It cut through my thoughts and emotions straight to the part of him that still lay in my heart. The reason the magic would keep him from dying. As much as I hated him for last night, I was still in love with my storybook prince. My Demon Spawn. My Soulless Prince. "My Little Witch-"

"Evana save him. Adriana will never forgive me if he dies," I whispered, before falling to Justin's right side. The betrayal, *his* betrayal, hurt as much as my fury at loving him so much.

We were *Soul Bonded, Soul Bonded by Blood,* at the tragically young age of six. We were destined from birth to be the divine match for each other, so neither of us would be alone. A guarantee there was someone who would love you no matter what. It is the absolute law of the land that no one can come between a *Soul Bond.* Yet, this ass slept with my foster father's *Sister-in-Bonding*, Roseden. Through the *Bond's* telepathy, I knew what was going on. I drew the line when she started to cut into his skin. Our matching Seabrooke crests. She was deter- mined to take it again. Our *Soul Bond* meant any damage one of us received, the other shared if we were within a mile of each other.

The same, devastatingly sad, smile he gave me when he saved me from the bullies was plastered on his face when I demanded this duel. I wanted so much to kill him for sleeping with Roseden. After everything Roseden did to me five years ago, he was naked with her in his bed. I had wanted to kill her. I tried to kill him for it. That sad smile hid his tears. I shed for him, instead. All because he thought I wouldn't love him anymore. I had loved him, truly.

In love because of the *Bond.*

The moment I felt him enjoying a woman who wasn't me, my inner fury burned that love away.

"Lys!" He gasped, wide orbs of summer sky shining up at me. He called my name again in full agony. "My Little Witch."

His father called me that in hate. Justin used it as a nickname. I always thought it was to annoy me, but he liked it. It made him happy.

I woke sometime later, feeling like I had been trampled by a flight of dragons. Breathing was hard. Muscles over my rib cage felt bound. The room started spinning the second I thought too hard. My right arm was pinned down. Looking at it, I saw a mess of dark blonde hair.

Not Justin's raven hair, as I expected.

Soul Bond by Blood shares injuries and healing.

Justin would have been the one sitting over me. This wasn't him. The Stowera royal crest on his shoulders. Wider shoulders than Justin's. This man could lift me despite my not-so-little form. My *Life Love*.

"Wren." I smiled. Wren Witwer never pushed, never pulled me in any direction but was constantly at my side. My cozy blanket. My boulder. I adored Wren. I curled around his head on my arm.

Absently, he ran his hand up my thigh to my hip before he nuzzled more into my chest. My flinching woke him. "Lyssie?" I smiled. He is so sweet. Wren had never moved so fast. Me and my sheet were now in his lap.

"Goddesses Lys, I was so worried when I saw you fall." Wren had not been the one to pull me out of Justin's room that night. He did, however, help me into my armor the following morning. Had he been the one to undress me when they brought me back here? "Evana said if you didn't share a room with Justin, you could die."

My left hand tightened on his bloody tunic. My blood? "I'm okay now. I'm safe," I whispered.

He just held me tighter. The pain was nothing to the warmth I got from my Wren. Sleep took me again until I heard my name once more. My full name. The thing I hated most in the voice I loved the most while I was cozy in Wren's arms. Gently, Wren placed me back in the bed. Rubbing my eyes, I saw Justin at the end of my bed.

"Justin, you may be my king, but I can't let you go near my *Life Love*."

My heart stopped. Wren had never admitted that. I was suddenly very aware this was the worst person to say that to. If it came down to a fight between Wren and Justin, Justin would be declared the winner. Not because he was the king. Our cursed *Bond*.

Wren could be jailed for going against Divine Law.

The king in question stood at the end of my bed, bandaged like myself in his formal black pants with the blue embroidery down his legs. The Seabrooke crest, my family crest, with two jagged ring scars around it. No bandages over it. Free like my own with the same scar. Justin's sky-blue eyes are sunken and dark. He hadn't slept nearly as well as I had. That is when our eyes met. I looked at Wren's back, my hand covering my tattoo. I couldn't look at his face. I would start crying again. The oh so familiar pull of our *bond* begging to help heal us.

"Lysandra is my *Soul Bound* wife, Witwer. The Divine Laws state that *Soul Bonds* have priority."

Soul Bonds are literally for forever. *Life Loves* are just for this life.

Bleen, Goddess of Love, has been said to believe the *Bond* was for the well-being of the human population. She didn't take into consideration that Elves and Dwarves were the dominant races on this planet.

None of them are included in the *Bonding*.

I groaned. He was going to play Law Keeper?

"You lost that right when you slept with Roseden." Wren's impossibly deep voice seemed deeper. My Wren was the one who enforced the laws for Justin. Annoyed by Justin. Angry for me. "I have not even kissed her lips out of respect for your *Bond*. Yet you blatantly bed her torturer? You, of all people, should know what the hell Lyssie went through with that bitch. Yet Lyssie still found you-"

Shivers spread through my chest. I didn't want to see it again. I didn't want to see her mounted on him as she moaned his name. Justin shifted, holding his biceps. The gentle brush sent chills through my skin as a rock on a lake.

"Stop," I said with a shaky gasp.

He was using our *Soul Bond*. My hands pulled from Wren to back away. Pulling back to the headboard of my bed, my own arms are wrapping around me. Knees tucked to the point of pain. Being this close, I could feel the bandages under his fingers. A reminder of what I had let happen to us. What I *did* to us.

Goddess, please stop.

Justin gazed down at me with a broken-hearted smile. I hated that smile almost as much as I hated myself. "Leave Justin. Please, just leave."

Wren returned to holding me. "Oh, and Justin, I'm no longer in your employ. I follow Arocana's Champion now."

Geez, Wren, there was no need to be an asshole about it.

The wooden door slammed as I pulled away slightly. There was self-hatred, pity, and sadness that filled the space between

Justin and me. I really didn't want to feel my own emotions. I really didn't want to feel his, on top of it. Honestly, I don't even know how my mental wall fell.

"Evana and Colin won their battle with the Noble Assembly, thanks to you."

I stopped breathing.

"You are to be their champion now. Everyone agreed you should be near Justin, only until you are healed. That is the only reason we are still in Knyght's Reach." Wren's smiles were always bright back then. Kissing the hand that covered my mouth. This was the only way he would kiss me.

I hated it. I wanted to feel his lips on mine. I had won. I got what I wanted at the cost of the thing that had always been mine.

I succeeded. The farce was finally over. 'Hallon' could sleep now in death. For the last six years, I have pretended to be my long dead twin brother. See, women are *treasured*. In being so, they may not take part in war, or warlike training. Queen Evana, my childhood friend, and King Colin of Arocana, her *Bonded,* wanted to change that after they were married. I wanted to help them. It was to be my gift to them. A hard-won gift.

The Arocana Royals already protected the Aldaina, the Warrior Priestesses of Daina, Goddess of War. Yet to allow women in the army, they would have to prove a woman could be just as good as men were at war. So, the plan was I would be 'Hallon' then reveal myself as female when I beat Justin. All I had to do was lose myself. Become the very monster I hated most. None of them deserved my love.

"They know the prophecy, so they won't worry when I leave for the mission." Wren's chocolate eyes turned to rocks.

It was an unspoken rule that we never brought up *The Destiny*. Especially since my own deaths, she saw, counted up to five. Three times she has seen me die in this lifetime. All of them this time next year. "Hey, you know what *The Destiny* said. You know she is never wrong." How can the High Priestess of the Goddess of Time be wrong? She had not been the first one I had known either.

"I know, my love. Eighteen months is hardly enough time to finally love you openly." I blushed knowing what it meant. We only had a year to be married. Even though I know he wouldn't go through with it. I knew he found his *Bonded*. At the end of the eighteen months, I would seek whatever mission called me. Then die finishing my mother's duties, even if I didn't want to. One cannot help it when you are the Pawn of Gods.

Being the Daughter of the Chosen of the Goddesses had gotten me nothing in life since no one believed me that Queen Tulora, the Red of Stowacana, was my mother. Back when she was just Tulora Seabrooke, mayor of the small town of Haven, I was just her daughter. Three hundred and forty-six years, three months and nine days ago, but who's counting? Back before the country split into Stowera and Arocana. I had to finish her job and destroy the last Death Knight, her twin brother Tabari.

A year to the day Justin and I met in the alley, I thought I could take on the Death Knight, King Justice Knyght, King of Stowera. My foster father, Dathon, had nudged me towards the king and his miniature duplicate. No one knew I saw the King's true form. The young prince was the boy from the alley. How he got there, I still don't know. I was in my time. I'm still sure of that. Mom found us after the fight. Hallon talked about it, wondering about the boy who looked like my doll.

My biological mother taught me Death Knights drain the souls of the living for a long life. The corruption made them ooze with black tar and smelled of a rotting corpse. I had seen a man like that; my mother's twin brother. I could still see that man's true face through the tar. However, the King was just bubbling black ooze. There was no man under all that. King Justice was powerful or ancient. Goddess forbid, he was both.

I heard the infant princess cry a second before her blue green soul drifted towards Justice. I remember only crying for the child before taking my foster father's dagger from his hip and running at the king. The one-sided fight lasted seconds. What had I *really* expected? I was a child. No one believed what I saw. My right hand had been sliced open when my crystal sword failed to defend me against the monster. Just as Justice swung his sword to dispatch me, Justin used his magic to create a blue dome around us. His blue lattice work was the most beautiful thing I had ever seen.

Even back then, his smile was lonely. I didn't think twice when he bent to help me up. The moment we took hands, his blue magic, my red magic, created a combined lattice work around us. Blue, and red weaving around two kids who didn't know what it meant. Stories and bards spoke of how our eyes glowed blue and green, the magic spinning around us, hands clasped so tight our knuckles were white before it seemed we had banished the demon from the castle. My last memory of that day was the heartbreaking smile he forced himself to wear when I cried for him, the first time.

That was the first actual memory I knew was corrupted with lost time. The memory I lost myself in often. Always getting caught not paying attention in class or with our friends. Now it was a nightmare that repeated in my mind. Just another nightmare to add to all the others that hound my sleep. The door opened again; I had missed the knock. This time it was my obsidian-haired Elven best friend.

Joy flashed on Evana's face before worry. "Maiona's breath, Wren. I told you she needed to stay warm." He pulled away. The only person he feared. It was adorable. He once said it was because she was so old. She had seen it all. I laughed at him. As much as I loved him, there was no need to fear my marshmallow elf.

Evana fixed my pillows so I could sit up on my own. "Justin came by after she woke up the first time." She gave me her sympathetic smile. "I must have let the blanket fall to the floor. Sorry Majesty." Together they tucked me in like a child. First, to have to be in the same room as Justin, to have to keep me warm? Had I really lost that much blood? Why was he perfectly fine?

I looked at my best friend. Healer, Queen, the wise, mixed blood elf, the only one who knew me from three hundred years ago. We had both found each other again when Evana was guardian of *The Destiny*. Justin's mother brought me to see *The Destiny*, after I saved her daughter the first time. We had to look at each other once, before Evana broke into tears. I had never been so happy for someone to know I wasn't lying about my family. I think I was seven. Ten by the old calendar.

"Oh no, don't give me that look." I feigned innocence. She smiled. "You did this to yourself. I told you it would work out, yet your inner Fury had to get revenge." A Fury? Maybe that was what my second soul was. One of Daina's winged warriors that righted wrongs on behalf of the Goddess of Justice. Maybe it was just a demon that wanted an excuse to kill the one person who could know she was in me. Evana sat next to me, looking at my half-destroyed room. I had done a number after I threw Justin's lover across the room.

I cast Roseden's own spell on her. The pain would have been worse for her. Roseden would force me to fight and kill others, then cast her new spell so I could feel everything I did to the other children. When I cast it on her, she screamed in near silence as I sat on her chest with a hand over her mouth.

That is where Evana found me. Astride a naked, screaming woman. "I was just going to ask why the asshole seems better off than me?" No one knew I cast the reverse of Roseden's spell on us. I took all the pain and damage. I learned things in The Pit. Roseden's Death Pit. "He ran all the way here, barely out of breath, yet I felt the room spinning from sitting up. Why is this worse on my side?" The healing should still be as quick. If Justin was fully healed, the magic would rush my own at that point. That is the way the *Bonding* worked.

"You were not together. You wouldn't have the healing magic work at full potential since you are a floor apart. Had you been in his room with him, you would have woken up days ago. Even after you used some *very* stupid magic," she said flatly. Evana's dark eyes on her darker face are not giving me quarter. She suspected what I did. I groaned. "I don't know what spell you used to do it, but you took all the damage you were giving to him. Only the *Bond* gave him injuries." Cursed *Bond*. She had been the healer in the ring. She would have seen my cut being deeper. She probably was the advocate for keeping Justin and me in the same room. "You must not have been *that* angry with him." I stifled a laugh. Guilt ate at me while anger waited for its turn.

"More like scared his mother would come down and beat me with her halo." Evana lay her head against mine. We both know I worshiped the ground Adriana walked on. She was the closest thing I had to a mother in this lifetime. Fear that she could ever be angry with me was very real. I was not following her teachings. I wasn't in Justin's room, after all. Adriana was the biggest fan of us getting married, even if I wasn't allowed to want that after *The Destiny*.

Wren had known I wouldn't want to be near Justin. I loved Wren for that, yet it was unfair that Justin bounced back so fast, spell or no spell. "Lys, you took most of the damage. His wound was skin deep, unlike yours, which cracked bones. With you being in the middle of your cycle, there was not much to spare. It's taking you longer to regain it. Thank Daina, I wasn't about to let you die. Just because the dumbass cheated doesn't mean you can leave *ME* alone." I laughed at that.

Being a girl is stupid. That was something I would not miss. Whoever decided females needed a moon cycle hated women. I am female through and through. I love pretty dresses. My favorite flower is a Lilac. As a teen I read romance novels. Justin and Wren were the most handsome men I have ever seen, and I crushed hard. I just wished we women didn't have bodies cursed with monthly cycles, emotions or slightly weaker bodies. It has always taken me longer to bounce back from injury. My moon cycle has never been normal, but this was ridiculous. I would be glad when it was over.

"Depending on how you feel in an hour, I will have a maid sent up with your formals."

Formals? Did she honestly think I was healthy enough for some sort of formal ceremony? "Evana-"

"Lysandra Seabrooke! It's your birthdays." Oh shit, I slept for a full week. We are nineteen by the new calendar, yet I felt the twenty-eight that was the old calendar. When I was a child, we used a twelve-month calendar. The year is eighteen months. Somewhere in the three-hundred-year jump, there were changes. One was moving to an eighteen-month calendar. This new one matches with the seasons, but the old one makes me older. I feel older than nineteen.

More tired. I don't feel lost anymore, not like I did when Adriana died, but exhausted by what should have been my young adult life. A time of hope and wonder. Others our age found what their lives would become. I found death and animosity. Poor Justin was dragged down into that hell because of a *Bond* that should never have been.

You know, she was worried and pissed when she used my full name. "The ball you worked so hard for. You are expected to be there." My hands rubbed my face. Adriana would never forgive me if tonight fails. It was the night Justin could formally take the crown of Stowera. Never mind that according to law, it was mine to claim. I had been the one to kill his father. We had been just two kids in love when Justice took that from us. "I need to get your blood moving without opening you up."

"Oh, I can think of a few ways." Wren winked at me. I knew he meant running laps. Had he been there the whole time? There was something in his voice that unnerved me whenever he returned from *HER*. Justin's birthday present. "I'll have her stashed away until the fireworks, though I think she is going to be in the crowd for most of the party. She wanted to see him crowned."

"If she is lost, we are screwed," I said, shifting to sit next to Evana. "You just got your wish, Eva." I stood up too fast, falling against my desk. The other three people in the room jumped up to help me. "I can do this," I said, more to myself than to anyone. The only piece of furniture that had not been moved in my anger, moved unbidden, helping me meet the floor. Behind it, the small chest Adriana bequeathed me on my sixteenth birthday. I had been ten by the new calendar. Inside it, something Adriana knew I would need for tonight. Our nineteenth birthdays. This is when our lives would change again.

"Do you need help?" Evana asked. I shook my head, opening the chest. Adriana's dagger, sitting back on the pile, as if I hadn't taken it out two nights before our duel. Only Justin knew this was here. Only because he could see into my mind.

"I had hoped to tell him the truth. The full truth. My mom is his hero. My brother's real fate. What *The Destiny* told me that day. What his father said to me when I avenged his mother. How I hid his sister to keep Adriana's blood line from going cold. That the man he thought of as his best friend was really his *Bonded* match. That I will be his wife, even if it was only for a year. I had been planning my confession repeatedly for the last month."

"Goddess Lys, I am sorry." I don't know when they left me to cry. For the first time since Roseden was finally banned from my life, I cried. I cried for losing yet another family.

Was I not allowed to have one?

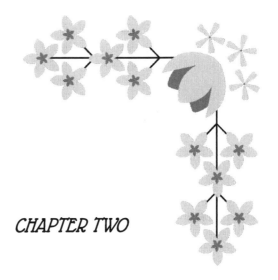

CHAPTER TWO

The 'gown' I had put into Adriana's Hope Chest was barely that. Leggings of silver-green suede with hidden reinforced shin and thigh panels, the skirt was hip to hip, along my back with the same reinforced panels, but made of Elven satin. The train was only a few inches long. The half skirt was attached to a cross overcoat. Its armored panel covered my heart while the armored collar was not fully around my neck. Under the coat a silk tank top. Both the coat and the top left my back exposed to show my black feather winged tattoo we had gotten one night after a tourney that left us very, very drunk. I got the wings, and Justin decided he wanted my family crest. Tulora, The Red, was his hero. It was her crest.

Jewelry came to my room sometime after the tears had stopped. Two boxes of black velvet with my family crest in green on the boxes. Evana found me in my outfit, staring wide eyed at the two boxes open on my desk. One was a silver simple chain with seven teardrop moonstones. Five of the stones, greener than the other two. The second, a circlet with an emerald, a moonstone and a sapphire, fanned out. Whoever sent them knew I didn't wear earrings. Not since my first encounter with a jealous courtier.

Chantara had always hated me for Justin's attention at balls or feasts. How was she to know we were *Bonded*? It's not like people our age ever found their *Soul Bond* as early as we did. I had been the only other child at the baby princess' naming. Goddess, tonight is going to be a fight if she sees me with him. To get through the night, I was going to have to let the magic do its job.

One last glamor to hide my scars and blood-shot eyes before I straightened. I swear Jeanevera hated me by how the city bells rang faster than normal. I was not ready. Not ready to let go of the life I had made myself. Not ready to follow in my mother's footsteps. Not ready to say my last goodbyes. The only people who knew I only had a year to live were in my room with me. So, you would think this would be easier. Wren holding Adriana's chest. Evana finished my red curls around the circlet. Colin frowning. My last gift to Justin, watching us as if I were a marvel.

"It is not right that this is the way you are going to do it." Colin grumbled. He and Justin are cousins. "I know he wouldn't have been with Roseden willingly." Colin said, bringing me back to the moment. Evana squeezed my shoulders. "I don't care. He has been in love with you since before the full weight of the *Bond* hit." The moment Justin first kissed me in the throne room. Both of us were sitting in his father's blood. Justice's head staring at me sneering. Their wedding rings cut into my left hand. My shattered crystal sword, forcing my right hand open. "Why can't you just stay?"

Why indeed? Years before I was trapped in Roseden's Pit, we had been the happiest two people could be. Then Adriana's death and Roseden happened. Part of me will always question if I wasn't just still trapped in her pit, waiting for the next boy to attempt to kill me. To shock me back to pain, she would send me images of Justin coming to rescue me from that hell.

I couldn't trust that. Then she had the nerve to put one last nail in the coffin. She was going to kill him to break what was left of me. Had she done it after Dathon first took me home, she may have gotten her wish. No, she waited until I had built my walls. Rebuilt myself into this broken angel. All she taught me was not to be the shell of a human. To not be what everyone wanted me. She showed me what my mother had wanted me to be. A warrior.

Even if I spent most nights crying, unable to sleep in my bed other nights. Picking up the sword had been to protect myself from the men I didn't know could hurt me as hers did. I mourned the one thing I wanted but could never be. I would never be Justin's wife. As much as I pretended I could have him before last week, I knew I would never have that. No use pretending now. All I could do for him tonight was play the champion.

I just left them to follow me. All the guests would be here by now. The room would be packed. When Daina's moon rose, the Mage Knights would begin the fireworks. Then I would leave.

Colin and Evana took arms at the ballroom doors. The herald called their names. Then Wren's. Lizzy looked at me suddenly, nervous. Every bit Justin's little sister. Her dark hair lightened from being in the sun all the time. Their sky-blue eyes sparkled in the candlelight. Elegant, despite her warrior training. I understood Wren being *Bonded* to Lizzy. We are weak to the Knyghts. "This is your home. He'll never take that from you." We said at the same time. She took my hands. "He will always be your home, Lys. No matter what the Gods have planned for you." I watched my friends bid the new king good evening. "Just for tonight, let yourself see that. It is your birthday too."

"It is not about seeing. I know this is where I was always meant to be. He has been with me in one form or another every day of my life since I was two years old," I said, looking at the bag hanging from my wrist. "If I leave now, it will give me time to get far enough to shield him from my death. I saw what it did to him when your mom died. I will not be the reason he relapses." The herald called my name. As ordered, not to call Lizzy's.

Goddesses help me if Justin wasn't gorgeous that night. The very image all the romance novels spoke about. Even the way the one curl hung down from his controlled mess of hair. The fae flowers twinkled off his sky-colored eyes as they widened, seeing me. Dathon was standing next to him when I saw his rosy lips move. With the band playing, I couldn't hear what my father said. Justin didn't take his eyes off me. I couldn't take my eyes off him. He was the king I had imagined he would be.

Even his normal formal black velvet coat with baby blue frog knot buttons looked even better on him tonight. I had seen his outfit so many times it was second nature to see him in it. Confident as he came down the three stairs to meet me in the middle of the floor. When he was five feet from me, I pushed back my half skirt to kneel before him. Lizzy, three steps behind me. Also on her knee in her Aldaina commander dress uniform with her hood up.

"Please stand, Champion," he said in a shaky voice. I looked up at him with a peaked brow. "Ever a vision."

"Thank you, Your Majesty." I released the bag from my wrist. My heart was trying to get out of my chest. Every voice in my head said my next action will get me killed. "If it is permitted, I have two gifts for you on your birthday." I returned my eyes to his feet. He was a king, and I was just a champion. No need to give Chantara more ammo.

"By all means, Dame Seabrooke." Less shaky. Good. We need to be nothing to each other. It will make it easier.

"Thank you, Your Majesty." I watched the Knyght family wedding rings fall to my hand with a small clink. "The late Queen Adriana bid me to give you these when you were crowned." I felt his heart stop through the *Bond*. Despite my walls really being up this time. It is an unspoken rule that we never mention his mother in front of the other nobility. Questions arose when her death was made public. Even more when guards found me 'unconscious' in Justice's blood. There is a sect of old law lords who would fight for me to be on the throne if it came to light that I was the one who battled Justice. Better to keep my mouth shut.

Yet his blue glove took his mother's ring from my hand. *I retrieved them that day.* His free hand covered his mouth. "Also, as promised to the queen, I have brought you your little sister, Princess Elizabeth Knyght." The spectating nobility rumbled as Justin stepped towards his no longer hidden sister. The woman he had not seen since she was a child. I looked at the assembled nobles. I really divided the nobles tonight—I can see it in the sneers and nods.

The first divide is over the question of me or Justin to rule. Me by battle. Justin by blood.

Only two lords ever asked for both of us: Lord Emeth and Lord Lugh. I think their interest lies because their wives were at Lizzy's naming. Rumors claim the Verity sisters can see the ribbon of fate. Lady Obelia Emeth once told Adriana nothing could break our ribbon. It was stronger than steel. That it was spun and tied to our pinkies long before the Goddesses even came to this planet. I couldn't see our *Bond* being that old.

The second divide was what noble house would find a *Bond* with Justin or me depending on which one of us would be crowned. Neither side of that divide liked the fact Lizzy was in the mix. The fabled missing princess Justin could look to for an heir. These are the same families who would have seen Justin and I *Blood Bond* at Lizzy's naming. That meant nothing. Their daughters and son would be the next consort to the crown and their blood would be tied to the throne.

The third divide had Lizzy on the throne. Justin and I were too complicated. Easier to have Adriana and Justice's young daughter. She might be controlled. To them I want to see them try. Lizzy has her mother's independence, defiance of social norms. Let them try to take the throne through her. We might have more trials. Treason ends in beheading. The thought made me smile. Just let them try.

"We thank you for your kind gifts, Dame Seabrooke." I turned back to Justin's feet. Polished leather shoes. He would have polished them himself. Lizzy is not the only one who was like their mother. "The return of our darling sister," he said, taking Lizzy in his arms. I simply bowed walking backwards. *I don't deserve you.* I smiled at his admission. I knew the truth was I didn't deserve him. Even if he had slept with Roseden. I have done and will do worse to him soon.

No, you don't. Yet I'm still hanging around this cursed castle.

Wren stood between the outside balconies' doors with Dathon. Both of my men were dressed in the Seabrooke green/blue. I smiled, stepping up to my father. "Never fails. You couldn't do your own tie." I teased straightening the three-inch piece of silk. "And you. Aren't you just dashing in my family colors?" Wren wasn't looking at me. I knew he was looking at her. "We have such weaknesses to those Knyghts. Maybe that is why we are *Life Loves.*" I whispered before moving out onto the balcony. Dathon took the hand that still held Justice's ring. "Leave it Dad. This is his night."

I don't know how long I stood on the balcony. I had found the fae blossoms to create a net of glowing flowers instead of using candles in the room. The Fae Blossoms bloom brighter and stronger as more oxytocin is released. I didn't want to be caught near a wall of them. It would be a clear marker that my thoughts were not at the party.

All I did was watch the moons rise, listen to the music, and fight the urge to punch Chantara Lian's glossy face in. She had noticed me out here, set herself and her gaggle up in hearing distance. Moving with me when I wanted to get away from her. The gentle tones of flutes and violins couldn't even block her spiteful voice out. We were once friends of a sort. In a time when Justin was trying to be one of those fictional princes in the book Chantara lent me. That was before her mother ordered her to win his heart. Like that was going to happen.

Old me wanted to have Justin dance me across the floor. Show Chantara and her annoying mother that we enjoyed each other's company. That he loved me, not Chantara. The new me wanted him to just stand out on this balcony. Be with me one last time. A year and a half by the old calendar could fly by so I wanted one last happy memory of us to take to my grave. After last week, I didn't even want that.

Before I could even finish that thought, I was spun around into a hard chest. Hand stretched across my naked back while his other was flat to the wall. Blinking, I saw the blue frogs and knots against the black. Looking up, he wasn't smiling. He was scowling while listening. So, I listened too. Were we in danger? Where was Lizzy? Dathon? Wren? The Wests?

"Chantara, how did you score a dance with the king?" Chantara? He danced with Chantara? That is what this is about? I started pulling back, but he held me tighter. Which, of course, set off our *Bond*. There was something in the dark parts of his eyes that begged. Years. We have done this for years. You think I could say no to him? I had years to perfect saying no.

Since we were eight years old, New Calendar, she claimed Justin for her own. At nine, she tore the earrings from my ears after Justin had spent most of the night dancing with me. Justin held me as I cried, and we healed. Nothing happened to her as punishment. Yet my dress was ruined. Every time she opened her mouth, she was seconds from having her painted face punched in. That is why I wanted to be away from her. This time she was pushing my buttons and Justin wanted me to react.

"It was easy. That beast of a witch Seabrooke can never be his queen." Justin covered my mouth before I could give us away. "She broke all the laws his father put in place. Plus, she humiliated him on the field. For his own image, he needs to find a noble and regal woman." Justin held me tighter. Now it was hurting. "He asked me to his rooms tonight," she whispered. Just loud enough that I could hear. She knew I was out here, sure. She didn't know that Justin was. "The way he spoke, it sounded like he was going to propose."

The deep rumble in his chest was the only sign of his dark amusement at what she said. *As if I would. I have you.* He turned back to me. *Time to make those bitter dancing flowers wilt in jealousy?*

We will kill some of the Fae Blossoms. I warned. He just shrugged. *What are you thinking?* I glared at the curtain. *Death is too good for her.* Justin's chest rumbled; this time lighter. I looked up at him to see a grin that could blind, before he kissed me gently on the lips. Despite what he did, the *Bond* made me still love him. Justin was still everything I wanted and couldn't have. If I keep telling myself that, maybe I won't feel so alone tomorrow when I am farther than a mile from him. When I am out of the range of our curse.

Just be regal. Just as Mom taught us. Justin's smile shifted to his cat with a mouse smile. He wanted to punish her. He placed his left arm out just high enough for my right arm to lie on top of it. *Come on, My Little Witch. Let's make her eat her words.* It has always been like this with Chantara. She insults me, him or both, and we get revenge by dancing as if we were king and queen. Adriana hadn't wanted me to destroy the balance she maintained.

Chantara always thought she was better than me. Just because she wore designer dresses over her tiny noble born body. Every time it would end with Justin showing her, I was all he needed. Even if I wasn't all that perfect highborn godly beauty. People our age didn't know we were *Bonded,* just that Justin favored me over other women. Chantara would always look like a fool to her friends. It always looked like we were taking the high ground, but in truth, we were slowly destroying her. Since coming back from The Pit, I have taken a sick pleasure in it. That made me hate myself more.

Lead the way Demon Spawn. In step we held our heads up, walking right past Chantara and her flock. All thoughts of Roseden gone, the second Chantara implied she was going to sleep with Justin then marry him. Chantara was the last person I would see Justin with. At least with me still alive. Once I was gone, I would like nothing more than for Justin to take Chantara as a *Life Love.*

Chantara wore an emerald dress that did nothing for her pale complexion. Even paler still, she had gotten her blonde hair dyed red just for tonight. She paled even more as we came off the balcony. Literally ghost white as I tried not to look at her. Even if she was trying to look like me. She needed to put on at least another hundred pounds.

Alivia Post wore yellow and black, while her little sister, Kendall, was in all blue. All three dresses, at least four feet across at the base. Sure, it was the fashion of the day. When Justin's wife or Lizzy set the fashion in the next few months, I was sure it would change. By the Goddesses, I hope it will change. How could you even walk in them? Never mind, on me it would be six feet around.

Adriana had this design in the book of plans for this very evening. I couldn't love this outfit anymore unless it was the Seabrooke colors. As it was, the fae flowers twinkling on the lattice work over our heads, reflected on my dress. The music arranged it just the right order that one song ended and began another seamlessly. Only the best for the new king. Only the best for my infuriating *Soul Bond* love.

I had not really noticed what song we were on next until the ney started. The Numarian flute took me away to more ancient times near an ocean. The song was called 'Your Love is My Cure' and is indeed my favorite piece of music ever. I have never really been .to Numar but someday I would like to sit by the ocean, in some market listening to street musicians. In my teens, I had hoped we would go together. As it came closer and closer to my mission, I know this is as close as I get.

My eyes closed, I curtsied low to Justin. Slowly, we swayed around the room. My left hand on his chest over his heart. His left hand over it. His right over my hip, my right on his shoulder. Neither of us wore our gloves. Our skin-to-skin contact burned white hot as the rest of me felt frozen in his arms. Our *Soul Bond* screamed to life. Blood raced. Bodies heated. Every raw emotion unfiltered in our minds. This song always seemed to make the *Bond* flare hotter.

For ten minutes of the twenty-minute-long song, it was only us. Us and the haunting melody of a time long forgotten. A seaside town, bustling with people and a warm cup of coffee. A memory of a place I can't remember. The start of a lifetime filled with joy. Everything was right in the world. There was only that moment. Justin must have felt the same, he slid Adriana's ring on my third finger. Then I did the same with his father's ring on his hand. I wasn't even angry that this basically made us married. The world was as I wished it to be. We were happy. We were together. We were dancing to something that bound us on a different level.

The pace picked up. Justin spun me out, then back, steadily parading us around the floor. Our *bond* pulsed in time with the music. All thoughts of the outside world were gone. *I want to see her real face.* My heart stopped. The music was quiet in my mind. My feet stopped. Seven words to destroy the mood. "Lys?" The scars. He wants to see the scars.

"You just had to ruin it." I snapped, leaving him on the dance floor as the song ended.

CHAPTER THREE

I was almost running as I left the ballroom towards the garden gates. More upset with how it ended than my night ending. Upset with myself for even thinking I could be happy for a moment. I had planned to stay longer. Wren had placed a hand on Justin's chest to stop him. I thought I saw Colin and Lizzy join them as I passed Dathon reentering the room. Dathon tried to take my arm, but I dodged. "Lys?" I just needed to get to the stables before Justin followed me. I didn't think they would hold him back long.

As my foot hit the gravel, the fireworks began. Plenty of time to get on the road. In the Grand City, I would ask for an audience with the current High Queen. I would ask for permission to live in her city. As Champion of Arocana, and now the queen, thrice over, of Stowera, it was protocol. Though I have never met her, Evana says she was related to me.

If I keep going over the plan, then I will not turn around. I needed to meet the High Queen. I didn't need to be Justin's queen. I needed to kill Tabari before he killed Justin and destroyed my home. I didn't need to be Tulora's heir.

The history books tell me Matix Seabrooke was my mother's *Bonded,* and they were married at sixteen. If that was true, I only remember seeing him once. The day the world went to shit. If the High Queen was really a descendant of my mother's other son, Hadain or even Hallon, I hope to find a haven. I was leaving my home with nothing but my gorgeous dress - my wedding dress, Adriana's ring and dagger, my Elven mare and the hope I could live my last year in peace. Maybe Tabari would come for me first. Save me time.

The fireworks were over. I should have been to the stable by now. Yet when I looked up at the sky, I saw the stars crying as the last blue green explosion lit the sky. Leila, Goddess of Stars, shed the tears she knew I couldn't. As I did as a child, I clasped my hands, offering a wish of health for all my friends. "Thank you, Goddess, for your sympathy. Please bless me and mine during my last year," I said before making my way again. The goddesses owed me. I was going to do what their champion couldn't.

A warmer, larger hand took my wrist. I whirled, dagger to the throat of the unwelcome man. In the moonlight, Justin's eyes began glowing as a summer day sky. The dark spots have turned to sparkling stars. "What do you mean, your last year?" He wasn't supposed to be here. He should be with his sister, not listening to me pray.

"Go back to your sister, Justin." He didn't let go of my hand, though. My body tensed at the wave after wave of *Bond* magic.

"Lizzy took Wren away to talk." I frowned. "You didn't see? Was it our wedding? Our coronation?" Wedding? "You spent most of the night taking compliments well. I thought you were in shock. This is not like you. I knew something was wrong." He released me, running the same hand through his hair. "I just never thought it was you leaving me alone."

I turned away from Justin, starting down the path again. I needed to get away before I lost my nerve. "It's this or Tabari kills you. Wren can tell you all about it in a year."

"Wren isn't meeting you." Crap. "Wherever you are going without me." I hung my head, shaking it. I should have known. Lizzy here would make it hard for him to leave. "We got married tonight. Can't you stay even for just tonight?"

"We are not really married, Justin." He held up his hand with his father's ring. He thought we were married. Coronation though? There was no real crown. Justin wore a circlet that looked like mine. The Knyght family sword on his hip. Oh shit! I had held Adriana's dagger. Justin was the one who sent the circlet and necklace. Our family colors and a moonstone for Daina.

"You officially made me a queen!" I held up my left hand. Shit. Shit! This was not me. I wasn't a queen. I am a thrown-away child. I didn't see that this night was supposed to be my wedding. I didn't see myself reacting that way to the comfort and love Justin gave me. I really needed to take a deep breath and relax. Yelling at Justin never got me anywhere, except the healer's room. Breathe as you pace, Lys. I told myself. The most frustrating part was that he was just standing there. "What the hell, Justin? We talked about this. I didn't want to be queen of anything!" He paced the width of the garden path with me. I would not force him into anything but saying goodbye. I turned back to the path. "Dammit Justin. The best part of you being crowned tonight was to make me not be queen anymore." His head tilted to one side as he eyed me. "What else did I miss?"

"Wren and Lizzy are *Bonded.*"

I snorted. Last to know, I guess. "I know you haven't seen her a lot, but why do you think he never touched me?" I knew one day I would be without Wren. He was Lizzy's. Being without Justin was going to hurt more. "Just like with me, he didn't want to act on it until she wanted him. He was even willing to give me my last year before he was going to come back for Liz." My hands relaxed. "I knew he would stay with her. Not everyone hates the *Bond* like I do."

"Lizzy told me you were going to be gone in a year, so she needed to get on with the heir making. I think she is crazy. She wants two pregnancies in the last year of your life."

"I think I gave her the idea. Lizzy was there when I found out I couldn't give you babies." I continued to walk. Justin beat against my mind wards. They fell when he was suddenly kissing me. My ancient magic spun the loose leaves and petals around us as Justin's barriers blocked out the outside world. It was just the two of us; Our goddess-given *bond* pushing our blood to lightning speeds. Walls crashing down. Hearts beating in unison. His hand brushed my scars, drawing me back from the power. "Stop touching my burns! What the hell, Justin?" I swung my fist, connecting with his shoulder. My injured right shoulder reacted violently. I gave out a scream of pain. Twice tonight, he made a point of touching the part of me I hated most. Proof I was weak and foolish. Now I was in pain because of it. A reminder that I am mortal.

"There is more news that you missed. If it wasn't for Colin telling me you were going, I wouldn't get to tell you." *Okay,*

38

fine, I'll bite. I looked at the gravel. "Dathon's investigator found out Roseden drugged me, glamoured herself to look like you. In my mind, I was making love to you. She's-"

Really? You think that makes this better? My mind screamed, but he didn't hear. "See, that is the problem, Justin. You didn't even think. Roseden is a whore."

"Yeah?"

"I'm a virgin, rat's ass!" I held my hand up to stop him. "I checked when I got home from The Pit. It is the only thing I can give you." I saw him force himself to stay upright. "I know the mechanics of sex, but lack the experience for confidence." Even if Justin never found out about Roseden's men, I had to know if they had broken me. The healer lady Dathon brought me afterwards, confirmed. I was still whole. For better or worse, if I allowed Justin to consummate our *Bond*, I would be wholly his wife. "After everything she did to me, I was still intact." He paled, "You like to believe that Wren and I were going at it like spring rabbits, he told you the truth." The angry laugh that left my lips scared me. I still cared about all of it. I knew then that I didn't want any of this. I didn't want to leave them. I didn't want to leave Justin. These people were the ones I loved. Who claimed to love me in return.

Even if he was an idiot, I knew it was just going to hurt more in a year. "He would never touch me that way. Even if he really met me tomorrow, I know he wouldn't marry me. He would never bed me." I shouted, stepping towards him. "Do you know why, Justin? He knows it would hurt you all. It would hurt Lizzy to know he was with me. Hurt you, I chose him over you. Hurt him for hurting her."

Behind him a sheepish Wren. Lizzy next to him, their hands clasped. Evana and Colin with Dathon on the stairs.

Chantara standing at the door just watching this mess. "I knew he found his *Bond*. It was when during my time with Roseden or that year I drove you all away, but I saw the change in him. I saw the way he looks at your sister."

He said nothing.

"It is the same way I *used* to look at you." I pushed him back, trying not to cry. "Before Roseden broke our hearts. We have a weakness for you, Knyghts. Sure he never said the words. It wasn't as if he ever hid it from me." I saw Wren's tears fall. Lizzy looked at the dirt. "I expected nothing from him."

Justin turned to where I was looking, "I didn't expect you to trick me into a wedding, or officially taking the crown." I held up the ring with my left hand as my right hand tightened on the hilt of the dagger and brought them level to my chest. "I don't want to be queen. I never did. That is not why I killed your father." I took a deep breath, willing the tears to stop. "Before Roseden, I was willing to do anything for you." I threw the dagger to his feet. The crown was harder. Evana had pinned it into my hair. The pins tore my scalp as I pulled. Justin stopped me. Eyes pleading for me to stop.

The tears came fast. "I didn't even expect to be arguing with you. I wanted to have one last dance in your arms before leaving." Justin just stared at me. He could at least say something, but I got nothing. "Goodbye, Justin." Then I started walking again. Nothing felt worse than telling him goodbye. That was why I hadn't planned on it.

My heart hurt with the sharp pain, yet it wasn't mine. "Why did you wear it, then? You could have worn anything. Why that?" Wearing what? He just pointed at me. He was crying. His heart hurt so much his face shone with streaks to match mine. His mother's dagger in one hand. My circlet in the other. I couldn't look at him, so I looked at the dress I loved. My wedding dress? Adriana designed it as my wedding dress.

"Because I'm as much of a fool as I pretend not to be." I whispered. "I remember our time before Adriana died." I walked back to Justin. "Adriana had it designed for me. I have been hoarding it with their rings since the throne room. She asked me to wear this tonight."

"The dress Mom wanted for you is not like this. She wanted you in a gown. The kind that Chantara wears." God awful. Wait if she didn't- "I designed it for you," he whispered. Figures. "Mom had been talking about our wedding for almost a year before my father demanded it of us." I, in no uncertain terms, denied that I would officially marry Justin. I wouldn't give Justice the satisfaction.

I would have done it somewhere quiet. I wouldn't give Justice the satisfaction of seeing me in one of those stupid gowns without weapons. "She showed me so many stupid puffy dresses. I laughed at all of them. They weren't your style. Back when I could feel you every day. I knew you needed to be free. Leggings give you freedom. Armor was better." Of course it is. I was in constant fear of his father. I only relaxed when it was just us, Adriana, Dathon, and Lizzy. Even then, I was in some sort of leather.

"You and I had just come back from the market where I saw you eyeing up some Aldaina troops in town, so I sketched you in different Aldaina styles." The art book I teased him about. "Six months before Tabari attacked her, I gave her the notebook you used for tonight's party." I looked at the ring. Again. He planned it all. He saw I couldn't have flames, so he wanted Fae Blossoms. All the songs I liked, the last one being my favorite of all times. That is why he came to find me. That was the real reason for asking me to dance.

I closed my eyes, trying not to break completely. Somehow knowing Justin had put so much effort into this and I wasn't here mentally broke what was left of my heart. I snapped when he wanted to see my scars. "It took me a full year to work out every detail that would bring you pleasure." His voice was barely a whisper. I had thought it was just Adriana's wishful thinking. Just wanted the best coming of age party for her son. "I wanted you to feel safe, yet beautiful. That was why there were no candles. I wanted Fae Blossoms to bloom over your head to prove to the world you were happy. Really happy for once. I wanted to dance with you to your favorite songs. I needed it to be perfect for you."

"Justin-" He took my hand as the other slid around my waist. I was going to fall to my knees. I have never hated myself more than I did at this very minute.

"The songs were all your favorite pieces. Then I wanted to watch your eyes light up as the sky lit up with colors. It wasn't hard to convince Dathon to add the green blue ones. I know that is your favorite color. I hoped you would feel safe enough to accept our *Bond*."

"I will never feel safe. This is the one thing your father demanded of us." My knees gave out. My fall was slow as Justin fell with me. "Tabari will come back when he hears about this. That is how I will die." In seventeen and half months I would die by my own uncle's new body's hand. "You do not know what you have done, Justin." He pulled my face to his. Our ring hands clasped. Our *Bond*, calling to us.

"Then tell me, my love. What have I been too idiotic to see?" He whispered in a strained voice. "Explain to me why

42

you are so scared all the time now. Why is Tabari coming back? Why are you going to die before me?" My forehead fell to his shoulder.

"Where to start?" I couldn't look him in the eyes. "My mother was Tulora Seabrooke. You know that. I've told you for years. You have seen my dreams. What I haven't explained to you is what happened with your father in the throne room." Goddess, help me. "Your father knew I was my mother's daughter. He called me by my Mom's name. I let my glamor fall. My scars were free for him to see.

"There is only one Death Knight that would know my mother, and the reason behind my scars." I let the glamor fall for Justin. "Tabari is her twin brother. Tabari held an eye in his hand the first time I saw him. Until he saw us. Tabari laughed at my mother as she raced to us, but it was too late, Hallon sent a fireball at Tabari, who batted it, and me, into a bookshelf. I was trapped, screaming as I burned. When he connected the dots, your father confirmed he was really Tabari." I remember the pain. I remember laying in the snow, screaming from the pain.

"Tabari was set free by me when I beheaded Justice. He wants to take you to use me. He has lived as the king of Stowera for centuries. I put a kink in that chain by denying our bond. Then I killed his body before he was ready. He needed to take over your body so he would force us into a child."

"I am married to Tulora's daughter." I groaned. That was not the takeaway.

"That is not the point." I turned our hands to show the rings up. "When I retrieved your father's ring, I learned Tabari knew me. The real me. He told me my Soulless Prince would be his next body. As soon as we were married, he would return."

"Because we are wed now, Tabari is coming back to kill us. To kill me. You are going to die protecting me." Thank you for seeing my point, finally! I nodded. His eyes lit. "Tabari is going to take control of me to force me to continue his line. To destroy everything your mother did in her time."

"That is my mother's failed mission. That is how I am going to die. I am going to die trying to kill him. To save you. In just under a year. Just as *Destiny* foretold. That is the prophecy Lizzy and Evana know about."

"Evana!" He called, pulling us to his feet. We were running then. This is not the response I thought I would get. "Where are you Succubus?" She was no longer on the stairs. None of them were.

"Demon Spawn?" My best friend scowled at his nickname for her. I called Justin Demon Spawn when I was angry with him. Just as he called me his Little Witch, he called her a Succubus when Colin talked about nothing but her. They were freshly *Bonded*, so Colin was right to do so. Justin just wasn't as excited. As far as I know, he never talked about me with Colin. Or at least as little as I talked to Evana about Justin. We had been *Bonded* so young that it was normal for us.

Evana's eyes widened at seeing Justin with me in tow. "What are you still doing here? Your great niece will not like it if you are late tomorrow." Evana saw me out of breath. I wanted to beg her to stop him. "Goddess Justin, why can't she breathe?" Evana tried to hold me up, but I was on fire. My body was so light but heavy at the same time. "Were you two physically fighting after we left? I told you she-"

"My wife will not die." He snapped. It sure felt like I was. "Not anytime soon. As for her niece, Lys gets an audience any time. She is the rightful High Queen anyway." Justin snarled.

Not another crown. That is not something I had ever thought about. My mother started Queensgate. A seat of power that would help her see everything. To help everyone. I was an heir to that throne, too. *NO!* Justin looked back at me as I stood wide eyed. "Just realized that, huh?" He sighed.

"I don't want - to be queen. Forget - about the High - Queen." Every breath hurt more than the last.

"Did your brother's gifts arrive?" Evana's nose scrunched. I tried to pull away from his hand. I had never known him to hold on to something so tight. The fingertips changed colors. He didn't want me to run away. As if I could. The exertion was too much, considering I just woke up this morning.

My lungs burned. My chest pulled uncomfortably at the bandages still wrapped around me. *Please Justin, stop.* He gazed back at me, folded over. "I am not letting you leave until you see your birthday gift." I frowned. No, instead he was going to drive all the air from my body. I will never make it to Tabari at this rate.

So instead you are going to let me die from lack of oxygen? My birthday was hours away and I didn't think I was going to make it.

"Evana, is it here?" This time, he seemed calmer and less in a hurry.

"Yeah, in the gallery." I saw her realize something. "It will not keep her here. She is my champion, Justin." But we were running again. "Eventually, she is going to have to live in Arocana." I was suddenly grateful I was wearing leggings. No skirts to lift as he pulled us to the second floor of his palace. At the top of the stairs, I gripped the railing so as not to pass out. Justin felt the tug. I was on my knees. Everything was spinning. It was as if I had run from Crystal Keep Tower to Knyght's Reach. That was a week long ride on horseback.

The rest of the way, he walked with me with an arm around my waist, the other under my arm. Every part of him hating himself for not realizing how bad I really was. *It was one thing to be told the woman you love is half dead; it is another to see her on her knees, trying hard just to breathe. I'm sorry.* I didn't even try to smile, everything hurt. I had to concentrate on breathing in from my nose and out of my mouth to hold more oxygen in my lungs. Which made my head hurt even more. *Breathe. One. Two. Three. Four. Out. Two. Three. Four. Again. In your nose, out your mouth.* Justin repeated in my mind.

We were in the completely dark family gallery. There was a painting for every royal Knyght family since the creation. I hated coming in here. There was little to no variation in the appearance of the king in each painting, until Justice and Adriana. It was almost as if Justice hadn't been taken over yet. He was the only smiling king in all those paintings. How had Justice stayed pure for so long? Then I looked at Adriana's face. She is the only Aldaina Queen. An Aldaina High Commander of Stowera wed to the heir to a Death Knight.

Was it Aldaina magic? Could it be that simple?

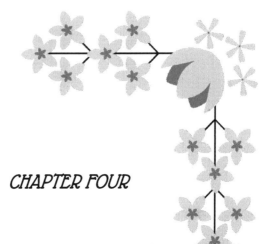

CHAPTER FOUR

Could it be? Could Adriana have found a spell that kept Justice safe for a time? How had Tabari gotten past it? When had he? Justin told me he remembered when his father had gone out as king, but because Adriana was pregnant, she had to stay home. Was that it? I turned to Justin, busying himself in the gallery. Could I find the spell she used? With my raw magic, I might be able to hold it longer. Not forever, just until I find a cleansing spell, ritual, prayer. Whatever my mother couldn't find. If we can't find one, maybe Dathon can make one. Adriana knew something she didn't tell us, yet it was protecting us now. What did we have that Justice wouldn't have had on that trip?

The man I hated and adored was smiling at his cousin. As if he was going to keep me here. His genuine smile was infectious, like something from years ago. Before all the bad. Before death. Before I pushed him away because of a prophecy. How could he smile, knowing I was going to die? Knowing that if I fail, he would cease to be? He would be food for an ever-growing Death Knight? Did he have confidence that I would succeed? Could I? Was the Aldaina magic the key?

Right there and then, I decided to stay. Tabari, usually at the forefront of my mind, seemed so far away. Justin smiled as he had done before the world went to shit. Tabari would come and I would be ready. Even if I had to dig Adriana from her grave to summon her soul to tell me what she did. I would keep Justin safe. I would keep that smile safe. Right now, in the middle of the night, I should have been more afraid. Instead, I planned. This was the man I needed to protect, just as Auntie *Destiny* told me to.

Justin was trying to show me some kind of gift. It looked too large for something I deserved. "Now, my love, can you light the candles? Only a few so you can see. I'll get you a chair." Even if this new plan was to work, would I still die? Would I never see his smile again?

Shaking, I lit the candles, though I could only do one at a time. I was still on the verge of falling over from lack of air. Nevermind my pyrophobia trying to call my elemental magic. I was falling over when Justin caught me. "I'm sorry. I know if you don't get to see it tonight, you would never get to," he whispered into my hair. *I need to be better for her. The rest of her life can't be grand gestures. She needs to know I am standing where she needs me to be. What will I do when she is gone? She had wanted to leave me tonight. Probably to save me from the truth. Seventeen months, she said. Was Daina going to take her away then? Daina, help me, I just love My Little Witch so much. Please don't let her walk away. Please, Goddess, don't take My Little Witch away from me.*

"Don't call me pet names." I groaned. Leaning back into his arms. He was so warm, and the *Bond* had such a pleasant hum. "Just give me a minute. Go prepare whatever your grand gesture is."

Justin froze, then sighed. *Yes, I heard all of that.*

I hated his sad smile.

Evana sat next to me, checking my bandages and pulse.

"I fell into his trap." I groaned, hiding my face in my hands. "I think we need to get to the Aldaina Archives. Tabari is going to find out, and I will have to kill us both. Or we can find whatever Adriana used to protect Justice."

She said nothing.

"Step back. You think Adriana had something to protect Justice from Tabari?" She blurted, looking at my left hand and gasping. There was magic on the rings, but I doubt something this little would keep Tabari away this long. Maybe it was a combination of items we had.

"Think about it. He is the only man in this room smiling. That was after he married her. Justin even said he remembered his father being playful, Justice left on a diplomatic mission and came back angry. There had to be something here in this castle that couldn't expel Tabari once he gained a hold."

"Could that be why Tabari hasn't come back yet?" I looked from her to Justin. "He could take Justin. You were *Soul Bound* at six. He could have just moved to Justin, when you were teenagers, he could have consummated the *bond.* You were more than happy to love Justin then."

Shit, she was right. Whatever was in this castle made it so that, once formless, Tabari couldn't enter a new host. This was his seat of power for hundreds of years. His throne room was almost completely covered in his black ooze. Yet when I took Justice's head, he didn't take me or Justin for a new host.

Why?

"So a wedding?" I groaned even harder. One problem at a time.

Evana just laughed.

"Yeah. The package that arrived after Adriana died held a notebook with some very thought-out plans, the detailed design for this outfit and a letter. The letter made me think the notebook was about his first birthday as king, so I followed the instructions. I had wondered why Justin didn't ask more than what I was wearing. Turns out he planned our wedding and gave it to Adriana."

"They were Justin's plans?" We looked at our men. "They were so detailed. Everything was down to the colors of the rug on the stairs. You are *Bonded* so a wedding would have been for show. I thought it being his birthday was weird." My oldest friend frowned. "The only detail wrong was the flowers. Calla lilies, not lilacs. Everything was something you loved. As if it was for your birthday, not his." We both groaned. "And I thought I got the hopeless romantic of the family."

"How can I leave now?" Evana held me. "Tabari will come. He will try to take Justin. I will have to-"

"No, don't think about that now." Justin was back pulling me across the room. "We will talk about it tomorrow in the Grand City." I could feel the blush drain from my face. I was not letting him come to the Grand City. What if Tabari was there? I don't think I can fail before I start this plan. Dathon might know or be able to find what enchanted thing was keeping us safe.

Justin looked from me to the white cloth draped over a painting. "Tonight, you are not a warrior. There are no Death Knights. No magic. You are just a daughter looking for her family." I frowned. He looked at a clock on the wall. It was ten minutes past midnight. My birthday. Justin just smiled, then kissed Adriana's - my ring. Together, they pulled the cloth off the larger of the two paintings.

I saw Hallon's face first. As old as I was now. Our father's toffee hair and green eyes. Burn scars mirrored mine. Dressed in modern Mage Knight's armor, just like Dathon. Next to him, an older, graying toffee color haired man missing his right eye. He wore a red and green leather outfit like Justin's style. Justin wore a black and blue version. Small crest of the Aldaina over my father's heart. Matix was Aldaina. History books say he was still a Templar of Leila when Mom defeated her brother. Were the Aldaina even a real force back then? I certainly didn't remember them. Not like now. Even Adriana dressed in Aldaina commander leathers whenever she got a chance. She wasn't the only Knyght who did.

Justin dressed as Aldaina. The same lines as the suit my father wore. The same placements of crests. But where the Aldaina triple moon should have been was the Knyght crest on Justin's. It wasn't right, though. On the knight's shield was the Seabrooke crest with the three moons of the Aldaina over the knight. You can still see the old Knyght crest throughout the castle. The old one was a tree by a stream, like the mage knight on the knight's shield. I frowned, reaching for the one on Justin's chest to see the Seabrooke crest tattooed there. I blinked, looking at what Justin was wearing. Was he even allowed to wear this style?

We were both in official Aldaina commander styles. I didn't remember him taking the training with Adriana. Adriana and I trained very early in the morning. It let Dathon sleep in. Back then, she spent nights more often than not at our home in the city. At noon, Justin would trade places with her. When I was tested, Justin, Dathon, and Adriana were there watching me. It took little for me to pass the full obstacle test. The oral test was harder. Justin wasn't allowed to be anywhere near Haven. Thinking about it now, could he have been somewhere else taking the tests? I wonder if it was the fact I was Tulora's daughter that got me commander at that age, or my actual skill.

My mother sat in front of my brother and father. Red hair free of the dyes we would use to hide our hair. Blue-silver eyes on the edge of tears. She was so much thinner than I remember. Certainly smaller than I am. I looked down at what I was wearing. My mother wore a red leather version of what I was standing in. The symbol of Aldaina on her left breast. She was Aldaina too. She was dressed as a commander. The history books mentioned it but didn't go into detail. They also called her a war monger. Matix's history was very detailed, but Mom's was practically nothing before she married Dad. Not a lot before she defeated Tabari. After that, it seemed like historians chronicled her every day, blaming her for every death, plague and famine over her thirty years as queen, then high queen. Everything but her twins, some denying we even lived at all. Only Hadain was her child.

In Mom's lap, a baby, maybe a year old with toffee hair, green eyes. That had to be Hadain. My precious baby brother, Hadain, I never got to meet. Mom holding on to him as if he too would be lost. I know after Hallon died, Hadain came to control the Mage Knights. My little brother became the God of Death when a plague came to the country. There is a debate in the histories if it was a Death Knight plague. All the books portrayed him as something both Aldaina and Mage Knight. The Seabrooke crest is the only thing on his chest in the form of a bib.

Did Justin design my wedding outfit before or after he had seen Mom? Had I even seen a commander in a team of Aldaina at the market? I can't remember ever seeing something like this until I was tested. That would have been a month before Adriana was murdered. I didn't see it again until Lizzy arrived in my room, wearing hers and holding my formals years later. Lizzy's coat was longer and overtly armored. The skirt was three quarters around and hung to her knees. Not at all like mine. The only armor I had was my red leathers and my wedding dress. Both of them with heel length skirts. Why was there a difference?

"I was at a trade summit with Mom that same summer, Evana's brother showed me this. He was showing me cohorts of the Starfall Nation as an intimidation tactic. When I found your eyes in another person's face," Justin said as he pointed at my father and brothers. "I thought they were some distant relation to you. Lero and Cael then informed me this was Tulora and family on her coronation day." Cael? Who was Cael and why did that name make me smile? "I asked right there and then to get a copy of it for your engagement gift." I groaned. Of course, he would flaunt this in front of his father. Tabari never really believed I was his niece.

"Cael tells me that as a friend of the Royal Seabrookes, Lero asked for a portrait of the savior of the Fae people. He told me she protested because they were not a whole family." Justin pointed to the small table next to her that held my flame burned wooden sword and two dolls. One doll with black yarn hair, black and blue suit. Though I remember blue buttons for eyes. The other was an orange yarn hair, green-eyed girl wearing a gray and green half skirt with a pants suit. Now I saw the resemblance of the girl doll. That ugly thing was me as I am now. Same dress and all. "What were their names?"

As if Justin didn't know.

My fingernails slid down the paint, smiling at the part of me I left behind. My first version of my Soulless Prince and me. Mom kept them. I had left them on my bed when I heard the shouting. "Was this who you rescued in the forest?"

"I was three by the old calendar when Auntie *Destiny* gave us to me." I looked up to Justin. "My Soulless Prince. I even named him Justin like Auntie *Destiny* said I should. Though you were forever the Soulless Prince." I sighed, tightening my hands. "She was so ugly to me I left her in my room. In my toy chest. Now I see she was me. You have to understand, I was three by the old calendar when I got them, so she wasn't cute like you were. She was half a person." I didn't look at her again until right before I came here. That was nineteen years ago for me. Was I supposed to know they were us? Yeah, no.

"*The Destiny* was my father's sister. She told me this was my Soulless Prince. That I would have to save him from all the dangers the world would throw at us." I paused. "She was the Mother of Deities." He took my right hand, pulling it to his heart. While my left touched my doll. "He and I would spend full days fighting back frogs and tom cats. While she sat in the chest ignored." I smiled, looking back at my dolls. "He would hold court over other woodland creatures. As his knight, I would stand behind him to his left. Hallon on his right. Protected from all evils."

"I was supposed to know your twin?"

"See, that is what I didn't get until I came here. *Destiny* said you would know but not know my brother. I wonder if she saw me as Hallon at the tournaments." I wanted to reach out for my twin. "I never thought I would have to defend my Soulless Prince alone. Until I got here without Hallon." Justin took my free hand. His warmth, trying to comfort me.

"Hallon was the brains. I was pure instinct. He helped me control my temper. Mom wanted me to control it too. I always had to be in the moment, so the bullies didn't jump him for being a mage." Had it been my Fury that made me jump at Justin's father? "You saw it in the alley." Justin laughed. I had almost killed him with the bullies. I didn't have control then. Based on last week, I still don't.

"Mom and *The Destiny* encouraged me to work with both my magic and my swordsmanship. I had an uncle who taught me to summon my sword. Everyone made sure I would be ready to protect the grown-up Soulless Prince. Since the king made it illegal to show any magic, Hallon had to figure out magic on his own. It wasn't fair to him. There wasn't anything I could do to help him. There was no way I will read all those books. They were all messed up, to me. Mom tried so very hard to keep me in check. *The Destiny* couldn't find anyone who wouldn't lead us to ruin." I wish someone would have told me my Soulless Prince would fall in love with me. Or that the monster I had nightmares about before Roseden was his father, and my uncle. "No one saw me ruined. No one told me I would bring the ruination of the kingdom."

I could almost imagine my family here with me. "My family moved on with their lives. They lived full lives. Never knowing what happened to me. How I would miss them so much." They were older. Even older than I am now. "How I had messed up so badly trying to do the one thing they asked of me."

"I am not sure if they really lived full lives." Colin released the second smaller painting. "I found this in Mom's room after she died." My brothers. Older, not by much. A woman sitting in front of them. The brass plaque under it, screwed into the frame, read "King Hadain, Lord and Lady Seabrooke." Lady Seabrooke looked as if I knew her. Alabaster skin with sun bleached hair. Blue-gray eyes that glared as if she was planning the painter's death. My brother watched her like a hawk. There was something about her.

"Cassandra." My body didn't react well to that name. It was excited for blood and scared of what Cassandra could do. Even if I shouldn't have known the name. It shut down at that. I thought it was just exhaustion, but this felt different. Something about that name felt almost like death itself had come for my soul, and it was frightening. Wasn't she part of my family? I shouldn't fear her.

In the darkness, I thought about Auntie Jean. She was *The Destiny* of my birth time. She had prepared me for death to save Justin. Only one death. Seeing the faces of my loved ones, after so long, with my loved ones from this time, crushed me. They were such a distant memory. As if I had already died and been reborn. That couldn't be true, though Tabari would come to take Justin from me. Probably try to take Evana and Colin with him. Maybe Dathon, Lizzy and Wren. That I was determined not to allow. If my blood family could move on without me. I could certainly do the same to protect my found family. I would fight for the life I created here.

This was my hope. From what I am told, hope is always more powerful than fear. Adriana had said it to me in a dream. A dream after my missing time had gotten worse. I wish I knew what that was all about. I was born three hundred years ago. I didn't have blackouts then. They started when I was put in this time. Something my Time Magic Aunt did sent me to the future and gave me bouts of black outs no one has noticed. I wish I had even a little of her magic. I will be in one place and blink, be across the city, or kingdom. The only time I didn't have blackouts was when I was in The Pit.

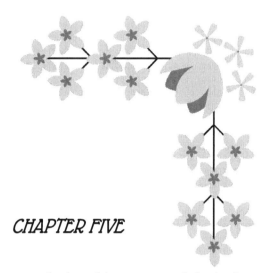

CHAPTER FIVE

I was up at dawn, gently knocking on my father's door. Luckily, someone put me in my old room. Too soon for me to be near my new husband. New husband. Such an odd concept for me. My room was cleaned up too. Small miracles. Not by my hand, though, which made me feel awful for the servants. Dathon stayed two doors down from my room when he was at court, despite being able to see our house from my room in the castle. I loved the room Adriana picked for me, so much sunlight.

Dathon, like me, would be awake as well. Not by choice. My natural awake time was five, so he learned to match my sleep patterns. Difficult when you are a night owl. Coffee would be a peace offering most mornings. Hopefully, he knew why I was there. The open door to no one on the other side, which told me he was working.

I showed myself to my bench by the window. My reading spot. I had picked it out unknowingly when Adriana was furnishing my room. "That was a lovely birthday-"

"Wedding," I said quietly, fingering Adriana's ring. Pulling up my legs, I stared out at the clear blue sky. The lighter side of Justin's eyes. "It was our wedding." Dathon gazed at me. I tried to smile back. My brother's green eyes stared through me. I had seen what Hallon looked like as a grownup. Now I could see new similarities in Dathon's face. Dathon's face was exhausted from holding it neutral. The way he raised his right eyebrow instead of smiling. Even the way he hunched over his desk. "Hallon would be proud of you." I blurted.

Yep, that brow rose. "It is horrible timing on Justin's part. He should have known better. Did he even talk to you about it?" Dathon handed me coffee. I took a sip, knowing it was black. Gross, but I needed that bitterness today.

"No. He wanted last night to be special." I laid my right side against the cool glass of the window. The morning chill felt nice on my overheated burns.

"I should have known your oath was not a normal one. Then he repeated it to you as if he was your champion. Kacie found me, so I didn't see you get her ring." Kacie, his second in command. A woman twice his age and doted on him as a mother. She loved us. She spoiled me as a child whenever I was in the Mage Knight offices. A grandmother I never had. She had no children living. Killed by Justice. "I wish I recorded it."

I stifled a laugh. "That would make two of us. I guess I shouldn't tell him I remember nothing from the time I arrived to the time Chantara started insulting us." Dathon groaned. Another episode of missing time. "I have so much to talk to you about, but considering how much Justin talks to you, I think you know what I am going to ask." He handed me a tan file folder. Roseden Seabrooke, written on the tag. "That is not the item on my list. Should you even let me read it? I am a witness."

Dathon sat at the end of the bench. I tried not to let him see that pulling my legs up caused me pain. The ache wasn't so bad after dancing and fighting with Justin for hours. Since he was fully healed, maybe that rushed my healing. Stupid magic. I deserve to be in pain longer. I tried to kill my divine match.

"The whole time you were sleeping, he helped with the investigation. He kept saying there had to have been a tell. There was no way he could have been so easily duped. There were other witnesses, so I won't ask you to take the stand if you don't want to." Did I want to? Did I want to see her face as I told the world what I felt when she was screwing him? How the knife blade felt as she tried to carve the Seabrooke crest off his chest?

"He told me what you said to him in the garden. About not sleeping with Wren and how you got a healer to check if you were intact." My eyes looked out the window. "It was too far away for me to hear clearly." I almost downed the steaming drink to not blush in front of my father. I had asked the healer not to tell Dathon about that part. Part of me didn't want him to know. That he wouldn't see me as his perfect daughter anymore. "He is really beating himself up. You were his whole life before Roseden got her claws in you both."

"Poor thing." Glaring at the coffee wasn't fair to the coffee.

"Are you ever going to tell me what happened to you? I know what you looked like when I got you back."

Same questions, same dodge. "Maclow will not be happy that his wife is on trial. Will he fight Justin over this? Will he come after me again? Will he be at her execution?" Six months after I got home, Dathon went off to deal with something with

Justin when Maclow broke down the front door. I was dragged halfway to a waiting carriage when Dathon saved me. I remember landing face first in the mud.

"I'm sure he is more pissed at her for getting caught. Neither of them knew this was the thing to break her control over you. We will try her tomorrow in front of a jury." Her seducing Justin? Or her trying to kill him? Forced intoxication. Rape. Attempted murder. The file said. Then I saw it. Kidnapping. Incarceration. Physical and mental abuse. Forced manslaughter. "Dad?"

"Roseden broke." My coffee fell to the floor. Cup shattering on the stone. Roseden admitting everything she did to me? Dathon knew. The old fears pulled me away from my father before he put a hand to my foot.

"There was no way." I was just the 'fanciful child' and she was the diplomat's wife. Her word against mine for nine years.

"She was telling Kacie everything she did to you during my three years away." I hid my face, trying not to cry. Kacie knew, too. She had been here every day to bathe and bandaged me. Now she knows why. Dathon continued. His way of telling me how much he knew. Why did he ask if he freaking knew? Five years is not enough time to face the B.S. I just finally have full weeks of not waking up in my bed screaming.

Yet not even my father could look at me. "Justin was there talking to me about getting audiences with *The Destiny*. He had questions about your prophecy. Evana told him about it. Roseden was screaming bloody murder in the interview room until she saw him." I froze. Please tell me she didn't tell him. "She laughed. Taunting him with how he didn't really know you. That you had kept him safe, even from her. You kept all of us safe from her. She was looking forward to eating away at my mind, but you-" Dathon stopped, looking at his hands. "Even when she used his image against you. She started talking about how she had her men rape you. Being careful not to take your virginity. How she tossed you in a pit to fight orphans on drugs she was creating."

Justin knew! He didn't stop me from saying it. *You bastard!!* I locked our *Bond* up tight. I had not wanted either of them to know or see any of that. How I murdered our peers all so she wouldn't beat me or have her men hurt me. The possibility that one might get the idea to go farther. Not in the details Roseden gave them. I let my fingers curl into my palms so hard they cut the skin. Pain made me remember I wasn't seeing the faces I saw at night. It also shocked me to hide the panic filling my mind.

"Justin heard enough to demand these charges to be added as his *Bonded* wife. As his *Bonded*, his queen, there were legal rights there. I couldn't deny him. As the man who loves you with his very soul, he wanted to skin her alive right there and then. I wanted to let him. Kacie literally held us back. We wanted revenge on the people who made you draw away from us. To draw as much blood from her and my brother as they had from you and the poor children there with you." My father was strangely open about killing his family. "We have to go through the courts, though. Longer lasting torment for the woman who flaunted her devilish freedoms."

I had been with Dathon for most of my life. This was the first time his soothing voice turned cold and venomous. Loathing dripped from every word. I had never once found myself scared of him. No, this was the turning point. Not when his *Life Love* was murdered. No. It was this. A crazed woman hurting his daughter.

"Call me." They knew. No use hiding it from the people I cared for if my villain has told them. Dathon's eyes came so fast to meet mine I thought he might get whiplash. "She told me what I was feeling was nothing compared to what she would do to either of you if I ever told you." My father took my newly jeweled hand. He didn't even flinch at the blood dripping from my nails. He turned over the hand to heal it. "We were all still hurting from Adriana. My walls went from sheer gossamer to as thick as a mountain to keep him safe. He didn't know half of what I did because she threatened you both."

"You could have called me. I would have come," he whispered. Dathon seemed so defeated. It was before Dathon gave Justin the ability to teleport to or from my father. He traced the pale curved scars on my palms. This was not the only place I clawed when I had to pretend to be normal. There was a reason I wore dresses with long sleeves more after I got home. Dathon kissed my palms as if I was a hurt child. That brought tears. He wanted to heal me, and he couldn't.

"Every night I had to force myself to not call for you in case she really hurt you. What was I supposed to do? Withdraw away from you to protect you both or have her follow through with the threat? She had made good on every other threat, she made me to that point. After, when people asked why I feared her, they brushed everything I said away as if I was lying."

I held my knees. "I remember that first week at home. I wouldn't sleep in my bed. It all seemed so unreal. When I got some sleep, it was like I was back there. One afternoon I had fallen asleep under my window in the sunlight. There was a meteor shower watching party that night Justin wanted to take me to. He was so excited he came into my room and found me on the floor. When I saw his face, I started screaming. I thought I was back in The Pit. I thought she wanted me to kill him. Either that or she had disguised one of her lovers as Justin again so he could hurt me for falling asleep. I couldn't tell what was real. Nothing he said could calm me. Not even with the *Bond* fully flaring for the first time in years."

"Goddess Lys, I hadn't realized how much I had failed you. I was a fool to not see it. I'm sorry. You were given to me to protect, and I left you with her. My goddess will never forgive me." I started crying. I couldn't stop. All I did to save them the pain and Dathon found another I hadn't even considered. Failing his Goddess. What was Justin feeling after Roseden's confession? The mountain was back, so he seemed so far away. Was this why he was being weird? Probably.

Dathon pulled something out from under the bench. I still don't know how he finds anything in this mess of an office. Guess it is time to file stuff away again. "Now that the worst is over, we can get her to trial. If my team and I have done our job, she will go to jail for a long time. You are stronger than anyone gives you credit for. My hurt, big-hearted daughter. Braver than I ever understood." On my lap, he placed a red leather journal and a letter with my name on it. I felt my brother's elemental magic. Hallon? "Lizzy brought it from the archives a month ago." Lizzy? "Before you ask, yes, he knew she was coming. He was happy to see her, but he knew of the plan." I groaned. "Happy birthday."

Seriously, could I keep anything from them?

Not the dark truth.

Not the joyful surprises.

My forehead hit the cover. It seemed like forever since I felt that cool tingle my brother's magic on my skin. Feeling

Hallon's magic was a slight comfort. One I needed right now. "So much for his birthday gift."

"Lys, you showed up dressed as an Aldaina commander on her wedding day. It nearly shocked him to death. 'Never thought I would see her wear that. My Little Witch is a wonder to behold.' He was beside himself with joy when you stood next to him for the Oath." I smiled. Still didn't remember that. Hopeless. We were both just so hopeless. "I had never seen him fight so hard not to rush to you after you moved out to the balcony. His job was to take the oaths of the crown. Forcing himself to be content with just having you in the room.

"I was pulled away for a moment and when I returned, Justin and Colin were arguing. Lizzy joined them. I have never seen him so miserable at staying with the others when Colin told him to run after you because you were leaving without saying goodbye. Lizzy told us more about the prophecy. His job meant nothing if you would not be at his side. His life seemed to boil down to his need to keep you near. I tried to stop him to find out what was going on. I was surprised to see him in tears."

I promised Adriana to protect him. "All he asked was if I knew you were leaving. When I said no, I saw all his sanity leave him. You hadn't even told me. He tells me everything. I think he thought you did too, however it was just like with Adriana and what Roseden did to you. He couldn't contain his fear, his loss. His world was vanishing with you. 'She is my everything, yet she constantly protects me. Lys is probably doing it now. How can I live with myself when she is gone?' He said before he started running." I tossed the file to the side table by the window.

"I wished on shooting stars to keep you two safe. When he caught up to me, I said goodbye to him. I knew once I got settled in the Grand City, I would tell you where I was. I would have told you the truth. The full truth. About Roseden. About Adriana's promise. About the prophecy, *The Destiny* told Adriana and me. I only told him part of the truth. Not about his mother or about what it felt like to be told that because my mother failed, I had to die. Then he told me about the party's true purpose. I failed to follow through with my own plan."

"Oh."

"A freaking wedding, Dad." I stood up, pacing. So angry at myself, I could feel the Fury coming to the surface. "A freaking, goddess-damn wedding that I wasn't mentally there for. As angry as I had been at not to piece it together, I'm overjoyed finally wearing this ring legitimately. I gave him his dream of a bride in green and silver. I gave him a chest of my mother's gold. Yet I hadn't been paying attention when I swore wedding vows to him. Then I left the moment he pissed me off by asking to see my scars. He just wanted to see the real me on our wedding day and I snapped." The candles flared. "How did we not see it while we were setting it up?" Looking at my hands, I felt the sparks. Which only made me pull farther in. My nails clawing into my arms this time.

Dathon stopped me to rub my shoulders. The magic relaxed. Either through him calming me or some magical suppression. "I never would have seen that as a wedding, but I guess that was the point. You have been against the wedding since before we lost her." Is that what they really thought? "You were becoming so distant."

"Dad, had he asked me while I was covered in their blood I would have said yes." He groaned. "Even with the prophecy

66

hanging over my head. Knowing I was going to never see him again, I would have said yes just because he had fought his way back through the castle to find me. I needed him at my side. I needed him to stand at my side as I killed Justice. Suddenly through the tears he was there, sword in hand, covered in as much blood as I was, saying my name. I was so tired. So scared to lose him, too. At that very moment, I would have said yes."

"Now?" I wanted to smile. Too late now, I'm wearing his mother's ring. Now was no time to think about what could have been. Now was time to find a way around a prophecy of a divine chosen.

"I have to find his soul before Tabari returns. I refuse to kill Justin as I did Justice. Now comes the time where I fight for what I want. I can't let fear take me. That is one reason I came to talk to you. I have a theory that Adriana has a spell of protection on this castle against Death Knights or against Tabari himself." Dathon frowned. "Justice is the only king in three hundred years who smiled. Not even my parents smiled in their coronation painting. When I killed Justice, Tabari could have easily taken Justin, but he was already in the castle. Justin has not been far enough from the castle or the town to be noticed by him. Justin should have been taken ages ago. Tabari threatened me with taking Justin's body so he could continue the line. He didn't need the rings." I held up my ring hand.

"So why hasn't he done so?"

"Exactly. The painting in the gallery Justice is smiling in his coronation painting."

"Interesting. I never noticed that." Of course not, Dathon only looks at Adriana. "He could have taken Justin when you attacked him and were *Soul Bound*."

"At six? I didn't want to think about him taking Justin that early. Thanks."

"So, you are thinking it is in the castle?"

"Yeah. If it isn't something like Aldaina magic, can you make something smaller to place on his person? Something that will always…" I reached for the dagger. It was hers. She gave it to us before I killed Justice. She handed it to me as she died. Adriana always made sure it was on one of us.

"Lys?"

"The dagger." Dathon took the weapon from me. "After I attacked Justice the first time, Adriana gave him the dagger. As teens, Justin and I would swap it back and forth. We were never very far away from each other. He had it when I was in The Pit."

"Who said you were not magic smart?" Everyone at the mage school Dathon tried to send me to. I still don't even know why he tried. I didn't like my magic back then. Even more than I do now. "Now, if we can get you to write this stuff down."

"Screw that," I said playfully, insulted. "I'm wishing for a magic solution, so I don't have to kill Justin or be the whore of my uncle." We sat in silence for the next two hours as Dathon prepared for the trial. I read an Aldaina book. Written by my brother. Hallon's grown up mind was more blunt and to the point. More like Dathon when he was at trial.

CHAPTER SIX

There was a knock. "Dathon, have you seen your daughter?" Dathon pointed to the window seat. I yawned, having moved on to Hallon's diary. Half asleep. It certainly is not thrilling to read bullet point events I had missed. One line caught me.

I thought I finally won her good graces again. Turns out, I drove her farther away. After Lyssie was gone, she was never the same. She claimed she saw her daughter all grown up at that inn.

This was not in my brother's hand. Written in the margins about an incident at a temple between my brother's wife and my mom that resulted in Mom's death. What inn did she think she saw me at?

"Hello, Little Witch, we are going to be late." Justin whispered. Late? I shut down the *Bond* a couple of hours ago. That used to be a sign not to talk to me. Why wasn't he heeding it now? "My queen needs to meet the High Queen." Did I really though? I no longer needed a place to live. I'm staying here. To save him. To save all of them. Hope is supposed to be stronger than fear, but right now, fear is winning.

"You know we can't be together." Reading all my mother's failures leading to her death made me fear the prophecy. I would die following in her footsteps. Considering the way Hallon wrote it, I would have made the same mistakes. Including letting Hallon's wife into the inner circle when they knew she was a Death Knight's *Bonded*. I had just said I couldn't let fear win. I was failing. "You need a queen who will aid you in healing the rifts between mages, elves and non-magic beings," I said, running my finger along the sentence. "If I'm not here forever. You need to find a *Life Love*."

He sighed, shaking his head. "Years forcing yourself to be someone else has made you forget what Mom saw in you." Gently, he pulled me to my feet, frowning when he saw the book. "Come on, Tabytha waits for no one." His arms locked around me. Our *Bond* hummed happily. No matter how much my mind wanted me to pull away, we both felt right where we wanted to be. "Did you need anything?"

"No."

"Take this." Dathon gave me a billfold and his - our Seabrooke crest. "Message me when you want to come back." Come back? Yeah, I would have to, now. Face one of my enemies, protect the people I love, and pray the legal system would take Roseden out of the equation.

"Lizzy and Wren can handle things for a few days."

"The trial is tomorrow." Justin grumbled to himself.

One day will not destroy everything. I narrowed my eyes. What was there to destroy?

"Lys has agreed to testify."

"No!" He pushed away. Eyes wide with worry. "Reliving for the defense over and over-" I smiled.

Don't worry about me.

"Don't worry she says." Justin snorted. Dathon patted the man on his shoulder. "After that first time, watching you cower as Roseden passed you. You have never cowered to anyone, yet you hid from her. Hearing you scream from nightmares. Feel the self hatred. I'm allowed to be worried. She -That was not my Lys." My glamor tingled across my skin, but the look in Justin's eyes made me stop hiding. "I couldn't stop it and Evana couldn't find the hell hole she took you to. It's just another time I failed to be what you needed. Even if she stabbed me a few times. I'm allowed to worry. Tomorrow is going to bring back that Lysandra."

Dathon's coffee mug pounded his desk. Had he seen me move to hurt myself again? If he did, I didn't do it consciously. "Lys, protected us all." Dathon then kissed my forehead. "Take this book. You both should read it." Then suddenly we were standing outside the High Queen's Light Crystal Palace.

Why did you want to come? I asked. *You and Tabytha have never gotten along.* Justin took my left hand, kissing it. There was still blood along my nails. *Are you making this our honeymoon?*

He laughed. "As if you were ready for that." That is what he wanted this week to be, but he had other plans. "I have years of dates to catch up on. What better place than Lysandria? A city named after her brave little warrior, the woman I love. My Little Witch." I shook my head. "Come on."

I remembered this version of Justin, from back before Adriana's death, Happy with the world, no royal matters resting on his shoulders. Just a boy in love with a girl who now barely gave him the time of day. His eyes sparkled, thinking about all the things he thought I would enjoy. I remember wanting to enjoy them. Not allowing myself. Trying not to fall in love with the boy who made me forget everything.

"Justin, don't leave my side." That genuine smile. Those blue eyes, shining so brightly. I know he was thinking I was accepting our marriage, our new life, accepting him. If it wasn't for the mountain I kept between us, he would see I was circling the thought of Tabari and Adriana's charm. I didn't know what the charm was, so it was just better for him to be in line of sight.

My mother failed to destroy Tabari. What the hell hope did I have? I am less trained. Twice her size. Slower than I remember her. So much less prepared. My only hope, keeping Justin near me. How far was the range on the dagger? Was it even the dagger? Did I have enough power to fight off whatever body Tabari had now? What would I do if I lost him? "I'm not sure what is keeping you safe from Tabari. I don't want to press our luck." His face fell. It broke my heart.

Justin was dressed to impress. He was trying to make today special. Black slacks, his black suede coat over the blue silk shirt that taunted me. Shortly after Adriana had died, we had been in the training ring when I ripped his shirt, flipping him. That night, I stole into his room to grab it. It was my first and last sewing job I ever did. The sleeve had an odd ruffle at the shoulder seam and the buttons no longer matched up with the holes. I hate that shirt, but he loves it even more.

Justin held his right hand out to me. No words. No big emotions. Just his hand. I can take it. Holding hands was such a little thing in the grand design. We were married. He could ask for so much more. He should be. I still hesitated. I could feel him begging for me to take his hand. If I took it, there would be a world of pain and loneliness in-store for him. If I just walked away, it would be less. Less. Could I walk away from his smile? Knowing he cried thinking about me leaving him? What happiness could I give him? Could I even walk towards my death in a year? Would Tabari be the reason I finally left him?

It was just Justin's hand.

So I took it.

Goddess, I thought I caused him pain when I saw his eyes fill. He gasped. I tried to pull my hand away, but he tightened on mine. "I never thought you would be so quick to take my hand again." That was quick? He rubbed his sleeve over his eyes. I just scared him. "I'm not scared. I am happy. Ecstatic. Overwhelmed with joy." His free hand touched my unscarred cheek. "I had forgotten that smile."

I smiled?

"A genuine smile."

I looked away, closing my eyes to let the glamor take hold.

"No, leave them. I love them."

"I don't."

Justin needed a beautiful woman to rule next to him. He deserved the perfect wife. Justin is the storybook love interest. Justin deserved the beautiful damsel in distress. Anyone but the scarred, scared, battle-sick, insomniac before him. He pulled me in and wrapped my arm around his. "Never going to happen." I frowned. "Those *sour candied flowers* could never be you." His hand fell to my hips. "I love your scars. Not because they mar your otherwise shining face, but because when you let me see them, you let me see the real you. It is an honor. A gift I would like to have for the rest of my life."

"Why are you like this?" He kissed my eyes. "Maybe we are both twisted."

"Maybe. I think we are two sides of the same coin." We were moving towards the city, away from the palace.

"I try to show all my emotions because you can never show yours. Which is your way to show love."

I groaned. Not showing I loved him meant I loved him? What logic is this?

"That and at the edge of your blade."

That I laughed at.

His heart fluttered. "I want to hear more of that over the next week. I want you to feel free before we go back home."

"Well then, fly me away to our first stop, my Soulless Prince." Goddesses, having my wall down could kill me. Justin wanted to kiss me, hold me, make love to me, run us away into the city, to never be seen again, fly us back to his castle and announce to the entire world I was his *Bonded* wife. Had he always wanted these things?

Had I once upon a time?

Could I want them again?

We had just under a year to see how much we could break each other's hearts.

Justin didn't want me to think like that. I needed to think positively for a change. I took a deep breath and closed my eyes—letting it go as I opened my eyes again and locked gazes with him.

Positive. "For now, just court me, Justin. Just let us be two young people. I need to remember how to love you." I had a year to live in freedom. I would make the best of it with the man I had forgotten how to love.

"Well, our first stop will be the hotel. I refuse to be seen with you while you are dressed like this." Shocked, I gazed down at my forest green satin and black lace gown. It was high-waisted, slim fitting, with slightly puffy sleeves. Short-sleeved for summer.

Too ravishing. I will want to just take it off you. Every man in town will want you. Every woman will hate you.

I glared at him. No. No other man would want me, as Justin does. I am hardly the ideal size, mental stability, or emotionally free. Never mind, I don't follow social norms. Technically, I am also five hundred years old.

"Maybe I enjoy dressing like a girl once in a while." He groaned. It was not out of exasperation either. Did Justin want me to dress like a real girl more often? Watching him, his face went from wide-eyed shock to a tight frown to a smirk. Through the *Bond*, he hid the thoughts that went with the faces. "Besides, I know this is your favorite gown of mine." I teased. On our birthday, ten years ago now, I wore it to supper with Adriana and Justin. Dathon had to turn to see why Justin dropped his glass. His all-black attire hid the wine stains, yet he didn't seem to care. His eyes were only on me. Evana had helped pick out the style and fabric. It was the fastest sewing job my elf has ever done.

"Oh, it is. I want to take it off you and put you in something better for the High Queen. You should look every ounce the powerful knight you are." The city bells went off at that very moment. Seven. Eight. Nine. Ten. We only had an hour to get changed, get back to security and be fully prepared for the High Queen.

"A week?"

"At least. Depends on the trial. Our vacation could be longer if the trial spans days. I have a list of things to do with you."

"Of course you do." I smiled, motioning him forward. "You could spread them out, you know? We could spend weeks dating. We are married now."

"Lys, in a month we are going to have a lot of work to do. It's the Summer Solstice. Tabari, then the Summit." I had to go to the annual trade summit? I'm not a diplomat. Why the hell did I have to go to that? That was for Justin and his ambassadors. Not me. "You won't take kindly to politics. That is what I am counting on this year." Justin explained. I sighed. He is using me as his impatient warrior queen to speed through talks. He better get me something to put me through this torture. "I'm not letting you out of my sight until the day I have to bury you." There was something so intense and encompassing. I liked it. "Even then, I'm going to find the loopholes in that damn prophecy, so I will keep you even longer."

Our hotel was on the Queen's Road, a marvelous red and white brick, three story building. Blue black slate roof tiles hung over balconies on the topmost floor. What the view would be from there. Justin didn't stop at the check-in desk, he just pulled me up two flights of stairs before I was winded.

"I'm sorry." For the last flight, he held me standing. Up to the door. "Evana said you took the brunt of the damage. That you magicked your body to take that cut, the pain and blood loss."

"Your mother would come back just to kill me." I rubbed my ribs. "Didn't help, all the girl shit was happening at the same time. Probably the reason I was so angry." I felt his hand tightening on my hip. I was sure he could feel the tape from the bandage under the satin. "I just need to get back to training next week and I will be right as rain."

He didn't seem convinced. "I will endeavor to keep that in mind, but if I get to be-"

I placed a hand on his chest. "Don't worry, Justin, I will endeavor to let you know more about how I'm feeling."

He smiled sadly as he opened the door. "I decided last night I would try for us. That I would let myself let you see what I am now, that I would let you see what she did to me, let you get close."

"I won't be too close. My room is right next door."

Seriously? Separate rooms too. He was really taking this date week to the limits. He clawed at his insides to touch me more. As if I was some drug he couldn't get enough of. Yet he held himself back. It was all for me.

"I'm guessing I have clothes in here." He nodded. "What should I wear?"

Nothing.

By the step back, I knew he didn't mean to think that. "We are meeting the descendant of one of my brothers. I don't think naked is going to be appropriate." I teased back.

"If you wore nothing, you could still outshine her any day of the week."

All I could do was roll my eyes. "You really are hopeless, Justin." I entered my room. He didn't move. He just stood there watching me struggle with the dress. "Well, come pick stuff out. It's going to take me forever to get out of this dress."

He said nothing. All I felt was self-loathing, Mine and his.

"Come on, did you really think that even in my Fury Form I would really let Adriana's son die?"

"Is that all I am to you now?"

I froze. This was a serious question. What did I really think about him?

"We were friends once. Before Mom, we were even in love. I was never just my mother's son to you then."

True, and that was used to cause us pain. We almost died because we loved each other.

"Since then, Roseden has destroyed the girl who loved you." That was my honest answer. "I was no longer that girl we saw so deeply in love. Roseden broke that girl. The new me has been hard won in lonely battles." It would have been easier to walk away before Roseden drugged him. I was so distant. A mountain stood between us. A mountain to keep him from seeing all I did as the monster. "I'm not even sure if the new me can love. She taught me love could kill me and those I loved. It is better to not love at all. You stay alive longer."

"Is that really living?" Justin just walked to the wardrobe, pulled out one half gown with leggings and boots. Green-silver like Daina's moon. High-waisted black coat over a corset style top. Matching black leggings and tall black boots. He laid it on the bed. More embroidery than my wedding gown. "Functional and still the girlish style, I think you might like," he said flatly.

"Did you design a complete wardrobe for me?" I laughed.

"Yes." Justin was so serious. He was walking to the balcony. "No one you have ever met has understood because you were just a female to them. I know you better than that."

I snorted. "Do you? Do you really?" The problem with my green dress was I couldn't get in or out without help. Lifting my arms that high caused me to gasp. Pulling the zipper required me to bend over and use gravity as my aid. Which just that morning had me almost face first into my bedroom wall.

"I do."

I heard the zipper, then felt the button release.

"I have spent years trying to study you, Lys."

I didn't miss that he was suddenly kissing the freckle on my left shoulder.

"Every curve and imperfection makes you perfect in my eyes. Every new broken, jagged, obsidian edge."

I reached up to touch his hair. *Bond,* lively as ever.

"I have never stopped caring for you. Not when I found you in his blood. Not the day Dathon brought you home, covered in layers of blood and filth. Not when I found you curled up in your room, screaming when you saw me. Not the day you drew your - our dagger on me in the pub. In fact, that made me love you more."

That I frowned at. I wanted to end his and *Hallon's* rivalry.

"The woman I loved and best friend wanted to challenge me for the championship. You were always better than me, but it was flattering you thought of me as a challenge."

I let the dress fall. Every word in his bedroom, whispered voice sent shivers throughout my body.

"If you really have forgotten how to love me, then we will take this even slower."

After that declaration, he wanted to go even slower?

"That is just the *Bond* talking."

Could be. That didn't stop me from reaching for him. Justin shook his head.

"Finish getting dressed. If you need help, just call."

So I got dressed. Alone. Record timing. Even with the three layers. We had very little time left.

CHAPTER SEVEN

At the main door where I met Justin, three women looked up at me. They could be sisters. All sunshine hair, black blue eyes, and the same height. From the stairs, I couldn't really tell if I was taller, or they were. All three wore a Seabrooke green with a black so deep I thought it would swallow Justin whole. The dresses seemed to be a uniform. Who were they?

"Nope, I was wrong," he said, smiling his sad smile, he motioned for the ladies to move towards a back room.

He then joined me.

"What were you wrong about?"

He just took my arm to escort me into the room.

"Do we have time for this?" I whispered, only to be seated at the head of the table. The arms of the chair were tight on my hips, though the cushion was soft. This was going to be torture. I had to remind myself to not stand up quickly. The chair would come with me—it was that tight. I think Justin saw that. He openly leaned on the chair.

"You understand that claiming you are *The Lysandra* will be taken seriously. Just not at court."

None of them looked anything like anyone in my family. So who were they? In front of me were two magic boxes that felt familiar. I knew the magic almost as if they were my own. "This is the test we give all claimants."

Claimants? What did Justin get me into this time?

"Excuse me, but I have been unwell. What am I doing here? Why is the thought of me some abstract thing? *The Lysandra*? I am not an ideal. I really do hate titles." The oldest woman groaned as if she'd heard that before. Justin didn't defend me. He simply moved to the other end of the table, took both boxes, and placed them in front of me. The wood was magically preserved. The same size. The only difference was the two branded crests.

The family crest, a babbling brook with snowdrops flowers. The other Dathon's order of Mage Knights. A river leading to an ocean surrounded by trees. Hallon's magic came off the Mage Knight box. The other was different. Where Hallon and I were winds, cool or warm, depending on the emotions, the other was all cold to the touch. Not as cold as a Death Knight, but close. I reached for them before I thought about it. First to the cold one.

Tendrils met my hand, pulling it to the crest. A sharp needle of pain seemed to make them tighten. "Whoever you belong to will hear from me if you don't let go of me." I was standing now. Justin held the chair down as I got out of it. Though that was the farthest thing from my mind. I had just wanted to look at the box before it feasted off my magic.

"I will draw it and scare your ladies." My fingertips started turning blue from the invisible tendrils of magic. Justin did nothing at my side. Though I noticed his hand wasn't changing colors. It was feasting on my magic rather than the *bond*. In my left hand, I summoned Adriana's dagger. "Want to try me? I will skewer you." The first box opened. The lid popping off into my hand inches above it. "Good boy."

What the hell was that? I have never seen magic like that. I didn't look at Justin because I didn't want my great nieces to see we didn't know what the hell was going on.

The dagger lay on the table as I opened the second box easily. No pin pricks. No icy, famished tentacle. As if Hallon trusted, it would be my magic to open the box. Hallon's well practiced hand was his name on a tome no bigger than a novel. I couldn't stand anymore, so I fell back to where I thought the chair was. Justin caught me. In the other, on a bed of cotton, my little Soulless Prince and The Mother of Deities. They were our favorite items before the attack. My dolls and Hallon's first magic book. My eyes could not focus. I heard a quiet whimper. Then I saw Justin pick up the boy doll. "Even has my eyes. The painting was black. These even have my highlights."

I gasped, yanked the doll from him, and slammed it back into the box. We - he had to leave. I took his arm walking towards the door.

"Lys?" Sudden fear the two were not allowed at the same time filled my mind with lessons of time magic paradoxes. The theory that if two of the same persons were to meet, one of them would cease to be. That would be the living Justin. However, I am not sure why I felt that the toy version of him would cause a paradox. It was a toy. It could be used for voodoo.

There was something else in the air causing me to retreat. Something that reminded me of The Pit. A magic that shouldn't be. It was coming from the end with the triplets. My eyes shifted to my magic sight. They were smoking as if they were on fire. The boxes red of Hallon's magic and the forest green from the other seemed to battle the black smoke. "We are going home."

I moved back to the boxes as their lids popped off again. Holding the lid shut, I glared at the women. Smoke moving across the table congealing into tar. "No. No. No." I heard myself chant. This is the test. To open the boxes. They wanted to know if I could. They were not normal. I have only seen this one other time. In The Pit. Something Roseden gave the kids made them smoke like this.

"Lys?" I realized Justin was holding me.

"Seeing them makes the time jump real." As if that explained why I was petrified of the women at the other end of the table. "We don't need them." Justin turned to me to face him. All to protect him. The real Soulless Prince. I needed to get him out of this room.

"Out of this city." I was not ready for whatever they were. Guilt crossed his eyes. "I need my mother's training to kill him, but the goddess sent me here to you. I don't need toys and novice spells. I need to get you away from them," I said, pointing at the women.

Power blended, creating a magic dome around us. Justin thought it was me doing this. It really wasn't, but I would not miss this opportunity. "I'm so sorry, my love." The forest green magic impaled a tar bubble, causing it to boil to ash. The magic on the boxes was protecting us. My eyes locked again on the ladies as they pulled back their smoke.

Justin wanted to hold me, but held back. "They will never know what happened to me," I said, more to them than to

Justin. "They got to move on with their lives. Mom became High Queen, had another child. A child who became the God of Death." I fell forward on the table. "It's not fair." I am only human. I can't fight this many enemies. I am not trained. There are so many of them. How do I get us through this?

"Your loss made your mother fight for her crown. Drove Hallon to create the Mage Knights. You were the treasure Tabari took from them," Justin said. The middle woman smirked. Oh shit. Were they descendants of Tabari? The Knyghts had no surviving female children until Lizzy, but what if Tabari had his own *Bonded*?

"The treasure they gave to me to protect." How could he? He couldn't see the dangers. The doll was suddenly in my hands. "Just as you used to protect me." And I couldn't. There were too many monsters for me.

I don't know how long I was huddled on the floor shaking, holding my doll the whole time. Another bout of missing time. At one point, Justin sat in my chair. Me in another. My doll was in my lap. One arm gesture to the ladies as he spoke in his diplomatic voice. His other, holding my free hand. His hand was cool. I had to look at him to see he was alright. Why were we even still here?

Justin couldn't see the tar with his own eyes, but why didn't he see it through mine? His own blue magic floated around us. The lattice work of the bubble encompassing the boxes. Mixing blue and green. That told me he knew something was wrong. Below my hand, the arm of the chair was seared with my handprint. He thought I was losing control, so he was protecting the ladies? Their smoke now slapped at the dome while the tar tried to eat away at the framework. *NO!* Justin's mind screamed. Shocked, I looked up at him. His blue eyes had darkened, narrowed. I snapped to the ladies. The youngest was bright eyed. The oldest glared right back at us. The third looked between them in shock.

"She is the rightful heir. She passed the test. Lysandra needs to stay here. To take the throne. The Seabrooke magic is weakening. She is the closest we can get to Tulora herself to recharge the wards on the continent."

"So, you would trap her here for the rest of her life just for her blood?" Justin tensed, tightening his grip on me. The free hand now held fast to my knee. "That is not why we came. She is my *Bonded*. My Champion. My queen. If she ever forgives me, the mother of my children. She is not some battery for this machine."

They wanted to siphon from me to keep them in power? Oh, hell no!

"With respect, Your majesty, highnesses, Lysandra, will stay with me. The Laws of the Goddesses overrule your need for magic."

"She only has seventeen months left. Not even you get her forever."

How did they know? Had I said it? Had Justin? How did they know? This refreshed my waning fear.

"Yeah, well, I'm damn well not going to let her spend the last of her life locked in another castle fueling some messed up magic. That is our last word." His grip eased. He kissed my hair. "I promised you courting. It's your birthday. I am not-" His eyes were dark again. "Not sending you to another prison." Another Pit? He was trying to keep me safe. Blue green dome, still protecting us.

I had to trust Justin. I was missing time. I was scared. I needed a grown up to decide for me since I couldn't see a path out. "Okay." My voice broke.

"Okay?" They all asked. Each one with an unfamiliar emotion behind it. I just turned to face the ladies. His hands no longer held me. Both sat on arm rests. I needed his strength. His confidence. So I lace my fingers through his left hand.

"What do you mean 'okay'? Isn't this your decision?"

"I came to this age not of my own free will. I was simply a child in pain. Tabari tried to kill me."

The oldest smirked.

"It was Justin who saved me. *Blood bonding* us." The Mage Knight box shifted. "We were *bonded*. Again, not of our free will. The next time Tabari," The box knocked over its lid. "entered our life, he took Justin's mother and my freedom. In beheading King Justice, I became queen of Stowera by battle. Again, Justin saved me from my grave decisions. I knew it was a temporary solution. That he was trying to protect me."

"Tabari," This time the box almost came off the table. Justin moved our laced hands to push it back. "is still out there. Now that we are married, he will return. No, she can't be trapped in her mother's crystal palace. We have to go wherever we can to finish our training. I had hoped to do research here. Research, we need to destroy Tabari before he returns." Again. This time, I frowned at the box. It was moving any time we talked about the Death Knight.

Justin kissed the back of my neck.

"One question, if I am permitted?" The youngest asked.

I said nothing. I could only watch her smirk grow with her smoke. Tar bubbles, getting larger. She saw my fear. She knew I could see their powers.

"Who is Tabari?"

Maybe I was just tired. Maybe it was a really dumb question. I laughed. Whole-heartedly laughed. Justin also chuckled.

"Sorry ladies," he said. His hand was now covering my hands and doll. "He has been a thorn in our side for so long. We forget he is not everyone's problem." Tabari would never be their problem. The youngest was enjoying my fear of him. Almost as if she was feasting off it. This was all too easy for them. Three against one. Use this test to weaken me. Suck the fear off of me when I realize what they were, then strike when I couldn't take the mental attacks. It was too early for me to die.

My left hand reached for the dagger. Adriana's cyan magic erupted to add another layer to Justin's bubble. I had never seen this from her. Runes, I have only seen my mother write in the dirt around our house, were now around us in cyan. Adriana was using my mother's own rituals. The runes created bands to join mine and Justin's powers, weaving through strengthening the dome. The boost in energies caused Justin to stiffen. Would this be what made him finally want to leave?

"Add to that my history. It's so fresh in my memory, I sometimes forget it has been three and a half centuries for the rest of the world." I smiled. I know how to protect Justin. I have a clue about my mother's lost magic. These three will never get either of us now. "So here is what I know. You all think you did a great job. That the creation of this test would make me fall to you. My mother taught me to see through the lies of Death Knight and their spawn. You will not eat me today or ever." Justin's hands clenched mine. The runes lit with my mother's green magic. The love of our mothers was a magic more powerful than Tabari's.

"Mom was scared. All the time. She taught us to be paranoid. Neither Hallon nor I were to step out of the house on market days. Festivals had a ritual around it. Mom spent days creating the dye we would use to cover our red. Just as she had done her whole life to protect herself from Tabari. The day I met my father," The box moved again. "Tabari held my father up as he tore out his eye. Being five, we tried to help but were thrown into a bookshelf."

Standing up, Justin assisted with removing my jacket. The cyan bands continue to spin with our magic. That means it is a trigger. I wonder if it was the show of bravery, I suddenly found myself gripped in. Justin and Dathon were the only ones to see my full body. Evana has seen my right arm. Yet this was the first time I had ever heard someone gasp at the sight. Even if they were spawns of my enemy. "I survived Tabari. I can survive you."

"We were taken from her. She failed to protect us. She failed to protect my father. She already held guilt over the dismemberment of *Destiny*. She never told us what he was. Just of his kind. In that she failed too. For me, it was a mere two years after he attacked our home that he tried to eat Princess Elizabeth's soul. My mother failed to teach me how to defeat him. To give the Death Knight his last death."

"Tabari will not fall to the likes of you." Hallon's book shifted in the box. It really needed to be free. Odd thing since it was never alive when we were little.

"Tabari is a Death Knight, sure, but also Tulora's brother. That means he can be killed, too." Again with the jumping. This time noticeably by more than just Justin and me.

"How can you be sure?" Goddess, they would not let us leave. "Tabari was the Red Eyes of prophecy." The book leaped from the box. Landing in my hands. Justin caught my doll as the book opened.

"Finally found you, sister." Hallon stood next to me. A full head taller than me. He was transparent. The room suddenly had no air. *"I didn't think Hadain's plan would work. He will never let me forget this."*

I snickered. "It's good that someone keeps my nerd in check. It's good to see you."

He grinned back. *"Likewise. I would love to chat, but I am not powerful in time magic. I need to make this quick. When are you?"*

"Five hundred years after our birth by the old calendar." He nodded. "Tabari is more powerful now."

"Wonderful." My brother groaned. *"So, did you find your Soulless Prince?"* Justin handed me the doll. *"If you find a way, Mom and Dad very much would like to meet him."*

"Hallon, you know Auntie said Mom never would." Wood slid against stone. "That doesn't matter. I should introduce you to your *descendants*." I motioned to the ladies suddenly huddled in a corner. Tar forming a wall around them. They feared Hallon. "This is the High Queen Tabytha and her family."

I watched as my brother went from happy to furious to scheming. *"Descendants of our family, but no daughters of mine or Hadain's. They are Cassia's Spawn. Which means they are really Tabari's Demon Spawn."*

"Dathon!" Justin shouted, taking hold of me. "We can talk later," he said to Hallon.

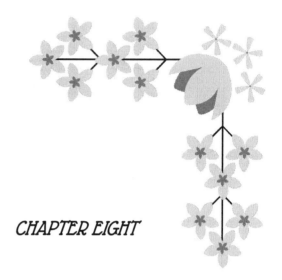

CHAPTER EIGHT

Suddenly we were in Dathon's workshop at the house. The book and dolls, still in my hands. "What happened?" Dathon asked, checking me over. I looked up at Justin. What happened? One minute we were talking to Hallon. The next Justin's mind rushed. To get us safe. We were, though. We were in Adriana's bubble.

Justin collapsed into a chair. "We were wrong. They didn't want Lys for peaceful reasons. They wanted her to power the magic. They're not Hallon's descendants." I handed Hallon's book to Dathon. Our red magic whirled around the room. Glass shattered. Papers fluttered around. Justin pulled me closer to him. "Dathon?"

"That is right." Hallon. He was back explaining everything. About time someone did. I do not know what is going on. This time not transparent. *"Cassia is Tabari's Bonded. The mother of his children and my wife."*

The way my brother and my father looked at each other made me feel out of the loop. There was something there. *"Are you* Her Bonded?*"*

"Yes." Dathon showed nothing. I couldn't imagine that in the whole time I have been with him, Dathon wouldn't be curious about my brother. There it was. They got to meet and there was aggression.

"Never leave his side, Lys." Hallon was motioning to Dathon. I blinked. What did my twin know I didn't?

Apparently, a lot.

"My soul is asleep in his mind." Hallon had been with me the whole time. *"The Soulless one said your name is Dathon?"* Dathon said nothing. *"Sounds about right."* Hallon turned back to me. *"Now to Tabari. Keep those blue spells. You will need them."* Hallon flickered. I reached for him. *"I am running out of power on this end. I don't sense a lot of my brand of magic in your time."* Someone knew magic like Hallon? *"To keep Cassia away from you, I hid my current book at the house. Get the key from grandfather's tower. In the meantime, look for the Death Palace. You will get your Soulless Prince a soul. Hadain and I hid it when we found it."*

"WHAT!" More glass shattered around me. "You are telling me I didn't have to come here? Justin's soul was in our real time!" My brother flickered. "Years of torture, of pain, of lying to everyone and I could have just gotten his soul with you beside me?"

"By now, you know Mom wasn't perfect. Heaven only knows what they say about us. We did everything we could to help you. You still can get his soul. You will still have access to me. I slumber in our patron's bonded.*"* I felt our magic fade. He was gone. Dathon scowled. I spun on him. His hand rose to

91

stop me. It didn't stop me from glaring at him as if I could kill him with a look.

"I was rather hoping that wasn't the case. My father hates you." More beakers broke. "Lysandra." He groaned at me.

"No, don't you dare. You lied to me, or did you not know my brother lay dormant inside you?" I waved my hand and all the remaining paper floating in the air slammed to the far wall. "You knew I wanted Hallon after I first got here. That I was alone without my brother. You could have called him to comfort me."

"I wasn't allowed to tell you. Laws of Deities." Dathon looked to Justin, who was trying to remain neutral by staring at the tiny toy version of himself. Moving its arm as if it would move Justin's arm. It wasn't a magic doll. It was my training doll. The doll that would remind me I wasn't alone.

"Bullshit." I walked to the door.

"Wait for me," Justin said, clambering after me. "Where are we going?"

"I don't know." Looking into his eyes, he was happy. Just happy to be in my orbit. "There is so much new information."

"Yeah, the High Queen, her mother and grandmother-"

"That is who they were. None of them looked old enough. They were not normal, Dad. part Death Knight. Something Roseden made me fight." Justin pulled me to where he sat. Holding my hips in a tight embrace.

That scared you. I am sorry, my love, I can't see what you can. I bent to kiss his head. Maybe when we get his soul, he can see things this way.

"Adriana's spell saved us." Justin's arms got tighter while Dathon seemed to relax. "They are not allies. Hallon said to search out the Death Palace. I don't even know what that is. Plus, he said the house."

"Your grandfather's tower?"

"Crystal Keep? No, Tulora's cabin." Justin offered. I nodded. Sounded right. "The house has a protection on it. No one can enter it. We went there for a school history lesson." And I fought our history teacher tooth and nail because he told her story wrong. "The one Lys nearly killed the guest teacher. Alun claimed to be an expert. He was an expert in pissing off Tulora's daughter on her home turf."

That was supposed to be an exciting trip. I was going home to Haven. The first time in three years of being in this time. Justin and Colin flanked me as our class stepped closer to the house. Colin put out our cushions as Justin organized our notebooks. I just walked towards my home. Mom's green magic swirling around the burnt husk. Then Lord Alum started talking about my life growing up in Haven. I was frowning the whole time. Justin was trying to keep me calm. Then Lord Alun said my mother was the whore of the town. Not the mayor.

Oh, I snapped.

The more he insulted Mom, the more my magic took over. The final straw was when he said Mom made a deal with Tabari to kill her children.

A wind sphere knocked the asshole into the barrier around the house. I would not let him lie about my mother. Not one second longer. I remember asking him how he could ever think that my mother, who wrote the Laws of *Bonding*, would sleep around? Why would she team up with the man who spent their whole lives to see her dead? Her paranoia any time someone new came into Haven? If he knew her fear when my uncle tore, my father's eye from his head? If he knew the panic in her eyes as her twins were burning to death? Knew she screamed when my uncle tore out Aunt *Destiny's* heart while she cast the spell that saved me and my brother?

With every question, a different element flew at him. In the end, it was Adriana who calmed my anger. All she had to do was tell me to stop. I fell to my knees, crying. Justin just held me as I fell. Mom was none of what that man said. She loved Haven. She loved us. Uncle Christoph and Aunt *Destiny* were her sounding boards when she felt she couldn't keep us safe anymore. That is what I got from my mom. The fear of failure that would lead to the death of our loved ones. She had *Destiny*. I don't. I can't stay ahead of Tabari.

"Zaidon, has the key." Justin stood to hold me as the tears threatened. Until this moment I hadn't realized I was following in my mother's ill planned path. "Your brother has given us some clues to follow. You know Mom's spell to keep me out of Tabari's hands. Let's go to Haven, and see what your family left you."

"Feel like a little midnight heist, Majesty?" I joked. I was trying so hard not to let that pain take hold.

"You know there are easier ways to do things?" He groaned. His hand massaged his forehead as I giggled.

"I could just get it." Dathon offered. My father went to get his broom. I did a number in his lab. Only the fourth time I have ever blown up here. I have been much better than that at keeping my magic back.

"Why not be the monster Zaidon thinks I am?" I gazed down at my hands. My magic calm now, but the panic was rising. Justin sighed, taking my hands in his. His forehead on mine. "You distract him. Moon and I will go to the balcony. Slip in, find it and return what is mine."

"I could just ask him?" Dathon repeated while sweeping up the shards of glass.

"Where is the fun in that?"

"My queen, a common criminal."

I laughed. Justin's arms came around my waist. Dathon chuckled to himself, pushing us out the back door so he could clean my mess. I needed to replace those beakers. Mari Gath should be able to order them. I will have to see what needs replacing. Or faster, just buy a full lab's worth. "In the meantime, we have a date to continue."

"Wherever my King wishes to go, I shall follow." I curtsied.

"Your king wants to kiss that delicious smirk off your mouth."

I shook my head, laughing at him. Part of me wanted that; the other part feared that would be the trigger Tabari needed. A mutual kiss. Our *Bond* got all excited about him kissing me. "However, I need you to like me again, so we shall go for lunch at The Lucky Griffin."

"The first place we met." Isn't he the cutest? Maybe It was Adriana's family that made Justin and Colin cutely romantic. If you can call going back to the place of our first fight, romantic? "We're going to go in the alley and beat the crap out of some street thugs, too? I should change if that is the case." I teased. "I'm sure you have more armor for me. Show me." I pointed back at Knyght's Reach.

"You are making it so hard to stick to my plan with all this teasing. I can't tell if it is hiding your fear of us or legitimately wanting to drive me to consummate our marriage."

The smirk on his face fell. I don't know what he saw on my face. "Fear it is." One kiss on my forehead and we were walking out towards the street. "Quincy has been telling me he has had more than his share of adventurers come through lately." Subject change. Thank the goddess.

Adventurers? That is exciting. Adventuring would be fun. Quests for royals. Missions for nobles. Debts to collect for the less wealthy. Beasts to slay. What would I give to go be like the books say? "Really? Was there a quest announced at Crystal Keep?" I was the Arocana champion, Queen of Stowera. I'm sure a quest would be fine. Justin has been ruling by himself for years. A few extra months won't kill him. Right?

"Even if there was, we have the trial tomorrow. That is what we are going to do when we are not on dates." Justin put his hands on my hips, walking backwards. I giggled. "You are so damn everything." I blushed. I am far too old to be blushing. Especially because of my husband. "You know I'm in love with you, right?"

"I'm sorry. I can't say the same anymore." I was enjoying our time. Teasing him. Love? I don't know. I remember loving him. I remember feeling this giddy and happy. I remember blushing whenever he even touched me. I remember many things. Not knowing or caring if it was the *Bond* or that I really loved him. I hold on to that memory like a lifeline to the world I once knew. All the while, Justin threw me a lifesaver for our new life. If I let go of the past and couldn't get my future, would I drown? However, they are like a dream before the nightmares set in.

"When did you force yourself to give up on us?" That was the question. "When Mom died?" We had stopped moving. His hands held my ribs as if I could slip away any minute. That stupid, sad smile reached his sky-blue eyes. I waited for a moment before answering, just to see if they would start raining. Why was it so easy for me to hurt him?

"Before that. When *Destiny* told me, I would never know true happiness. That my death was a mere ten years away. We were still so young. Too young to get married. Even then, I didn't want you to have to live with knowing we were not destined for happiness in this life. She told me three different ways I was going to die! All while drinking tea. She was so calm. As if me dying three times was the norm. Adriana was pissed at her. I had never seen your Mom so angry, Justin. I guess the last time she was there, *Destiny* told her we were going to be married. It wasn't even why we were there."

"Mom wanted us to be happy. She had been talking about our wedding over lunch when we were attacked." My hands tightened on his biceps. "Right until she died."

"I know. She wanted me to look after you, Lizzy and Dathon. She made me promise to love you and keep you safe." He kissed my hand. "Sometimes I wish I had just let you consummate our bond before she died." Now I was crying. "Then I remember The Pit. That hell no person should know. Even second hand. It was bad enough that some slipped through. Roseden used my feelings for you against me. I am sure she didn't know about the prophecy."

"Had you called one of us, you wouldn't have been in there that long?"

"Maybe, but she would have taken more from me. She could have killed you. Knowing eventually she would have to give me back to Dad was enough. I fell into a routine. Only when I got too complacent, did she use you against me. She wanted the fire. She wanted me to use my pyromancy more and more. Her favorite way for me to kill. How sick is that?"

"My Little Witch." There has been so much pain. There will be more. Even if I ran away from him now. Would it really be so bad to have his love? I have to let myself dream. I want to be happy. I want to remember what it was like to have his love. "I don't want any promises. I just want you to be happy."

"I am." Even the playful smirk was unsure. "I swear I am. Teasing you is fun." He held in his laugh, making his chest shake. I pulled away to look up at him. "Neither of us laughs that easily anymore."

"Just another thing Roseden took from us." His three years were closer to five for me. Time seemed so fast now that we were together again. I was rushing towards something. I was told it was my death, but was it really?

The Lucky Griffin seemed so full. The Mad Queen right across the street had a lineup. The Blue Moon and Sunshine cafes were fulfilling takeout orders. I saw Layla's son running with a sack on his shoulders. A sign of a delivery. Were that many adventurers passing through? Why hadn't Justin been informed? Were the city guards prepared for this? Both of us were confused. Getting up to the bar, Quincy's eyes lit to see us. No one in Stowera called a quest. There was no war. Why were there so many mercs here?

"All hail the conquering Champion." I had not been into the pub since the tourney. "On the battlefield and in love, I see." I love Quincy, but his teasing us about our relationship always made me blush. He would just laugh. "What can I get my two favorite royals?"

"What do you want?" Justin asked.

"The usual." Quincy smiled knowingly. I had said it out of habit, but I had never been here as a girl. Justin started telling Quincy what he wanted when I felt a tug on my sleeve.

Two young ladies were behind us. One never meeting my eyes and one with crossed arms over her chest. Both were dressed in tunics, leather pants, and vest. All the clothing, ill fitting. Maybe a year or two younger than us. The bold one, full elf, sharp ears, ash gray hair and eyes. The other has the same facial features but half-blood. Less pointed ears. Like Evana's shorter ears. Black hair and eyes. "Lady Champion, can we and our party ask you some questions?" The sheepish one asked. I could barely hear her, so I moved closer.

My hand left Justin's and suddenly the world was louder. I heard the entertaining music over the chatter. When had Justin learned to block out the sound? How often did he use it? Was that why he was so touchy feely? I'm not as freaked out about crowds anymore. I was glad to get away from the bar. The three other girls sat in the corner closest to the door. Scared of something if they were trying to keep an escape open. All three looked like the sheepish girl. They were all sisters. The bold girl stood leaning on a corner, just watching. The sheepish one sat next to me. Around the same age. The full blood elf was certainly the oldest.

"Champion-"

I held a hand up. "My name is Lysandra. Please call me Lys. I don't do titles." All the girls relaxed. "I hear there are some questions?" I smiled. Two of the girls looked at the bold one. "Okay, how about telling me your names?"

"This is Lily, Rose, Calla, Iris." The bold one went around the table, putting a hand on a shoulder as she said the name. I'm Venus." Justin placed a mug in front of me. The Flower

Girls all eyed up my beer, as it was amazing. Venus paled. "Majesty." Venus made eye contact with Justin and blushed, moving back to the corner. Funny how random girls could have crushes on him, but Chantara pissed me off.

"I'll hang with Quincy unless you need me."

He was going to leave me with strangers? Why was that in my mind? I'm a grown-up. I can be unsupervised. So why was I so scared of five young ladies in ill-fitting equipment? "I'm sure we can all sit."

I think Justin felt my brain spinning. "When was the last time you girls had something to eat that was not a ration?" Lily and Rose looked back at Venus.

"We left home two months ago." Venus looked at the ground. She was their protector. They were all malnourished, wearing armor made for a man looking at someone else for help. I saw she felt like a failure. I know that feeling well. Every time I bled in The Pit. Justin tightened his hands on my shoulder. He knew that look well. Colin says I wear a similar face. I have seen Justin wear it when The Pit is mentioned.

"Love, I better get two more chairs and order five more plates." Justin vanished as the rest of us got snug. The tables hardly sat five comfortably and now we were seven. Venus then sat between me and Lily, while Justin sat on the other side of me.

When he was gone again for drinks, I leaned into her. "You are doing a wonderful job. They are still alive and not injured. That alone is amazing. There are still plenty of people in this kingdom that would kill a half-elf where they stand. Never mind a woman half-elf in armor. That is the trifecta of prejudice."

I passed her the bill-fold Dathon had given me. "Get some paper from their books. Make some notes. I'm going to give you places to go. People to see. It is not safe for them as they are. I will help you get them safer. It will be less strain on you." Marlene, Quincy's daytime server, started putting food down. Venus' eyes were wide. "Where would they be if you went down? Let's get them so they can take care of themselves. I will help where I can for as long as I can."

"So, why don't you ladies tell us why you left home?" Justin asked.

Lily seemed to be the voice of the group.

"Venus's mom died over two centuries ago, so when our father found his *Bonded* again, they had us. Our parents were killed by a black oily-" I spit my beer into my cup. "Blob."

Well shit. Shit. Shit!

"The Tri-Cities got more and more attacks. Some say there was a plague."

My cup came back to the table. That far south. I would never make it there in time—even with magic.

"The High Queen sent no one to help us, so a plea was sent to the Mage Keep at Crystal Lake."

Of course, she wouldn't. Oh shit. Shit. SHIT! I am not ready for a fight with him yet. Justin's hand covered my cup as Marlene came by for refills.

"The Mage Keep sent out summons, asking aid in their search for a way to end the attacks. We decided we needed to help since we had seen what it did to our family and farm. Not even the local barracks were left standing. We took what we could to be safe." Rose said, trying to hurry the story. My uncomfortable form must have seemed like aggravation. This plague needs to be dealt with. These girls would not be the answer.

"You know what this thing is?" Both Venus and Justin asked me.

We really needed to get the girls safe. As far away as we can from Tabari. Where could we send them? Safe. Trained to protect themselves from Tabari. Dathon could train the girls, but they needed to fight, too. Who does magic and physical training that takes girls?

I felt so dumb some days. "Ignore Crystal Keep." They all blinked, then frowned. That was not at all what they were expecting. My hand tapped the table in time with my quickening heartbeat. "We are heading there in two days. We shall tell Mage Master Zaidon what you saw. You need to stay as far away from Tri-Cities."

Justin touched my hand.

"I'm fine."

"No, you're not. Lys, what is it?" This time, I gave Venus the family crest. I need them protected until I can come up with a better plan.

"I have a different mission for you if you will take it."

Eyes lit around me. "Lys, they-"

"It's Tabari," was all I had to say.

Justin didn't question my jump in logic. He just trusted me. He started dishing me a plate of food. "This is where the notes come."

Venus dug paper and a pen from her pack.

"Go to Estrid's Blacksmith. It's just down the road. Get the armor sized properly. Good armor, well-maintained, is a great second skin," I quoted Adriana. I don't know how many times she said that to me as we cleaned armor over lunch.

"What are your skills?"

I frowned at Justin. It was a good question, and he beat me to the answer. "I'm excellent with my sword, okay with magic, crappy with a bow. Lys is a wonder to behold with any blade, okay with a bow." He said nothing about my magic.

Two of them were mages. One had a wand and a dagger on her hip and the other a staff as tall as me.

"Lily, Rose and Iris have elemental magic and powerful minds."

A psionicist? Who did I know that could teach her?

"Venus is great at pole arms, and I can summon *creatures*." The way Calla said it made me think the creatures were not normal.

Where do we even start with her?

Justin pushed my plate closer to me. "Eat up girls. You are going to need all the energy this afternoon."

I frowned at Justin.

"Trust me," he shrugged and pointed at my plate.

I took a bite of the pork sandwich.

"Before we take you to Estrid's, I'm testing you all." Venus and I coughed and choke as Justin muttered the words.

Venus was as red as my hair.

"Have some water." He passed our drinks, then eyed me up. "We should know what your abilities are before we arm you properly. I don't want a fire mage covered in meltable metal."

I coughed again. Yeah, we did that. Once. I wasn't expecting my fire to surface. I didn't call it. The melted steel just added one more scar to my arm.

"Lys?"

"We were just surprised." Venus nodded. "What about our date?"

"Even between us, the kingdom will have to come first. Tabari beats even that."

I nodded as Justin answered.

"We are investing in the future with these five."

I wanted so much to kiss him right then.

"Careful, Little Witch, someone might think that you really love me."

"Demon Spawn." I snapped back, smiling. He laughed. I turned back to Venus just as a tear fell. So strong to be looking after her sisters, but she, like me, wanted someone to be there for her. To not have to be the strong one all the damn time.

Just once, someone needs to take the burdens.

I grabbed her hand tight. "Once the Demon Spawn has tested you, get a good night's sleep. I want you to head to Haven. There, find Biane. Tell her I sent you." I tapped my mother's crest. "Biane is a trusted friend of my family. If she knows I sent you, she will keep you safe."

"Biane? You have a lot of faith in these ladies, my love," Justin scoffed.

That scared them, so I kicked him under the table. Our ankles would be bruised.

"Okay," I turned back to Venus as Justin tried to clarify. "Biane doesn't like me."

"Cause you are a pain in her ass. Now hush so I can give these ladies instructions." He motioned forward. *You're an ass.*

You forgot adorable. Adorable Ass.

I rolled my eyes. "Biane is a harsh taskmaster who can train you in weapons, magic, and powers of the mind. She also is the Master of the Archives." Justin nodded, getting where I was going. "This is my mission to you. Learn to fight. Learn to protect those around you. Don't fear the gifts the Goddesses have given to you." Calla looked at her hands. I saw dirt around her fingernails. Scars on her palms. What was she? I could tell Justin was just watching me as I watched them. Listening. "Your mission there is to search the stacks for any mention of the Death Palace, Death Knight, Death Knight Plague, and train. When we get there in a month, I hope to see five much more confident Knights."

Rose and Lily both placed a hand over their mouths to hold in the sobs. Calla couldn't look at me. I have seen that look in the mirror. She didn't like her powers any more than I did. Iris just stared off. Blank to the world. Adriana had a friend who did that when she was just learning about her telepathy. Was this girl talking to someone? "After the tourney, we were sure you would tell us to go home. That this is no life for a woman, but you are sending us on our first mission?" Rose stated. Wholly unsure how to feel. "How can we repay you?" I don't want to be repaid. I want help. I can't fight Tabari on my own, knowing as little as I did.

"Be my weapon against the Death Knight. Help bring his destruction. Help me save the world." Calla stiffened. Rose and Lily held each other. Venus tightened on the crest. Iris held a hand over her mouth. "There is a possibility no one will believe you. This life is hard and lonely." I looked at my mug. "No one ever believed me." Why would they believe five random girls from Tri-Cities?

"My mother lived in fear. I have let it consume me on more than one occasion. That is what true bravery is. Isn't it? Waking up every morning knowing it is bearing down on you then fighting your way through the day, anyway." I glanced at

Justin to smile. As if this was a secret, I had never spoken aloud. In a way, it was. This was my life since The Pit. A life I didn't want him to fall into as I pulled myself out of it. "It will eventually become second nature to you. It will seem less like a threat, but it will always be there. You will always have to fight it. So ladies fight it." And this is where my mother would end with something silly. "Be my Thorns in the world. Let's not let the monsters at our door win." Tulora, The Great ended all her speeches with that. I don't even know who the Thornes were. There is no other mention of this after the war with Tabari.

There was complete silence. No music. I felt the whole room staring at me. "And that is why I love her." I groaned, sinking further into my chair.

"To King Justin and Queen Lysandra." I heard Quincy call up.

The crowd sent up an "Aye."

"To the Queen's Thorns." Another one. "Long may they reign." The Goddesses cursed me, didn't they?

"Shit." I covered my face. Justin just laughed at me. "Why didn't you tell me they were all listening to me?"

"Who was I to stop that heartfelt speech? It was thrilling." My hands clenched on my clothing. Justin just pulled my face to his. "I felt for the first time in a long time, that is how you really felt. I saw the girl you once were fighting to come home. That stubborn girl who never wanted help, who thought she could take on the world alone. The girl who became the woman I eventually fell in love with."

Goddess, he is sappy.

"*Bonding* or no, I would have fallen in love with the woman who spoke about fighting fear." I sighed. "So much

106

stronger than you give yourself credit for." My ring hand touched his face. Out of the corner of my eye, I saw Quincy lift a mug for me.

This. This was me. This was the moment I felt most myself. This was the moment I knew no prophecy would win. I would fight what was done to me. I would fight to love Justin. I would fight to be the queen Adriana saw in me.

Careful Little Witch. I might throw you on the table and consummate our Bond *in front of your Thorns.* I back handed his shoulder, which only made him roar with laughter. *I love you.*

If you did, you wouldn't have let me embarrass myself in front of fifty strangers. Fifty people I had planned at one point I would be. Fifty warriors, men and women, who were free of Fate's design. Even if I couldn't live that life free of all my fears, I wished these girls could.

CHAPTER NINE

The rest of lunch was less eventful. I spoke about supplies they would need. We talked about what they had. Three old plow horses. Two short swords, miss matched daggers and a quarterstaff for Lily. Nothing for Calla. That made me even more curious about what she could do. We left to cheers of good luck from other adventuring parties. Life of adventure is the only true equalizer.

I'm sure that is why older adventurers came to the table dropping small bags of coins, books, notes of introductions for shopkeepers in other towns. The Blacksmith from Yorktown, Demir Mire, brushed past Venus, dropping a set of Elven designed amulets made of metal. One he pulled closer to Venus, and she blushed. Justin greeted the man we knew well. Adriana went to him for all our weapons and armor. Venus smiled softly at the amulet. My eyebrow rose, and she wrote me a word. *Bonded.* I looked at the dwarf. He was smiling and talking to Justin as if his *Bonded* wasn't just sitting right here needing a comforting hold.

Maybe I am spoiled with Justin as my *Bonded*. Unless forced, he is never over five feet from me. My story book king tells me, hourly, that he loves me. The smallest request he fulfills, even if it is not spoken aloud. Demir barely even looks at Venus. Was that why she blushed when Justin dropped off my drink? There were laws that *bonds* came before anything.

I took her pen. *Why?* I wrote back. She frowned, then sighed.

Race wars. She wrote back. Justin took my hand. One did not have to see magic to see they were protective charms. Or that Venus was trying to ignore the flare of the *bond* from this Dwarven Blacksmith. He kissed her hair before vanishing into the crowd. I went after him, but Justin shook his head. What the hell?

"I can't believe he followed me." Venus was as pale as her hair. "If anyone from Starfall sees us, one or both of us will be killed." I took her hand to comfort her. Ours was not the same situation, but I knew what it was like not to be with my *Bond*.

"The *Bond* makes us do strange things for your other half," Justin said. His mind spun in spirals. I know his legal mind was working out laws to get Demir to Haven. In Stowera, the *Bond* was high law. Nothing but direct influence from a god could break it. In Dragongut, second souls like Demir were second class. Even if you were born to another clan, you were sent to them. It wasn't a life I would want for anyone.

We just need a safe place for them. Justin nodded. We are king and queen. If we can't get a *Bonded* pair together for the sake of laws, what good are we with bigger issues? *I will do anything.*

I'm working on it. I knew he was. I should trust him, but I knew politics would get involved. I am not Adriana. I couldn't sweet talk anyone into doing anything. I am a doer, not a talker. Justin took after his mother. *I'm working on it, Lys.* This time he sounded like he knew I wasn't planning on waiting.

After lunch, Venus walked with Justin discussing types of blades. Calla walked to my right, Iris linking arms with the other girls. "Lys?" I looked at Calla. "I know I have seen you fight using elemental magic. It is impressive. Yet, His Majesty said not a word of it."

I chuckled to myself. "I came from a place where magic meant death. The king didn't look too kindly on mages. Or red-haired women. Think Justice with more targets. People were murdered in the hundreds daily when my mother was young. Whole cities were slaughtered to exterminate those who are magically inclined. My family included." Justin and Venus stopped. I looked at him for reassurance. He gave me that sad smile. "The day I was taken from my family, he and his soldiers came to Haven and slaughtered almost the whole town before he got to our house. Mom didn't take kindly to him trying to kill us." I took a deep breath, holding my hand out to Justin.

"Only when I came here, met my foster father, Justin and his mother, did I understand magic was not a death sentence. Yet Goddess Daina still bound my gifts. To lessen them, she said." I ran a hand over the family crest under my clothing. This has been a day of opening myself up to near strangers. "A few years ago someone got a hold of me. She wanted to see how much power I had. Forced me to murder other children using my magic. Magic became something I feared again. I only use it when my emotions are high." I turned to Calla, calling fire to my fingers. Watching the flames flicker like candle flame on my fingers tightened my chest. My breathing was harder and shorter. Justin, not letting me go.

"She has something the Mage Knights call rhabdophobia." He offered.

"I fear my magic. This is part of the fear I face every day." Justin's hand covered the flames in mine. Since we were so close, the blisters healed almost as fast as they formed. It didn't stop smoke leaking out from between his fingers. "For years my father went through lessons with me to help me not go catatonic. I still do the exercises from time to time, when the power is too strong from being unused." I tried to smile at her. Lines still formed on my cheeks that Justin dried.

"I shouldn't have asked." Calla pulled away from me.

"There is a breathing exercise that works for her. I can show you what we do?"

I reached out to keep her from shrinking away. I didn't want her to be scared like I was. "You were shaking right then," she whispered.

Had I been? Probably. My left hand was indeed shaking.

Breathe. One. Two. Three. Four. Out. Two. Three. Four. I closed my eyes to Justin's words in my mind. Adriana figured out that this helped me when I was about to freak out. Concentrating on something other than the topic took years for me. Truth be told, I think it was Justin's voice trying to calm me that did it. It has always brought me to a calm place.

Justin kissed my hand. *Thank you.*

"My daughter should never be ashamed of her magic." Dathon was suddenly there. "None of you should be. Magic is a gift given to mortals." Dathon pulled me into his arms, kissing my hair. Lord Mage Knight Dathon Seabrooke's daughter was terrified by magic.

"Dad?"

"If we are going to invest in training, I need Dathon to test the girls. How are we to train them if we can't tell their limits?"

I nodded.

I'm sorry, my love. You'll have to use your magic when you are with me. If you need to stop, we stop.

I nodded again. I said nothing.

"Lys, tell me you will not fight it farther than need be." He pulled me back to him. Holding me at an arm's length. "Promise me, Lys."

"Justin-"

"Lys," he warned.

"I don't know when that point is. You'll have to judge for yourself. At a certain point, I lose myself. You know that." He sighed, pulling me into his chest. "I could freak out from lighting my hand or from erupting in fury. I don't know what my limit is." That alone was horrible.

We went to Dathon's house. The backyard was warded against magic. "So, Lys doesn't strain herself. I'll have her show what I am looking for." After almost breaking down in the middle of the sidewalk, he wants me to call more magic?

"You hate me don't you, Dad?" He smiled. What could I do? Refuse my father. Justin and Dathon were there. We are in the warded magic bubble. Wren and Lizzy were not too far away if things went too far. It was safe. Nothing will go wrong. Right?

"I don't know if this is a good idea, Dathon. She has pushed herself a lot today," Justin said, and I nodded. At least he understood. The man who could know my mind with a look at my hands. The man who had access to my soul strangely knew my limits more than I did.

Yet I called my crystal sword. The tip, drawing a circle around me. I reached my power into the soil where I cut the grass. Willing it to rise. The wind then came to cushion it from the ground. I looked at the water in the horse troughs, easily three feet under me. With my left hand, I called half of the water there to wrap around me. My eyes closed again. Silently begging the fire to not be needed.

"Fire, Lys." I could feel the fire spark with the very mention. I didn't want to. Everything pulled at me to end it all. If I add my fire to the mix, it might break me. "Lysandra." I was already at more elements than I have controlled since The Pit. I heard the screams already. Faces flashed in front of my eyes. All of them seconds before my magic hit them. Killing them.

Breathe. One. Two. Three. Four. Out. Two. Three. Four. Again. In your nose, out your mouth. Justin said. I followed the instructions as my hands flared to life. *One. Two. Three. Four. Out. Two. Three. Four. In. Two. Three. Four. Good my love. You are safe. I'm here for you. I love you.* I smiled, looking down at him. I was certainly over three feet in the air. I was so high up I could feel the shielding bounce my wind back at me. That was easily twenty-five feet in the air. Knowing I was so high up made me lose control. When the flames engulfed me. I saw the ball of orange and screamed. "Lys, drop it all." It was out of my control.

Faces, one after another, flashing. The girl with one eye, silenced by a wind so strong it ripped off her head. Her little brother, maybe four years old, billows smoke from his eyes, nose and mouth. I pulled a shard of stone through his back as I pretended to cower in front of him. The boy, my age, begged me to end the poison in his veins, taken down when I lit his

113

clothing on fire. The man, three, four years older than me, stabbed me in a mad craze. His charred remains whispering thank you as I was attacked by his drugged out, very pregnant wife. I was forced to cut the baby out of her after killing her with her husband's dagger covered in my crystal. Even the baby was dead.

Their faces were gone in a blink as I collapsed. The long forgotten feeling of a Templar of Leila wrapping around me. Silver and chilled cage sealing the powers in my chest. The even older fear that the Templars were there to kill me gripped my heart. They had been a constant threat to Mom and me. Even after I came here, I could still feel them watching me. Waiting to pounce and kill me. Now it was their magic that suppressed my own. Were they finally going to get their shot?

Justin caught me before the ground did. "That is all from her today, Dathon. I warned you it was going to be too much." Justin kept counting in my head while yelling at my father. The other girls look petrified. Calla at our side with water to drink and a towel, mopping my forehead. She, too, was concerned.

"Have I hurt anyone?"

"No." I relaxed slightly. Magic was still humming in my veins. "I have you, Lys. Go ahead, cry. We're here." Justin placed Calla's hand in mine, then kissed them both. "You both will be fine. I have you."

"It took control." I could feel him rocking me as I held on to him for dear life. "I saw them. All of them."

"Only for a second, Love. You could shut it off with a thought this time. You didn't fully lose control. Nothing more breathing won't help."

"I didn't though." I let him curl around me. That wasn't me who shut my magic off.

114

"I won't ask you to do that again." Dathon patted my head. As if I was five again.

I hated him right then. I know why he asked me to do it. I didn't have to like it. Justin was right. I pushed myself too far today. I didn't have to. I just had to watch the girls do it instead. I could have said no. No. No. I had to trust my father knew what he was doing. I knew I was being spiteful, but shouldn't a father protect his daughter from these sorts of attacks?

Justin never let go of me. Not making me watch them, either. Holding my face in his chest as he held his new silence dome over us. Until we got to Calla. I was just too curious. I also knew Justin would keep me safe. He had given her an encouraging smile as Dathon called her name. "We have faith in you," Justin said.

Calla stood up and walked to the center of the field. She closed her eyes with her palms facing the dirt. "I have little to pull from here, Master Dathon. I don't want them to walk through main street." Them?

"Do what you can." A dagger came off her thigh, hidden in the folds of her oversized tunic. Sliced open her arm and then back into the sheath. She knelt in the dirt, blood creating a puddle. She wrote runes in the mud created with her blood. I felt a pull to her, and she looked at me in shock. Justin frowned. The pull got stronger as animals in different states of decay gathered around us. Each one kneeling next to me in front of her.

"Daughter Death, daughter of mine, who has harmed you?" I heard myself ask. The hell was I saying? The hell was I doing? Daina, why was I tied to death?

"I'm sorry, Mother. This was just a test." She pointed to Dathon, and I was suddenly very annoyed at him. How dare he force her into this? He is just a minor god. "Thank you for coming when I called. I shall not call you again unless I am in danger."

"Know that your mortal father is so very proud of you, daughter. Though this is our first meeting, know I, too, am proud of the lady you have become." Calla's eyes filled. "Someday, I hope to get to know you better."

Honestly, that was the best rest I have ever had. When I woke up, the girls were gone. Only a note from Calla apologizing. I didn't know what happened. How was she supposed to know? That was new, though. I have never spoken like that in my life. I had never felt power like that encompass me. Justin kept close tabs on me when I woke.

Seriously, what in Daina's name was that about?

CHAPTER TEN

First day of the trial of Roseden Seabrooke dawned to find me pacing. Dathon was trying to tell me about the witnesses he had lined up. One of my guards had turned sides. He was the one who found Dathon, it would appear. I didn't recognize the name. Then again, I called them numbers, except for Fluffy. He had been *nice*.

Justin came in later as we were about to teleport to the courthouse. Which made no sense to me. Justin could have just met us there. He has to pass it to get to our house. My husband was here just to hold my hand. Gentle but firm. He was there for me. I needed him there for me. After yesterday I was walking on the balls of my feet ready to run. *Breathe. One. Two. Three. Four. Out. Two. Three. Four.* Justin was repeating in my mind.

"Can you tell us in your own words what happened to Dame Lysandra Seabrooke?" Years I spent trying to take Roseden down. Yet it takes Roseden trying to kill Justin for me to get her before a judge.

Kacie wore one of her silver armored formal mage knight uniforms. It matched her hair and eyes, making her seem twice as scary as I knew her to be. My adoptive grandmother wore her silver and emerald ring. The one she wore when she knew she was going to win. On her wrist, her silver bracelet I gave her when I was sixteen by the old calendar. She had been wearing it a lot since the moment I told her, Roseden scared me. Her braided bun was held with her bun cage and a poisoned pin. That told me she was expecting a physical fight. Kacie was ready for anything. She leaned on the table. She was confident in a way I never have been.

Breathe. One. Two. Three. Four. Out. Two. Three. Four. Screw the breathing. This was not fair.

"Objection!" So it starts. Maclow's lawyer was a slimy guy I had seen at Crystal Keep. A mage knight who didn't make it high in the ranks or the legal section. Just someone Zaidon would have kept around, so he had to be Maclow's man. "This has no bearing on the charges brought forth by the king."

"Oh, but it does." I shot up to the voice. I hadn't wanted to look at the man on the stand, so I looked at my ring. Our eyes met. I knew him. The only one of Roseden's men, who was kind to me. He locked eyes with me and smiled. Fluff Master. He had massive dogs bigger than my horse. The babies were so fluffy they didn't look like dogs. They were adorable balls of fluff that waddled when they walked, which made me smile. I don't know the breed's name. This jailer also could turn into one of his dogs, using a magic ring. "Had Dame Lysandra not escaped, Roseden would not have gone after her *Bonded*. To know why she targeted the king, you need to know how bat shit crazy she is."

"I will remind the witness that he is not to answer out of turn." Fluff shrugged. The judge was one I had never seen before. An elf, full-blood by the points, easily a thousand years old. Green hair in a braided bun held together with a gold twig. Black robes making her pale skin almost translucent.

"How about we start with your name?" Kacie began her pacing. Which gave the other side false confidence. I know Kacie enough to know she thought she had the Jury on her side. Even if it was so early in the trial.

"Caleb Brekker." Caleb? Has he ever told me that? I had a feeling like I was supposed to know this. Justin rolled my ring on my finger. He was watching Caleb. Neutral. Not even thinking or feeling anything that I could peek in on. What was going on in his head?

"What do you do for a living?"

"Dog breeder. Malamutes." Hence Fluff Master. "And I was on Roseden's lover rotation." That was more shameful for him.

"How did Lady Seabrooke bring Dame Seabrooke to your attention?"

"Roseden said her *Brother-in-Bonding* had a foster daughter who needed us to look in on her from time to time. I was more than willing. I met her when she was seven. She called my dogs Fluffers." I smirked, Justin chuckled next to me. "I asked where to find Andra and she showed me the Oubliette."

"Were you unable to get the Dame Seabrooke out?"

"Andra wore Mage Metal Manacles bound to the oubliette." Justin flinched.

I hated my magic, so I was fine with that noise. The constant humming suppressing my flames was a relief.

Justin had a unique experience with them. Tabari, while he was in Justice, tested the limits of Mage Metal. These were Justin's nightmares. Watching humans and elves waste away into nothing as their magic and life was drained from them. Tabari had no less than six in his 'test' chambers. When we were young, Justice would take Justin down to watch and brag that he would have me in there one day. Destroying those rooms was the second thing Justin did after I took Justice's head.

"I needed to get the key. I am not magic, so I couldn't do it myself. I feel Rose knew what I wanted and started taking me to bed more frequently. I was ordered to sexually abuse Andra as a punishment to her." The entire room gasped as Caleb shifted forms to look like Justin. "Always in this form. Always to draw blood. She always knew I wasn't her Soulless Prince. Even being drained of all life, bloody, bruised, exhausted from using too much magic, she knew I wasn't really him."

Justin let go of me. *I really don't deserve you. Knowing you knew the difference in that state-* His hand covered his mouth. The man who clawed at his insides to touch me slinked away into a dark place I couldn't follow. I took hold of his left hand with my left.

Yet here we are. Married. You are at my side when I need you. I'm sure if we weren't in the middle of court, he would have kissed me.

"In the last year of her captivity, I started shifting into one of my dogs. A massive one for her to sleep on. A small comfort for her, I had hoped. I had come to respect the woman Andra had become." Caleb smiled softly. "I just couldn't find anyone powerful enough to help me get her out of that pit."

That was after he had me moaning. Justin's eyes widened. *When we get back to the castle, Justin, I want you to do to me what he used to do to me. I need to know the difference between torture and safe. You are the safest person I know.*

As much as I would love to, Little Witch, I'm scared for you. After yesterday, I'm reluctant to flip anymore triggers. I leaned on him, our left hands still locked on our thighs. *I will always worry, Lys.*

"I was out checking a new batch for my pack when I found Lord Mage Knight Seabrooke. He was looking to get Lysandra a puppy." I involuntarily gasped. Dathon was going to get me a puppy? "Her very own fluffer. I didn't know who he was until he mentioned Andra. Within the hour, we broke her out. For my betrayal, Roseden killed all my dogs."

"She did what?!" I stood hands on the pews. Slight smell of burning wood coming from my hands.

Breathe. One. Two. Three. Four. Out. Two. Three. Four. Rose turned back to me. Crazy wide grin on her disturbing face. "Bitch, they are just dogs. Helpless animals." Justin held me back. I didn't know what I was going to do when I got there, but I knew Kacie was going to be right with me. She loved dogs. I was out with her when I found that they even existed.

"Dame Seabrooke, please sit down. I don't want to remove you." The judge said. The judge's name plate said Moonblossom, she was old. There was a shift in naming babies around the time Mom took the throne to more human-like names. Kacie signaled me with her eyes to sit with Justin. I sat. Dathon turned to look at his brother on the other side of the room. The sneer on his face was priceless. I stood up again, moving to the door. Justin, I knew, followed me.

Yell in my mind, Lys.

That bitch never threatened to kill the dogs. Never to me. How dare she do that to Caleb? He was only ever nice to me.

Breathe. Relax, my love. She will get what is coming to her.

Will she? Justin raised an eyebrow. *Three years she tortured me. Longer to the kids, she was drugging to madness. She tried to kill you. Many times through me. Sent her husband to bring me back to her after Dad found me. Then has the gall to kill the thing Caleb loved the most. Just for being a decent person. No, decapitation is an easy out for her. No, give her to me. Let me use her own spell on her again.*

You know I have no power over that. I gave him a shriek. *Come on. Dathon tells me I'm after lunch, and I know you need to burn off some energy.*

Do you need me there? I seethed. *If I see her again, I will kill her.*

"I always need you near me. You are the very air I breathe."

My face warmed.

"That is my girl. Red as your hair."

I elbowed him. "We will go get food in the market." Walking hand in hand with Justin in the market was another thing on his list of dates. I really enjoyed it. Sitting, eating with him at Sunshine Cafe a block from the courthouse.

Dathon had to ruin it by saying we had to go back.

Justin was called to the stand.

That was the last thing I remember of that day until we were home. Justin took a shower in my room, wanting to get Roseden's filth off himself. While he was in the shower, I changed into a nightie. I couldn't understand the filth he talked about. So I closed my eyes with my arms braced up as they were in The Pit. Did it change the way I felt about my body? Did I know what it was like to be clean?

No. I still hated my skin. The memory of their touch on my flesh. No water and soap would take away those feelings. Even before that, I hated my body. The scars. That I was chubbier than most girls in our class.

Lys, why are you standing like that? I looked at Justin. *I will do nothing to cause you fear.*

Everything I do causes fear, Justin. I'm trying not to fear you. Caleb is not nearly as tall as Justin. *One hand on mine.* He did as requested. *Caleb never kissed me. He said that was for lovers.* Justin locked eyes with me. *His hand would be gentle as it slid down to my nipple as he kissed my neck. Then it would go between-* The groan told me to stop talking about Caleb. "Erase his touch, Justin."

"With pleasure." His free hand pulled me to him. "My darling, this is not the way I wanted to show you how I wanted to make love to you." A tear fell. Mine matching his. "I will gladly take those memories. I hope it is enough." The kiss was firm and asked me to open up to him. So I did.

I lost all sense of myself. Our *Bond* hammered in our veins. We felt liquid and hard at the same time. Justin's tongue caressed mine and my head turned slightly to get more of him. But he took it as a request to move to my neck. The second he took my pulse in his lips I moaned softly.

Ah, My Little Witch, you sound glorious. Justin picked me up to sit me on the bed. I fumbled with the mismatched buttons on his horrible shirt. With his scars visible, I had to kiss them. "Lys." He groaned. "You are going to make it so hard to stop if you want me to."

"Who said I wanted to?" He was kissing me again. Rougher this time. As none of the men had ever kissed me like this. It wasn't triggering anything. I half expected it too. This was my Justin. His eyes were the right shade of blue. Our *Bond* made every touch echoed in my mind. This was nothing like with the other men. His black hair shining in the Fae Flower light.

In The Pit, it was dark. Almost pitch except for the torchlight around the edges. I could barely see the men. That was not the case now. Fae Flower light bloomed over us as a canopy on my four post bed. The hearth held a moderate sized fake fire. Every mage light in my room was lit. It was as bright as daylight here.

Justin knew it was so I could see him and what he was doing. He also knew the Fae Flowers were a warning of sorts. I never drew the curtains on my bed anymore. The state of the vine would be withered most days. He looked up at them as a confirmation I was happy. Then he came back to kissing my mouth.

You're beautiful. This time his lips went down the flame marked side, causing me to stiffen. Justin wasn't rough. The kisses were feather light. *Remember, I love them. I love seeing the real you.* The scarred breast tightened under his touch, causing me to gasp. Blue eyes shot to mine. Fear. Genuine fear shone in them.

It was just a shock. No one touches that side. Not even my rapists.

Good. I love it even more. The fear didn't fade, so I took his face in my hands. *I never want to hurt you, Lys.*

I don't think you could even if you tried. You love me too deeply for that.

I love your faith in me. Justin nuzzled the scarred side of my neck. *I wish I deserved it.* That was where our night stalled. Gentle nuzzles mixed with feather kisses until I fell asleep on his naked body.

When I woke to the sun, the Fae Flowers were still shining. I smiled up at the rare sight. Justin was even still in my bed. His hand on my stomach over the sheet. His other arm was under my head. I turned to him. His hand tightened on my hip, before sliding to the small of my back. His other arm wrapped around my shoulders.

Last night wasn't a total waste. I found I really enjoyed the way Justin's voice strained, saying my name when I was kissing him. So it was the first thing I did. *Maybe I should start calling you my Dark Temptress.* He whispered, rolling on his back.

"Stop groaning and I'll stop kissing," I said. Which got me a groan. I had to smile. "Such a magical sound." I kissed all the way down his chest and back again. I was rewarded with strained groans of my name.

When I lost time, I sometimes would be in a black void. Sometimes I would see Adriana's bed, Justin sleeping in it. He was safe. More than once, I would walk over to his sleeping form just to have him hold me. His groans would drown out anything else I heard for days. The way he said my name sat in my heart. I knew it wasn't real, but it was a safe place.

None of the men ever said my name. Strained or not. Just beastial grunts. Making my normally very composed king melt under my hands was empowering, intoxicating, addictive. I was enjoying every second of the pleasure I was giving and receiving. *That was nothing like what they did to me.*

Wren didn't either? Surprising. I have wanted to have you like that from the second I was bathing you after the throne room. I stretched, feeling my bones reforming. *We have missed so much.*

"Justin."

"Say it again," he whispered in my ear.

"Justin."

"That is the ticket." He groaned. "The best sound ever." I giggled. I was trying to tease and be sexy. I felt like a fool, but Justin smiled. That was all I could ask for.

"I will not push nor deny you, Lys." For that, I kissed him.

I don't know how long I was engulfed in colors, just that when I surfaced, Justin was breathing just as hard as me. He was over me. Flashes of a face started. Number four. His toothless smile before he would gum my breasts. One's fangs was biting my thigh. Maclow smiled as he turned my naked body to face the wall. With each one, a sharp pain jolted up my spine.

I found myself face first in the toilet in the next breath. Bile being the only thing in my stomach. I chastised myself for not eating supper. I had been so angry with Roseden; I paced my room for an hour, went down to the training ring to beat up some helpless recruit before deciding I wanted Justin to make me forget.

I'm sorry. I whispered.

He held me as I tried to regain my breathing.

"I saw them. I'm the one who should be sorry. I wasn't thinking." Justin held me on the floor as I moved from memories of Number Four to throwing up.

He was still there when I had nothing left. Cold cloth in hand, water glass in the other. Tears covered his face. "I swear

I will never top you again. We will stick to the positions you start. If you ever let me touch you again."

I relaxed. I wanted to kiss him, but held back. I didn't like it when they kissed me smelling like vomit. Instead, I placed my face to the side of his neck, arms holding his head. "I didn't tell you. You wouldn't have known."

His arms tightened around me.

"Thank you."

That got him crying. Hard, full sobs. He hated himself, and the men who did this to me. Part of him hated me for not letting him know the darkness I experienced. That only made him hate himself more.

I joined in his tears.

Our *Bond,* raw and open.

Dathon found us like that. Naked in tears with sex and vomit in the air. He cleared his throat to let us know he was there. "We have to leave in an hour. Will you two be ready?"

Justin pulled back to look at me. He let me wipe the snot from his face. "Have someone bring Justin some fresh clothing. We will shower and meet you at your room."

"Okay." My father said nothing else.

"Dad, thank you," I said as he closed the door. "Now come on, my love. We have to go face the bitch and her harem."

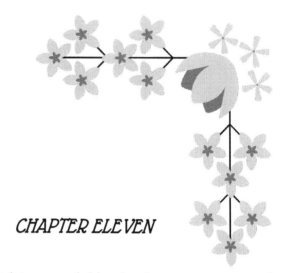

CHAPTER ELEVEN

Justin wouldn't let me wash him, but he was ever so gentle with me. After he was done with me, he stayed in the shower longer. The mountain grew between us and not of my building. I was out in the main part of my room, reaching for a shirt, when I felt the pain in my knuckles and wrist. The bruising was almost instant over my knuckles.

Justin punched the wall. So hard it cut open two of the knuckles. I wrapped my hand, getting dressed in leggings, a peasant blouse and a short-collar vest. Mine in green and white. Justin's clothing was white and a navy blue so dark it was almost black.

I brought in his clothing. I hung them on my door. He was leaning on the sink in only a towel wrapped around his waist. "Sorry. I forget sometimes you can get hurt, too."

I said nothing. He sounded so defeated. There was nothing I could do for him. Simply washed his hand.

"Lys, please talk to me." It was almost begging. "Please, I can't take it when you are silent. It's like when you came back."

"I just don't know what to say." I washed the growing bruises.

"Then tell me all the thoughts." His left hand gingerly cupped my scarred cheek. "You being quiet like this makes me remember how helpless I was. I want to help. I need to help. You are the other half of my soul." I wrapped his hand as I had done for my own. By lunch time we should be healed.

"I thought five years was enough. I thought with as close as we are trying to be, maybe I wouldn't see them. That your love would break those memories apart." My voice cracked, so I went back to dressing his hand. "I am sorry I did this to us. It was not what I intended. Especially not while we were making love. I should have known I can't have nice things."

Justin's hands were on my shoulders. "This is not your fault. This is not my fault or Dathon's. The fault lies firmly with Roseden and the bastards she ordered to hurt you." I didn't look at him. I didn't believe it. Every part of me knew we could never repeat last night.

"Then let us get revenge," Dathon said from the door, this time with food. "Come on Lys, I need you to eat something." Dathon back to being a dad. He brought Justin a fruit bowl, omelet, and toast. I got toast and honeyed water. Probably because I had been throwing up. Justin frowned at my sparse breakfast and put the fruit between us. When Dathon's back was turned, I would pop a grape in my mouth. Justin even got me to bite down on a strawberry. The juices dribbled down from my lips. Which got a chuckle from Justin. Dathon sighed.

"Do we need to get a healer for Lys when we get home?" Justin pulled me closer so we could openly eat the last of the fruit.

"She is fine, Dathon."

"Physically, I can see that. I'm thinking about the future. How are you two going to deal with children?" I must have never told him about meeting his Goddess.

"Lys can't have children unless the Goddesses heal her womb." I blinked. Wait what? How does Justin-

"The *Bond*." I sighed. "You know cuz I know what Daina said to me." A sad smile. "Birth control will not be a problem. Daina told me I won't have kids in my lifetime."

Dathon scowled. "Hence, you want Wren and Lizzy on baby making duty."

"Yeah. That is why I'm pulling all the stops for their wedding. Once Lys' time is up, I'm passing the crown to my sister." I stabbed a grape with Justin's fork. I always knew this was the plan. There was no way around Justin not having a child of his own. That didn't mean I didn't feel like a failure for not giving him any. "This is not your fault, either. I will always be here for you."

"I adore you." I smiled.

"I will be adorable any day of the week if it means you smile like that." He kissed my hair.

"I am happy for you two. It has been a long road for you." We both turned to my father waiting for the but. "We are calling Lys today." We both stiffened. "I can't promise they will be gentle." That slime ball won't be just so Roseden can see a rise out of me. I was looking forward to it.

"I had a relapse this morning. I'm already in an awful place. Maybe if I break down, it will help more." Justin held

130

me in a hug while Dathon teleported us to the courthouse. We were met by Caleb at the door. He and Justin acted like they were old friends. "Fluffy." I greeted.

"My Queen." He bowed. Oh shit, people knew. I guess they would after being called Justin's *bonded* a thousand times. "On Saturday, I wish for you to come to my home. I wish to gift you a little fluff for a late birthday/coronation/wedding gift." A puppy? I looked at Justin. He would have to take care of it once I was gone.

"Mr Brekker, we will be delighted. Is there a specific time?"

Are you sure, Justin? He waved me to go with Dathon.

"Whenever my King and Queen would like to come. My day is free." I didn't hear the rest, though. Inside, the courthouse was not like the day before. A person could not walk for the news reporters asking me questions. They were very close to me. One man even took my arm. Expecting to see a man. Yet I saw Justin's back. The hand dropped from my arm.

Justin and Dathon were there. Justin got the man off me and threw up his protection dome. I couldn't hear what they called me. I closed myself so I didn't see them. The three of us made our way through the people to the same room we were in yesterday.

Maclow and Roseden's laughs were the first things I heard. I didn't have the benefit of Justin's silence dome. They were standing on her side of the room. Dathon sat behind his team, whispering something to them. Justin and I sat on the edge of the pew.

I'm here if you need me. Pinch us if you need a break. I will get Dathon to ask for a recess.

"Therefore, I don't deserve you." I got the sad smile. "I hate that smile." He kissed me.

"Okay Lys. You are first. I got the judge to allow a garbage can in the witness box." I nodded. "Kacie said they would be gentle as they can but I can't vouch for the other side."

"The sooner this is over, the sooner I can go home." Justin kissed my hand. "Find something on your list we can do safely at home, please."

"Done." I watched the same jury members sit down. Today was different. Today I would have to tell everyone, not just my *Bonded* and my father, what happened in my own words. "Don't look at them. Look only at me."

"We call to the stand Queen Lysandra Seabrooke-Knyght." We both shot a glare at my father. But I stood, took a deep breath. With all the confidence I could muster went to the tiny box. Yes, there was a garbage can waiting at my feet. That didn't stop the wave of nausea crashing against me. The box was tiny. Justin said something to Dathon, and my father turned to me apologetic. They hadn't thought about my new claustrophobia. One of many of my new phobias.

"Can you please confirm your name?" Kacie asked.

"Lysandra Enya Seabrooke-Knyght." Justin was fingering his ring. So I repeated the movement at my name. "Queen of Stowera by blood, battle and *Bond*. Heir to Queensgate by blood."

"Thank you, Your Majesty." My hand twitches. Titles. "Can you please tell the court about your time with Lady Roseden Seabrooke?" I felt my right hand tap with my heartbeat.

"My father had asked his brother and *Sister-in-Bonding* to check in from time to time as he had to go away for a while."

"Why did he leave his young daughter alone?" Young? Would have only been fifteen by the old calendar. I guess that was young.

"Because his *Life Love* had just been murdered. My father needed time away from me." I didn't want to look at Dathon, but I knew it to be true. "I was the reason she was murdered. I held him back from her last moments. Then I left them both in a bubble while I confronted her murderer. He wasn't able to say anything to her before she died." Adriana was dead because of me and Tabari. I denied them final words with her. Then I denied them revenge. Some loving daughter I was. Tabari was always my issue, not theirs.

Tabari. He would come for sure after this. Repeated in my mind. My hand tapped faster. "Dad knew I would be fine. I was ten. That is fifteen by the old calendar. The crown prince came by every day and our own staff was there if I needed anything." I tried to force a smile. "I had decapitated the king in single combat, just days before." The jury let out a collected gasp. "I could take care of myself. Sometimes a girl just needs a woman to talk to about things she can't talk to her boyfriend or father about so he asked Roseden to be there for me. I really wasn't taking my new titles well. I knew someday I would be Justin's queen. I just never thought I would be a queen in my own right. I don't deal with titles well."

"How did you get from your comfortable home to the oubliette?"

"To this day, I don't know. Auntie Roseden and I were having tea, talking about Justin's birthday celebration. What I was about to wear. How I would do my hair. All those girly things women talk through before balls. I was a real girl back then. Like every other girl my age.

"Next thing I knew, I was twenty feet underground in the pit. I couldn't call my magic. I was chained to the floor and a wall with five Mage Metal cuffs." Kacie glared, tightening her fists. When she turned, both my men sat back at the glare. I adore Kacie. "She was leaning over the edge in the gown I was going to wear." You could tell who the mages in the courtroom were. Each one wincing at the thought of Mage Metal. Some made the realization five was enough to kill anyone, but I was sitting there scarred.

I took a pause. Justin rubbed our arms. "She said she thought I would be out longer. Said it was a shame." I looked at my scarred wrists. "She told me that if I told Justin where I was, she would know. As if I knew where we were. Then she shifted into me. She said if I said anything to Justin, she would kill him." My eyes filled. "She left me with my own dance partner. I called him Number One. He cut my tattoo off. The tattoo Justin and I got of my old family crest. The one from my mother's time. Number One enjoyed cutting open the wound so he could drink the blood." I placed a hand over our matching tattoo. "He shaved my hair completely. Hitting me every time I fought back. If I would die, there would be no markings on me to say who I was."

Kacie passed me a tissue. "Did you try to contact Prince Justin?"

"At midnight, he searched out for me. When he connected, I was pinned to a wall half passed out and bleeding. Number One had finished beating me when I heard Justin. I could feel his panic. I heard him call his cousin and my best friend. As promised, Justin was stabbed within minutes. I knew we were within a mile of each other when my gut bled. When she returned, she had Number One anal rape me while sinking his teeth into my neck. She made sure he knew I had to stay a virgin. Just as she told all her men. She had a plan for that."

Justin was no longer looking at me. He glared at Roseden, who winked at him, blowing him a kiss. She turned to me, smiling, when Justin just glared harder. She was enjoying this. "If it wasn't for Justin, I wouldn't have known the passage of time. I saw his every dream. Until it was too much. A month after being in The Pit, the trials began. Mage Metal was released. I sent a warning to those I loved. Prayed to my mother's goddess."

"Where did they take you?"

"A fighting ring, wrapped in fire. She knows I have pyrophobia, and she had Number Four push me through the fire to the ring below. My clothing was burning. I didn't have time to react when the first boy ran at me. Justin was faster, though. The boy bounced off Justin's shields. I forgot about the flames high above me looking for the boy I loved. Praying he wasn't there with me." Both my men frowned, then something hit Justin's mind. A second of pure joy that was eclipsed by loathing.

"Thirty minutes in the pit and the boy hadn't even so much as gotten within three feet of me. Roseden didn't take it well. She killed the boy herself. When I got back up to her, she took my promise ring. She laughed at me for not knowing Justin's magic was on the ring." I watched Kacie bring me the ring. The ruby and sapphire ring shined at me. I hadn't seen it since that day. I reached for it, stopping. I was not that girl anymore. I had Adriana's ring now. I didn't deserve it. That girl was pure, innocent, and loving. That isn't me. "Three years my week was exactly the same. Sundays were the day I was given food. Fluffy - Bekker would be there to give me some peace.

"Monday I would be beaten for sleeping or not sleeping. Whichever, she decided. Most of the time, it was just a beating day.

"Tuesday was a new boy or girl around my age. Drugged out on something that took their reason. I would be raped again if I didn't allow the fight to go long enough for her to derive pleasure from it.

"Wednesday was food again and the release of some of the Mage Metal cuffs so I could recover. I was no use to her if Mage Metal drained my life.

"Thursday was a fight with some sort of beasts. A mix of animal and human. Same punishment.

"Friday she would come to sit in my pit. She used her torture spell as she told me what my friends did as I lay in her Pit. I knew it was not true. That Evana didn't rest looking for ways to get me free from wherever I was. I could feel Justin trying to break the mountain I placed on our *bond*. I did not want him to feel what I felt. It would be unfair to him.

"Saturday, she and my uncle would come to the edge of my pit to have sex. Maclow would look like Justin. I knew it was Maclow because Justin's eyes would never be that cold to me. None of her magic could make his eyes just right. Plus, I didn't feel his pleasure. Especially when Justin was beating on my walls trying to find me."

Kacie noticed something and moved away from me. "Do you remember your rescue?"

"There was sharp magic in the air. Number Four had just been in my Pit. Roseden was not happy with the length of the match I had that day. The woman was a giant, I took down in three moves. A battle with her wouldn't have been worse than anything her men could do to me. Except then she sent One,

Four and Six as punishment. I watched Number Four and Six be impaled on the stone walls on either side of where I was hanging. Dad was covered in blood. Secretly, I wanted it to be One's blood on my father, but I knew I wasn't seeing him. It was just a dream. I didn't want to go with him because I feared what Roseden's plan was. She had never used Dad against me. Of all the people in my life ,she never touched Dad's face.

"The next thing I knew, I was in my bed in my home. The sun was shining. Justin, Dad, Queen Evana and two different healers stood over me." I covered my mouth. I was going to be sick thinking about that day. Swallowing, I looked up at Kacie. "I attacked them. It was a trick. Roseden wanted me to fight them. One last thing that would break my mind."

"Well, shit." Roseden exclaimed.

"Justin's protective sphere saved them. Not him, though. A knife flew, but Justin caught it. Our left hands were bleeding. It wouldn't happen if it was fake. The *Bond* wouldn't have let me feel his pain if he wasn't there. I think he knew that." I held up my palm showing the scar. A crescent moon of white that filled most of my palm.

"That was when I knew it was real. It just took me almost killing the one I loved."

Just another reason to feel like shit.

"It took a year before I left my room. I entered the tournaments. Not for any noble means. I wanted to die. I was going to die. All I was doing was causing pain. If I entered the tournaments, I would be killed the first time I faced a guy stronger than I was." I rubbed our twin scar. "I was not myself. I was my twin, my brother. He was free of all my baggage. I found that even without my magic, I was skilled in combat. I didn't die. No matter how much more difficult it got, I was winning. I even won the top prize. I was named champion. All I wanted was to end my life at the hands of my foe." No matter how much I tried.

"I found something I could live for. Soon it was just Justin and me at the top. Bouncing between first and second place, match after match." I looked at him. "I knew I couldn't die by his hand. I also knew I could never beat him. He needed the following for his crown. Having a woman beat him would have been too much. Lords could have started a rebellion." Looking at Adriana's ring. They might still, but I wouldn't let them defeat my king. I smiled, then remembered Roseden. I felt my voice go hard. "I was five years free when she came after Justin."

Kacie paced the width of the courtroom. I tried not to watch her as she passed Roseden. "I understand you and the king were not on the best of terms."

I laughed. "That was an understatement. I was not the girl he remembered. I don't think I will ever be again. Roseden took that from him, and I felt guilty for letting it happen." He sagged in his seat. He felt the loss of that girl while he claimed to love the woman I had become. "I was cross dressing as a brother, he would never meet. The girl-me, only went to the balls after tournaments or castle events. I wouldn't have gone to them, but my father is very fond of reminding me I am the true queen. That meant I had to be there for Justin, who was ruling for me because I hate titles. It would show confidence in his rule. Blah blah blah. We were both trained by Queen Adriana to rule. She knew one day our *Bond* would be the thing to save us. I had confidence he could rule without me." Fury came to the surface. "I never thought I was mean. I just never wanted to be queen."

"I was planning to tell him the truth. Plotting with Queen Evana when I felt Justin's breathing change. It was stronger than any other intimate *bonding* I have felt from Justin. I knew something was wrong, but I tried to ignore it. Secretly I had hoped he had taken his *Life Love* to bed. I was leaving in a few days. Then my chest started bleeding again. My tattoo was being cut from me. AGAIN! Roseden delights in taking our mark off each other."

"What did you see when you got to the King's room?"

"Roseden trying to cut the heart out of the man to whom I was *Bonded* while she was astride him." Flames came to my hands. Now she looked scared. I wasn't. My flames were not scaring me. Was it because I was angry?

Had Roseden finally made me snap like her?

"Using my wind magic, I threw her to the far wall of his room. She laughed. It didn't take much to subdue her. After three years in her Pit, I learned her spells well." I watched her pale, remembering the spell in question. It would be so easy to cast it right now. Watch her scream in pain. Dathon couldn't stop me.

"I hate my magic, but I used her own spell on her. All the pain she ever gave to me had inflicted on me or to Justin rolled over her body." Goddesses, it gave me such joy to watch her in all that pain. "I held her down as I ran a heated silver candle stick through her palms. That was when Dad pulled me off her. The next day, Justin and I had our very public duel. I almost became queen by battle twice over."

"Those are all the questions I have."

Half-way done, love. Calm down. Just breathe. One. Two. Three. Four.

I was already angry when the defense asked their ridiculous questions. Why didn't I escape? Why didn't I refuse to fight the kids? Why didn't I call my father, Justin or even Evana?

"What part of not knowing where I was didn't you get?" I snapped. "I didn't know where I was. Roseden had proven to me time and time again Justin was at risk. I wouldn't put any of them in danger. As for escaping myself, didn't you hear the part where I was cuffed with Mage Metal? Do you know what it does to mages?" Silence. Even from Justin. I didn't look at him. I glared at the slimy lawyer.

"To a mundane mage, one cuff could make them catatonic. Two would kill, draining their life and their magic. A Mage Teacher could survive two, maybe three. If they were lucky, four. Mage Knights die at four. Five if they are as powerful as my father. This has been studied deeply by King Justice before I beheaded the man. The sheer number of mages Justice killed is sickening. Just to test his new toys. New toys developed by his second soul, a Death Knight." Gasps. "I am glad I killed him. The lives I could save will never counter the ones he took, but now they will live. I'm still in this kingdom, so when he comes back for his prize, it is protected. Then I will take the head of the Death Knight."

"What makes you think you have the right to take the king's head?"

"My mother was the soul daughter of Daina." I snorted. "Daina herself feared my magic could overtake me, driving me crazy, so she placed a lock on me. That is the only reason I survived The Pit. Tulora the Red's one failing was that she couldn't kill her brother! Even after he tried to kill us. She left that for me. Her brother was in control of King Justice. It was my divine job to rid the kingdom of that ass."

"Who was your mother?"

"I am the daughter of Tulora Seabrooke." I created a crystal version of my mother's crest. "Tulora The Red. Tulora The Great. Queen Tulora, First queen of Stowers. High Queen of this whole damn peninsula." I gave it to the judge. "I have all the powers that my mother had with the gifts that my father learned as a templar. I have been trained by a templar, an Aldaina and the highest-ranking living mage in the world. Oh, I have the power and the divine responsibility to kill him before he kills more people. It is still here. I don't have the will to access it." I heard crackling that felt like it was coming from my back.

"Five Mage Metal cuffs were enough to keep me weak, but not kill me. Justice learned that a month before I took his life." Justin snapped to me. "Where did you think Roseden got the Mage Metal?" He groaned. Did he think I wouldn't keep track of a weapon to use against me? "Justice caught me when I was visiting Adriana. For three annoying hours Justice tried to add more and more Metal to me. He wasn't fast enough. I broke free with three cuffs." I gave them an evil laugh. Looking at the bitch. "The sad thing is you could have gotten away with just the fire. I would have been cowering with a wall of fire."

"Why fire?"

Don't let him bait you. Justin said. Too late.

"Listen to me, Jackass, I'm only saying this once, so you better listen. The Death Knight Tabari Seabrooke, the demon that Roseden worships, tried to kill me with fire when I was five years old!" I dropped the glamor. The people of the jury pulled away. I heard gasps seeing the melted flesh down the right side of my body. The judge did too. Kacie looked at my father, who held his head in his hands. Justin was at the edge of his seat. "It is the element that comes easiest, and it is the one I fear the most. A wall of fire would have stopped me in my place at ten years old." I stood.

"I'm twenty nine and you can't find me cowering in fear of the gifts my mother gave me. I have taken back everything Roseden and her master took from me. If my husband wasn't constantly in my mind I would be just as bad as his father. Mages, just like my aunt, would be in prison or dead." Flames engulfed my hands. Burning my shirt sleeves, revealing more of my scars. I couldn't concentrate on the asshole asking me questions that should be obvious.

"There is nothing to lose when you are bleeding and broken. My only interest now is showing this corrupted mage I'm more powerful than her. That she will never beat me into submission. I'm something more than she can imagine and she will know my wrath!" My hands were completely covered in green flames. Just as my mother's flames were.

LYSANDRA! Justin was standing. *Listen to my voice. You need to calm down. Just breathe.* I closed my eyes. *One. Two. Three. Four. Out. Two. Three. Four.* I don't know how long I stood there. When I opened my eyes. My eyes wide at my hands. The flames were on my fingertips. Yet they still didn't frighten me. *Just breathe. One. Two. Three. Four. Out. Two. Three. Four.* I fell back into my chair. What the hell was that? My spine cracked. My jaw unclenched. I closed my hands. Just breathe and I will return to myself. Everyone was looking at me.

"I'm sorry, this is the monster she created. My king keeps me in check, but when triggered by my Aunt, I'm a bomb." I tried to smile sweetly but smoke came from my hands. It smelled like burning apples. That was new.

"If Lady Seabrooke had wanted King Justin dead, why would he allow himself to be intimate with her?" I took a deep breath, looking at the bitch.

"I don't know why? It is something I will never forgive him for. Even if she used magic, he should have known she was not me." I wouldn't look at him. This was the truth of my heart. I was still truly hurt by that night. "Even if he just wanted someone, not me, he could have chosen any other person. It didn't have to be the woman who caused us both so much pain." Staring at the ring, I felt like crying again. Screw them all. I don't like feeling like this.

"Are there any more questions?" The judge asked. I glared at the slimy mage.

"No." Now he feared me. He wasn't the only one. The jury huddled in the corner. The judge was the only one who stayed in their spot.

"Your Majesty, may I offer you some advice?" The judge looked down at me.

"Please do, Your Honor." I forced a sweet smile. Just like Adriana taught. The smile of a queen not affected by the world she hated.

"Maybe find someone to talk to."

I looked back at my hands. "I have tried." The judge touched my shoulder. "During that first year free. I was told I am delusional. I am a liar. Roseden was a respectable mage and wife to an ambassador. I was attention seeking. Making up stories of my mother and the torture I faced. That there was no way magic worked the way it does for me. I am anything but what I was. A destroyed woman looking for help to rebuild myself after I was torn down to the foundation. I have had to build myself back up, but as you can see, I didn't do a great job. If you can offer me someone who understands the crap I have had to deal with, then I will gladly see them."

"I think I know someone." The judge smiled.

"Then thank you. I know my husband and I would be grateful for any help." Justin sat back down. I was back talking in the Adriana voice. Only the charred stand, the evidence of my outburst.

"I am calling a recess. Please see me in my chambers." The gavel hit the desk. I saw the damage I did to the stand. Very ashamed of my outburst. I held my hand up to my men. Earth magic took a lot of concentration for me. Moisture came back to the wood from the pitchers of water on Kacie's desk. The ash flew away in the breeze. When I opened my eyes, it was like I wasn't there.

"Now." Justin was holding me in a heartbeat. "I am calm, Justin." He held me tighter. "Thank you."

"I thought I was going to lose you to the Fury. I didn't realize how much rage you hold inside." I held him to me. "I should have been - done something."

"You can now." He pulled away. "Let's go see who the judge thinks can help me." I turned to Dathon. "I am sorry if I hurt the case. You know how I hate to repeat myself."

"I think you proved our point. Invoking Justin as your balance, you have proven you are more broken than you let on. I don't know if you saw it, but you had your combined barriers between you."

"Thank you, Justin. I don't think I would have taken it well if I had hurt any of them."

"I have studied you for years. I saw when the self hate turned to outrage." He pulled us towards a back room. "If this

144

person still doesn't understand the way you need them to, we will find someone who will."

"And this is when the Queen of Stowera started therapy." Dathon took my hand, and Justin squeezed me. "What will the history book say about me?" I knew mentally I was going to pay for my outburst tonight when I was alone in my room. It was stupid to let her see me that way. I ruined the case. There is nothing that could fix me. I was broken beyond repair.

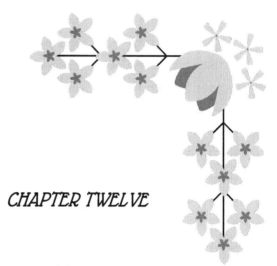

CHAPTER TWELVE

The second I saw one of the Elven men, I knew who I was looking at. I reached a hand out to one of them. Our Uncle Christoph. His sunshine hair. Christoph's gray-blue eyes were like Mom's. Christoph's playful smile. The other elf looked hopefully then sighed. I knew him. The sight of him lifted my soul. I couldn't tell you his name, but I knew I wanted him to kiss me. "Uncle Christoph!" Christoph's arms engulfed me. "I thought he got you, too."

That was when I noticed the other three people in the room. Another tall, full elf, with white hair, gray star eyes that were in anguish. There was something he wanted. I knew that face—though I didn't know where from. The couple with him seemed just that. They wore the crest of the Royal family from Starfall, but not similar.

She was my height with her hair cut short on the sides and longer pulled back into a braid that fell to the small of her back, dyed blue. She had some elf in her, but there was only the hint of a point to her ears. She wore a bow across her back and two short swords on her hips. She wore clothing designed for adventurers but made of Elven silk. Layers with pockets. Functional and gorgeous. Bonus, I think I can get it made for my size.

The man next to her was a burly man with a broad sword across his back. Brown hair in the same style as she had but pointed ears. He was a full elf, though he had brown hair instead of the characteristic blonde hair.

I was confused.

He wore the same clothing style that she did with an oversized pouch on his hip. Full blood elf gray stars for eyes.

Who were these people?

The white-haired elf looked me in the eye and then went to Justin, who hugged him. That sad, slender, full elf wore no weapons or armor, only the flowy, Elven silk robes of a Royal of Starfall. They had to be his bodyguards. Knowing this, my mind spoke to me of how they were a threat. Justin didn't seem cautious. Yet there were so many weapons in this room. Moonblossom's office.

"Your Mother and Aunt knew he was coming. I fought to take you with me, but Jean said it was my destiny to be here when you needed me. After what I saw the last few days, I see more of Tul in you than they thought." This man spoiled me when I was a child. I was the child he wanted. I think he knew I was on edge from the others in the room.

"Few days?" He was the templar who shut my magic off when we were testing the Thorns. "What took you so long?" When I pulled away, I punched him in the shoulder.

"Hey. Your mother told you never to hit first."

"My mother always said family would be there when you needed them." He smirked. "You, my dear uncle, are very late." I punched him again. This time not as hard. I was so happy to see him.

"Ow." He took me in his arms. "When did you get so violent?" He whispered into my scars.

"That is how she shows affection now," Justin said, coming over to me. A hand slipped around my hip, pulling me away from Christoph. I shouldn't be surprised. Justin didn't know him from a hole in the ground. The other three elves left the room, letting me fully relax. Finally, something good from my old life meets something good in my new life. "I look forward to you being with us. I hear so little about her early childhood."

"I must admit, you are not quite as I imagined Lyssie's Soulless Prince." Justin's hand tightened on my hip. I was getting the feeling Justin wasn't okay with that nickname anymore. "You handled her breakdown with her magic, as well as her fury today. Her temper has never been a simple thing to control. Matix would have even been impressed. Tul was like this too, after we lost our little warrior girl. Matix never knew how to hold Tulora calm."

"I had the blessing of history. Tulora was my hero growing up. I think that is what I loved about her daughter first. That she was so much like her mother in the early years." Justin pulled me closer. "Trauma changes their flames to bonfires."

Was that what I was now?

"A bonfire?" Dathon smirked. "Yeah, that is my Lys."

I gave him a dirty look.

"I should be angry with you," I said to Christoph. "I could have used you so many times. Where have you been? When my teachers didn't believe what I told them about Mom. Trapped in that Pit. When I started losing control after I was rescued. You could have trained me when I was in the tournaments. There would have been no question of who was better. Templar training would have given me an edge. I could have shut his magic off. You promised me you were going to show me how templars shut off magic."

Dathon stiffened at *Templar.*

I froze. Shit.

Dathon's magic felt sharp in the stale air of the office. The last time this happened, Adriana was teleported into his workshop half dead. The Mage Knights were built to counter the templars who hunted down me and my mom. Dathon being the head of the Mage Knights and Christoph, the only living Templar in the same room.

"Lyssie?"

I looked back at my father. Justin followed my eyes before moving to Dathon's side. Dathon glared at Christoph, who just smiled playfully back. Oh Christoph, either too stupid to see the problem or too arrogant to care that he was in danger.

"Dad-" Justin and I were no longer in the judge's room. We were in my sitting room in the castle. "Oh shit. Shit!"

"Why did he teleport us away?" Justin asked as he glanced around the room to catch his bearings.

I didn't stand still to answer Justin. I needed to keep them from killing each other.

"Lys, where are we going?"

"Christoph is the second in command to the Templars of Leila."

Justin frowned. History nerd that he was, he should have known who they were, right?

"The people who hunted Mom when she was young. Then they came to kill me." Things were still not clicking, but the threat towards me got his attention. "Fire and Oil."

"One head of the templars was your mother's friend and brother-in-law. Surely that would keep Dathon sane." The explosion that bloomed through my balcony doors proved my point. "Shit."

"That is what I said." I was running then. "There is a law hidden in the Mage Order that if a Templar is found, they are to be killed on sight. Only a Mage Knight of Dad's power can go toe-to-toe with a templar on his worst day. I don't think Christoph was looking for a fight today. So the worst day."

"Why the hell did your mother keep him around?"

"I don't know. I know my brother and Christoph didn't get along. Now Hallon is in Dad. Two powerful mage souls against one templar who wasn't expecting a fight." We were on the roof when Justin questioned where we were going. I whistled. "If we don't stop them, they will destroy the city."

Our Elven horses, Moonlight and Warrior, were there with us on the roof—Moonlight's feather wings already out. Warrior didn't trust Justin enough to show him the wings and appeared annoyed at the expectation.

Justin was shocked.

"No time. We need to get to the house now," I said, jumping on my Moonlight. "Warrior, please, people could die if we don't stop the magic battle."

The horse reluctantly bowed to me.

"Thank you. I will make sure that you get some extra apples for this."

We were airborne. I blinked at the sight of another explosion. This time, the fire was blue. Barely contained by the wards on the property.

"Hallon is awake."

Moon circled over the field behind Dathon's house. My father and brother stood side-by-side with full plate metal. From where I was, they could have been twins. Across the field, Christoph stood alone in his full crystal plate, his crystal sword in his hand half laying on the ground. I felt the drain of my magic.

Moon must have felt it, too, cuz she landed.

"Goddess, stop it." I called, placing a wind wall between my mages and my templar.

"Lyssie. It appears your brother still hates me." Christoph fell to a knee. Blood dripped from his sword arm. "Maybe I should have tried more with him. You needed more help controlling your powers."

I got under his arm to help him stand.

"Christoph, I will make him stop."

The older elf smirked. Arrogant.

"Hallon has to listen to me. I have saved his ass more times than I can remember."

"Your brother stopped listening to anyone after being raised by my father. Call it an odd sibling rivalry. He didn't even tell me who he was growing up, but he knew me. When I saw you two for the first time at three, I knew that was my little brother."

"*You were never my brother. You were his favorite son. I was just the lost child he could mold into a weapon.*" I heard over the wall.

A chunk of earth flew at us.

A smaller wind wall shattered the boulder.

Part of it still hit me in the left side.

"*I saw you corrupting my twin.*"

"Hallon, please stop. You will kill me, too."

His hand stopped for a heartbeat. "I'm not as good as you with our magic."

More earth flew.

I waved my hand up to knock him off his feet with the wind. That didn't help. The next wall I used was with fire. The orange shifted to green, and I was not losing control.

"Please Hal, stop," I begged.

Christoph saw me shaking. His free hand touched my shoulder.

"You know the laws, Lys." This time it was Dathon's voice.

Where was Justin? I could really use the assist right now. My fire and my wind vanished with a wave of Dathon's hand. In the years that I had been in this time, I have never seen Dathon glowing as he was now. The green-blue that I loved, an aura around him. Eyes shining like Daina's had when I was with her.

"Shit, your foster father is a god," I heard behind me. "Leila protect me."

What? Dathon is a god? Of all the stupid things for me to do I am facing down a god to save a rival deity's templar.

"Leila's armor!" Christoph ordered.

My crystal sword formed in my right hand as crystal plates formed across my body. I had never tried to do this until now, and wasn't sure it would work. But if he could do it, so could I. I just needed calm, even breathing. My crystal didn't look like Christoph's, though. A green flame danced in each crystal plate.

I saw Hallon scowl, and Dathon's glow dimmed.

"I don't want to hurt either of you, but I can't allow you to hurt Christoph either. He is family. Just like you."

"You were always weak to him. Now look at you. An abomination."

My heart stopped at the sound of my brother, Hallon, my twin, calling me an abomination.

"What would mother say if she saw you like this?"

I refused to cry, holding back the tears stinging at the back of my eyes. I refused to let him see me be hurt by his words.

"That I finally got the sword right." I launched at my brother. Was this what it was like for Mom when she fought Tabari? She wasn't given the years to grow up with him. Nothing in the world hurt more than locking swords with my twin, whom I missed. The brother who now thought of me as an abomination.

A monster.

Hallon didn't have a weapon. His green eyes glaring at me with such hate.

Dathon had a metal sword I had never seen before. Blue and green steel, a green stone in the hilt as if the metal was poured around it.

"Stop it, both of you," he yelled. A snap of his fingers and Hallon was gone. "Lys, you know the law."

"Laws written by a man who hated who he grew up with," I snarled back, pointing to where my brother had been. "He hated me." Flames surrounded me. "I loved him. I have missed him every day of my life and he hates me, Dad!"

Dathon dematerialized the blade.

"Does that mean you hate me, too?"

Dathon said nothing.

"He was raised by the bastard who wished our family dead. He got to learn firsthand the monster the history books tell us

Templar Max Crowley was." As if that justified the look on my twin's face. How the sweet nerd had changed.

"Christoph left his father's order to join our mother. I remember him being the gentle one that helped my mother train me. Hallon, my brother-" My voice broke. I finally got my brother back, and he wanted me dead. Twenty years of wishing I could see him again and he hated me. "My brother holds hate so deep in his heart that not even I am free from it."

I stopped fighting back my tears, which flowed freely. "I shouldn't be surprised. Tabari is my mother's twin brother, and they hated each other. I guess it is only fair that mine hates me." The look Dathon gave me destroyed the thought I could get back with my brother. That he would help me defeat Tabari. "Tabari corrupted my brother against me, too."

"Tabari? He's here?"

"Now is not the time, Christoph. I need to get my father out of god-mode before he kills us." Dathon dropped all his powers. "Thank Daina. Where is Justin?" He was suddenly next to us. Eyes wide. He was covered in snow.

I smiled, seeing that he was okay. He saw me on my knees crying though. A second in my mind and he was holding me as I cried.

"My wife needs help. She used too much magic," he said calmly, though I know he was just as heartbroken as I was. He had hoped that Hallon could be key to defeating Tabari forever.

"Did not." As I fell face first in the dirt. "Okay, maybe I did."

The darkness was as cold as the grave. The *bond* void there. There was nothing but me and the tundra cold.

"So, you married my foolish son."

I knew that voice. Crystal would not come to my hand. No armor to my skin.

"This is my domain, girl. You cannot call your corrupted defenses."

Corrupted? Of course, Tabari built the Templars. That is where Hallon got the idea for an army of anti-templars from. A way to fight the corruption, all the while falling to hate.

"She is still mine, Tab. I will let you have her when I am done," the new voice said.

I had never heard that voice before. Shrill. Grating on my senses. Yet familiar. And coming from me. "I have a year."

I don't know how long I was out, but it was midday so I estimated at least a day had passed. Justin held me on his lap as he read Hallon's journal. He was searching for something. Dathon on one side of the bed, Christoph on the other side.

"Seriously, you both love me so why fight?" I grumbled.

"Polar opposites, my love." Justin pulled me tighter. "Do you have any idea who she was?"

"Thank Daina. I thought it was a nightmare." He kissed my head laying the book on my lap. "I didn't have very many women in my life as a child."

"It's probably Cassia." Christoph sighed.

Justin wrapped more around me.

"She is the only player I haven't heard of yet," Christoph continued "Your mother couldn't hurt her. She was your replacement and Cassia knew that."

"I saw the page," Justin said with a growl as he nodded to the book. It was on the page with the note. I wanted to show it to Christoph to find out who wrote it. Dathon reached for my wrist. Justin pulled me away from him.

"Tulora was killed because she couldn't kill her own daughter-in-law. Can you blame her? Knowing her daughter was taken away from her, Tulora couldn't handle another loss." Justin was keeping me away from both.

Justin?

They said that they were going to kill you. I glared at my father. *Your brother is more adamant about your death than Dathon, but he is still inside your father.*

"Is my brother locked away?" I asked. I didn't want to think of his eyes glaring at me. "He hates me. Just like Tabari hates Mom."

"Yeah. I spoke with Hadain last night. He is keeping Hallon for a while. He is not to be reborn until he can calm down. Justin doesn't believe it."

"Honestly, neither do I." I pushed Hallon's book away. "You didn't see what I saw."

"I know I didn't tell you the truth. There are laws," Dathon said.

"Laws?" Justin and I scoffed. "We have been with you for fourteen years, and you never once told us you were a damn god." Justin was just as upset about this. Different reasons. "Were there laws that stopped you from saving my mom?"

"Yes."

I knelt between Justin's legs. He just glared at Dathon.

"Hey look at me," I said to Justin.

He didn't.

"Justin, look at me please," I asked more in a whisper. "We are not needed today, right?"

He sighed.

"Okay, let's go away somewhere for the day. We both need to be away from all this for a while."

He pulled me in for a hug. "Dathon was going to kill you because of a law that has been void for too long. There is only one templar left."

I held him close. Yeah, I felt that betrayal too.

"He loves you and yet he will kill you because of the last templar." The heartache was real. The man who raised me saw me as the same monster my brother did.

"No, he is justified in wanting to kill me." Christoph sighed. I didn't look at him. "My people killed his followers by the hundreds for Tabari's pleasure. My order is still alive, though I am more of an advisor now."

"Not helping."

"In this, I don't think I am not supposed to." I groaned. "Tabari is back. Cassia is looking for revenge on your mother and has somehow claimed you. Even against her own *Bonded*." If that is really what was happening. "Back when your mother fought them, it was only her family. The Aldaina backs her as the Soul Daughter of Daina. To defeat them both, I think you are going to need all three factions."

"Three?" Justin asked.

"Oh Princeling-"

"He is my King, Christoph. My *Husband-in-Bonding*." I snarled. Pride danced in Justin's heart. "Watch what you call him." I was not pleased with either of them right now.

"I tease. He is very protective of you. I watched him carry you off the field yesterday. Your love is deeper than that of your mother and father." Christoph sat up in his chair. "As I was saying, I saw more than you both did. Leila's crystal vestiges took the form of Aldaina armor, filled with the flame of the Mage Knights."

I blinked.

Justin nodded, showing me what he saw. Me kneeling, covered in clear crystal plates as if it was commander Aldaina armor. Each one held a dancing green flame at the center. I looked terrifying and beautiful.

"If it comes down to a war, Lys is going to need all three orders."

"How do I recruit three different ideologies to my side in the face of a war? I can't even get my own family to stop fighting."

"I still have the ear of the templars. I am guessing you are the Master of the Mage Knights." Dathon's glare softened. "Who is her connection to the Aldaina?"

Justin and I both raised our left hands.

"Both of you?"

"My mother was. My wife and sister are Aldaina commanders." Justin brought my ring to his lips. "Maiona, Bleen and Daina."

Christoph laughed. "No, my boy. I will agree that Lyssie is Daina, but your sister is not the maiden. I know for a fact that Hades hasn't found his wife yet. Hadain still talks to me. The only one in the family who doesn't glare at me."

I sighed.

"I get in your case, Lyssie, I have rather been absent. I should have been here when you made that rather dramatic entrance into society. Whatever you attacked made me take a pause. I have started a war with your current family. I insulted your husband, repeatedly it seems. I am the bearer of bad news."

"Yeah, so you two need to work out whatever the hell this is. I have a lot to deal with, so I am taking today to be with my husband. Get out of my room."

Both men sighed and stood.

"I don't want to see you until we have all calmed down."

They left without another word.

"Am I cursed? Is my family line cursed?"

"I don't know, my love. I can see how he looked at you. Something changed in Hallon between contacting us through the little spellbook and when he died. I was trying to figure out what that was. The lucky man we saw was not the same man I saw yesterday." I sat back on my heels. "Why don't you go take a shower? I will pick out something for you to wear."

"We will have to go get you clothing."

"No. All the clothing we had in the grand city is here now in my room. I will just go shower too. Meet me at the stables?"

"Warrior is going to be so mad at me."

"He tried to buck me off twice yesterday." I laughed.

CHAPTER THIRTEEN

Warrior and Moonlight were both at the gate and saddled when I got there. Justin wasn't anywhere to be seen. We also had no stable hand, as these two were normally held in the royal stables. "What is going on, guys?" I asked them. Moon looked to Warrior, expecting him to do something. He just pawed the ground. "Whoa dude, did you not see what happened here yesterday?" He huffed. "I didn't know Dathon was going to send Justin away. You can't blame me for that." Moon nuzzled me.

"He's still pissed?" Justin asked. I sighed. "Can we talk about this later? Lys and I need to spend the day away from people angry with us. Can you please not try to kill me? I have had enough of that for a lifetime." Moon nudged Warrior, who huffed in reply.

"Thank you, Your Majesty," Justin said in mocking. For that, he got head-butted.

I laughed. "Justin, our horses are the royalty of all the horses in the area."

"What?"

"Well, I guess I know what we are doing today," I said, mounting Moon. "Come on. We are getting a picnic worth of food for the four of us and we are going somewhere to talk."

Moon set off in a happy trot. Warrior and Justin were still in a standoff.

"Alistair, save me." First one of fire and horses was a patron of Matix's family. Well, I guess a friend of my godly father too. "Warrior, if he doesn't come, I will revoke our deal." I have never seen a death glare so sharp from a horse as the look Warrior shot me at that moment.

When they finally followed us, I was in the market. I found a basket vendor for two baskets. She was a sweet, frail looking woman who was teaching her grandson to weave. The boy's mother, I want to say, sold me two apple baskets that could be attached to Moon's saddle. Plus, a smaller one with a lid to hold our lunch in it. We were about to go when a young woman, maybe ten, rushed out of the shop.

"Majesty." She bowed. Bowed, not curtsied. That caught my attention. The Mother looked shocked as if she didn't know who her daughter or I were. "Wait, you don't like titles. Sorry. Lys? That is what the king calls you, right?"

I tilted my head in confusion. I didn't have to tell her. Was she a fan? "Yes?" Her eyes lit. Silver the size of moons, brown hair that hit her knees. Her dress reminded me of the leggings and coat with a half skirt of the Aldaina commanders.

Oh shit. I started a new fashion trend?

I laughed at myself. I had wanted a new trend. "You are?"

"Maribelle."

"Good morning, Maribelle. I am happy to meet you." I tried to sound calm and regal as I put my hand out to shake hers. Adriana drilled this voice into me for this very reason.

I was petrified of what this little girl wanted. "What can I do for you?" My other hand tapped my leg in time with my heart. Maybe I could keep it slow.

"Can I ask you to start a training school for girls to enter that tournament next year? I will be of age by then." I bit my lips to keep from laughing.

"Mari!" Her mother gasped. "The tournaments train boys for war."

"They also taught me how to survive. How to relax and have fun. They gave me friends I will never forget and a home in the ring that I can never lose," I said with a smile.

The girl lit even brighter.

"I will talk to the king about it on our picnic today. How about that?"

She literally bounced. Justin chuckled behind me. I was trying so hard to be calm. So very hard but I could feel the corners of my eyes welling. Girls' training to be the best they could be.

I should have known you would start getting a following.

"I know at least three of us who would be interested. Even some boys who agree girls should train. Two of them want to go to the girls' school."

"Justin and I will see what we can do. There are more issues than just a location. I see nothing being started until the fall though, so you are going to hafta be patient."

"Yes, Lys. Thank you for considering it." The mother glared at me. Why do people glare at me all the time? "I am done with my chores and the three orders for tomorrow. May I go see Julia and Cate now?" Her mother waved her off. The girl kissed her mother's cheek, grandmother and brother, then came to hug me. "You are my favorite person in the entire world." Then she bowed to Justin before running off. Now he was laughing.

"I don't mean any disrespect, Majesty, but ignore my daughter's foolish request. Women don't belong fighting." Really? "Not even in the Mage Knights." Dathon might have something to say about that. "Nor the ridiculous Aldaina cult." Cult? What the hell? "Not in the tourneys. Women are meant for child bearing and shop owners." Justin stepped closer. I know it was to back me, but to her, it looked like he was getting the horses out of the way. "I mean, look at your scars. The king must be very forgiving."

What am I forgiving? Does she think your scars came from the tourney? Do you get this a lot?

"You may not have meant to, but yes, you have disrespected someone. Your daughter." She blinked. "She has seen she is not meant for just popping out babies. There is more to life than that. She is looking for something that will make HER happy. Too often, people ignore the brains of young ladies have. Saying they are just silly, but I will have you know your daughter is looking for a way to be her own person. If taking part in the tourneys makes her happy, allow her to do it. Even if I hadn't spent a third of my life in them, I would still have encouraged her to follow her dreams."

The little boy looked amazed that I would talk to his mother that way. Where the old lady just laughed.

"As for these scars, these are because a man decided I was not even worth the air I breathe. I was five years old. There is nothing for my husband to forgive except because I nearly killed him in that tournament ring."

"I told you our queen follows her own path. It is an old path. Hundreds of years old. It is a joy to see a balance back to things." The older lady said, not taking her eyes off her weaving.

"Thank you for your wise, kind praise." I tried not to sound growly. She laughed harder. It came out in wheezes and coughs. I made a move to help, but the boy gave her a glass of water.

"Queen Adriana, given a chance, would have adored the queen you are becoming, Lysandra." Justin took my tapping hand. "Now, go, girl. You have a new school to discuss with your king." She waved us off. The mother gave me one more glare for good measure. "Oh, leave the queen be. This is her divine path." The old lady muttered.

"You didn't snap. I am very proud of you," Justin said when we were out of earshot.

Everything in me was bright as sunshine. "She said Adriana would love the queen I am becoming." I smiled at the thought. Justin grinned back, and I wiped my eyes. "She implied Adriana would have been proud of me."

"High praise indeed." For us it is. "You sorely needed that." I nodded. "It is one thing coming from me. I am the other half of your soul. I am supposed to praise you." I stifled a laugh at that. That is what the terrible voices tell me. "Seeing her take your side. I don't know, it was like we are finally doing something good for a change." He took my hand. "We can talk about the school later, but I think it is a good idea. That is eight girls you have recruited, in something like three days. You have only just started real queenly duties this week."

"Just think, when I really know what I am doing and not just reacting to things." He laughed.

"Goddess, save us all when that day comes." I gave him a playful squeeze to let him know I knew he was teasing. "You are gorgeous today."

"I'm gorgeous every day you are just blinded by it to compliment me," I said playfully, moving to the fruit vendor. He was all too happy to sell us a sack of apples. He just didn't have the green ones Warrior favored. So we got some Golden, which was Moon's favorite. As Justin paid, I took an extra apple and bit into it. Today may not have started off the best, but I felt amazing.

My next stop was the tack master for some feed. Even our horses needed something other than apples. I didn't get there. Someone slammed into my shoulder and the world went black. *You are not allowed to be happy, daughter of Cordelia.* That odd female voice said. The one that claimed me against Tabari. When I came back, Justin had pulled me into an alley.

"I think I know what your missing time is, Lys." He looked scared. "After lunch, I am going to have to give you back to Christoph. Dathon and I have something to talk about." It is concerning. "I would love to tell you, but I am not sure and need to do some research, my love."

The rest of the shopping was quiet. My apple, long since forgotten. The picnic basket was filled with all our favorite travel foods. Looking at the crowd, I looked for signs of what had happened and saw nothing. No glares. No scared faces. The far side of the marketplace, the basket weaver's shop, was bustling with people, though I couldn't see what was going on. What did the voice inside me do? Did I hurt someone?

"Hey. Hey. None of that. Nothing went wrong. I just need to confirm something magical with your father," Justin said, taking my hand again. "It was only twenty minutes."

"In twenty minutes, we were married. In twenty minutes, I could decapitate your father. In twenty minutes, someone innocent could have died. I don't know what will happen until after I come back. There is so much of my life I can miss, good or bad, in twenty minutes."

"Evana said something about you not looking right when we said our vows. When you moved back to the balcony and said nothing to Chantara on the way. I thought you were hiding behind a mask. You had done that a lot since The Pit. It was even hard for me to see if it was really you in those moments. I think I just saw your tell."

"Are you angry with me?"

"Why the hell would I be angry?" He was shocked. "Lys, whoever your second soul is has been popping to the surface. That is what I need to talk to Dathon about. I am not angry you missed our vows. Those were words. You were fully with me when you placed the ring on my hand. Then when we made love. That is what I cared about." He pulled me into his arms. "I love you. If I have to deal with two of you to love, I will figure it out. In the meantime, I will keep watching and learning."

"You are far too good a person to love me." I smiled, and that got me a kiss.

"You are too adorable not to love." The uncertainty still gnawed at me. Until we got back to the house. Christoph was mucking out the stables when we landed.

"I know that face," he said, coming to get me off Moon. "What happened?"

"You start by taking care of the horses. I will go see your father," Justin said, kissing me on the head. "It will be okay. We can figure this out." So, I did what I knew how to do. I stripped down Moon and Warrior. Counting my breathing to keep myself calm. Stay on task and breathe.

"Lyssie, talk to me." Christoph finally said when I was brushing Moon. Warrior was happily eating his oats. "I am here for you to talk to, remember?"

I was in full tears when I looked up at my uncle. "I think Cassia is hurting people and I think she is inside me." Christoph took me into his arms. "I think I am a Death Knight." I had tried so hard not to kill people. Five years I hadn't killed a single person. Injured sure, but it was nothing when you had healers on standby. I didn't hurt anyone bad enough that they had more than a bruise. Until the last day of the tournament. Now the thought of being a Death Knight myself scared the hell out of me. "How can I fight the demon that has anchored inside me?"

Christoph was still holding me when an arm pulled me from him. Dathon bent down to look me right in the eyes. "I think you are right."

That got me crying again.

"I can block her for a while, Lys. She will not cause any more lost time."

"I'm a Death Knight." I felt my whole body shake as I lost all emotional control. I was the thing I was sent to the future to kill.

"No, you are not!" He snapped. "Do you want to know why I know that?" I said nothing. "My daughter is still talking to me. Still crying out of fear. Cassia hasn't taken over yet and I will be cursed by all the goddesses if I let that happen." My body shook. "Do you really think my Divine Wife would let me fail you a second time?"

"Daina is your wife." I groaned. Today was a day of revelations. None of them I was prepared for. "That is why she gave you to me. Is that why she gave you Adriana as a *Life Love?* Was that the magic she blocked? Did she block Cassia's soul drain?"

"Yeah, I think so. I think that is why she was crying when I found you two at Alistair's tower. She has no power over the Death Knights." I hugged my father. For the first time in a long time, I was the little girl again, scared of the monsters she saw. "It is okay. Let's get in the workshop and I will get started."

CHAPTER FOURTEEN

The rest of the day was a blur for me. One minute I was crying, the next I was in pain, fighting to keep control of my body. Cassia fought back for every inch Dathon was trying to take from her. Until dark fell and I was back out in the stables. Justin found me in Moon's stall, leaning on my sleeping horse. My eyes locked on my new set of matching bracelets Dathon wanted me to wear. When Dathon showed me the new collar, he wanted me to wear. I was justifiably freaked out. The bracelets were the same. They were to block Cassia from doing anything to me. I knew the reason, but they were made of Mage Metal. It took five, inch thick rings to hold me in check. How would two flimsy bracelets do the job?

"Do you think he could just make me a crown of this shit?" I said when Justin leaned on the gate. "Something powerful enough that I could block her and take away my fire."

"I asked him about that. He said there is no precedent for something like that. As your father, he is looking into it. He thinks the idea of a more powerful object could keep me safe from Tabari, too." I leaned back.

"We are the best couple ever," I said sarcastically. "I am a Death Knight and you have her *Bonded* trying to get in you." Justin sighed. "Who did we kill in a past life to deserve all this torture?"

"I don't know, love, but Dathon and Christoph are on it. In the meantime, are you ready for your heist?" I snickered. "I know I shouldn't encourage you and your criminal tendencies, but we need the key to the house and Zaidon will not let you in wearing those." I stood up. Moon followed suit.

Warrior was already getting his saddle blanket. "Will you let me fly with you?" Warrior looked over at me and Moon.

"Yeah, we love them."

Both man and horse sighed.

"This is your understanding," I said. Elven horses are smarter than anything in the world. Which makes them picky about their riders. Even more so for the ones who know they can fly. "Moon and I understand we are here to help people. Warrior and I understand that sometimes protecting people requires us to hurt others. You two seem to understand that you would do a lot because you love us."

Warrior huffed at my explanation. That was when I knew I was right. In Justin's case, I have always known. He knew I was being tortured, and he stayed in the one mile. "Yeah, well, loving you is easy as breathing, but so damn hard when you are hurting." He took the bracelets. "Would it help if I put them on your wrists?"

"I don't know. I don't know if it is having something on my wrists again or the fact they are Mage Metal, or even I don't really believe they will keep her at bay."

"I won't force you, Lys. I will stand beside you no matter what you decide." I put them in my saddlebag. "We should get going. The old man will want to sleep."

We flew in silence. I just wanted to breathe. I didn't know what my brother wanted me to find. Could I trust him? He wanted me dead. What if my second soul took over before I could find the cleansing? What if I can't do this and I die? Who would take up the quest to kill Tabari and whatever I became? Would I become a Death Knight, just like Tabari?

"Lysandra." It was Justin's voice. He's been saying my full name a lot lately. "Love, please stop." He was at my knee. We had landed. The silver cylinder that is Crystal Keep was a mile away. I love flying and I missed the entire flight. New fears entered my mind. Shit. Did Cassia take over? "Lys." My shoulders tightened. My breathing grew faster, as did the tapping on my leg. "Lysandra, you were you the entire flight. I had us land because you were thinking in circles."

"I don't know if I can do this." I stared at the steel tower that once belonged to my grandfather. There was a time I knew every curve, nook, and room in it. After the fight in Haven, Dathon brought me here. The formerly simple tower now had five wings hanging off the central tower, a stone wall two stories tall, and guards. We never had guards when I was with Mom. "I am sure we can find another way into the house."

"Come down, my love."

Moon knelt down.

"Thank you, Moon."

He took my left hand as I was some noble lady, not the panic induced woman that could not stop staring at our destination. "Lys, look at me, please."

Slowly, I did.

"I know this means very little coming from me, but you can beat this. We will get in your home, we will get this spell book from your brother, we will cleanse Cassia from you and save me from Tabari. There is no way around it. You are your mother's daughter. I am her biggest fan. We have so many books written from her time, telling us what she did wrong and how she did it, so we can avoid doing them, too."

"My mother had the soul of a demigod. She was the champion of said goddess and she still failed. How am I, her broken and bruised daughter, supposed to succeed where she failed?"

"Your mother didn't have me." That I laughed at. "Your Aunt sent you to me. There has to be a reason. Your brothers found my second soul and hid it. Why?"

"Cuz they hate me." Justin glared.

"No, I am the deciding factor here. She taught you to protect me, right?" I nodded. "Then she sent you to me to really protect me, because she saw Tulora would fail because she loved her family. You no longer have those ties. You never met Cassia and Tabari has done nothing but try to kill you. We just need a spell to cleanse that bastard from this planet, and we are golden. I'm the key to that."

"You think I'm panicking when I just have to prove you are my magic button to solve all our problems?"

"Yes." I laughed. I couldn't help it. It was mean of me. He was trying to help. Trying to take the weight off my shoulders.

"No offense, Justin, but if that was the case, they would have sent Hallon, who could do magic, not the warrior."

"But I am your warrior, so you can embrace your mage side."

That made me freeze in his arms. Embrace the thing that I feared the most? Why in all the Goddesses' and Gods' names would I do something like that? "Because we both know I am the only one who can keep you from completely losing control."

"Christoph can just snuff out my magic." I snapped my fingers. "Are you going to learn that power?"

"I have plans to start with him in the morning during your crystal training. I don't think I need the templar magic, but he thinks having me in your head is not always going to be the solution. You have panic mode on speed dial."

I placed my hands on his biceps.

"You have learned to place that mountain, as you call it, so fast I can't keep up. If you did that and blocked me out while you were in panic mode, the templar magic would be the only thing stopping you from destroying our kingdom."

I tightened on him. The courtroom came to the forefront. I nearly destroyed the stand. Probably the whole room, if Justin hadn't put his dome on me.

"I seem to have two modes, Justin. Panic and irrational rage."

"Yeah, that was new. I have seen you angry. You nearly killed me, but what I saw when that slime ball questioned you was like nothing I had ever seen before." He moved his hands to my hips. "I wonder if your magic isn't growing or if it has been unlocked. Because you haven't summoned that much magic around you ever, either."

"What if not even you can stop me and I burst like Mom did at the Battle of the Reach?"

"Hence the new training." He laughed at me. "Your mother needed that. She needed to cause all that destruction. She killed all her brother's monsters, destroyed his power and his base. Had she not done that, he would be more powerful than she was, and it would not have ended very well. I have theories about all of that." Theories? Really? What more could it be than my mother lost control of her powers? "That is for another day. Tonight we need to break into Dathon's father's study, grab some shit and get out. Dathon will tell us if they need us."

"So from here, are we going straight to Haven?"

"Maybe not straight." I eyed the smirk. "Lys, it is two days on the ground. It will be the middle of the night. I think we can stop at an inn before we get to Haven. Hell, not even your Thorns are going to be there yet." I relaxed. "I know you worry, love. I know Roseden did a number on you."

"I am sorry too."

His fingers flexed.

"The other night was great, Justin. I'm willing to try again." I thought he would kiss me, but no, he pulled completely away from me. "Justin?"

"I want that, Lys. I really do. I just can't get your fear from my mind. I have never, ever seen you that scared." His hand covered his mouth. "I have seen you face my father twice. Face me near death, and you were not nearly as scared as you were when I was on top of you."

"They say to conquer your fear, you need to face it, right?"

"Not at the cost of losing your mind. Lys, I love you. I hate she made you fear me." He was crying. My big powerful protector was crying because Roseden hurt me, hurt us so deeply. "I will not feel right making love to you again for a while."

"Justin, we can't let her win. I have seventeen more months to live. If we let her take this from us, then she will truly have

174

won." My hand cupped his cheek. "Please help me not make her win?"

"I love you."

"I know."

He kissed my hand.

"Now, should we do this? Heaven only knows what my evil twin needs me to find. Or how I am even going to find it."

CHAPTER FIFTEEN

Getting in was the easiest part. Zaidon met Justin at the door. I think it was him. I was on Moon near the very top of the tower. This had been my grandfather's office back in my time. Now, in this time, it was the personal study for Dathon's father. I had never thought of Zaidon as my grandfather. I was some magical deviant who knew more about his home and the first Seabrooke mage than he did. For some reason, he hated that. That didn't stop me from coming into his study through the secret door behind the painting of what I know now is my brother, Hadain. Those days made this place feel like home. There was no cinnamon in the air. No warmth of his fiery magic. Zaidon was nothing like my grandfather.

Not that hard to feel for my family's magic. It was picking through to find the right item. Seabrookes resonate as the wind. Everything in Zaidon's office resonated with the wind. He was a pure-blooded Seabrooke. So I tried auras. Our family's color is mostly green. Hallon was greenish blue. Nothing in this room was greenish blue. Then I saw the glass case. *Destiny's* locket, the size of my palm, glowed blue. The dagger next to it is red. That was Mom's inner fury's color.

Mom's dagger looked like Adriana's. So much so that side by side, they were the same. Where did Adriana get the dagger? I reached for Mom's magic with my left hand. I thought Adriana had created the rune spell—converted it from something that Mom put around the house. I was wrong. A red dome surrounded me. Runes dancing all around me. The same ones in Adriana's spell. I spun to read them all.

I missed so much more than growing up with them. Mom's magic changed. Drastically over the time I was gone. Where she could breathe a plant to life, now she protected that life. Green magic. Now it was red. Had she embraced fire or blood magic? Why would she? Maybe that is why mine is red. I understand why my magic was red. I am very close to fire magic. I had seen nothing in the books that would prove she, too, had changed to fire only.

"My God." Zaidon and Justin stood at the door. The old man, still, looked like the fabled wizard with the long beard and the pointy hat.

My dark-haired story-book king shared the same shocked expression.

"Lysandra, what have you done?" The mage asked.

In my left hand was Mom's dagger, and in the right, Adriana's. Both extended with crystal, so they were three feet long—closer to the length of my full crystal sword. One blue. One red.

"I don't know." I shook off the crystals, sheathing both daggers. The locket and three books now stood out to me. All the items that had my family's magic were silent. I grabbed the locket. Going for the books. I could see the mage move to stop me from taking the books. Hallon appeared to stop Zaidon.

"That is my sister, son." Justin rushed to my side. *"You are mine. You look like our grandfather."* Hallon sounded shocked. He turned to me. *"Lys?"* Neither of us spoke, and Justin pulled me to the balcony. *"I see. I have turned. Go. Destiny will have words for you when you get to the house."* So we turned. Moon and Warrior were waiting there for us. *"Lysandra, for what it's worth, I'm sorry. Whatever I did to you, know, I did it out of fear for what you are going to become."*

"What am I going to become?"

"The Mother." I turned to see the sadness in his eyes. *"In the next life that we are together, I will most certainly like to grow up and know more of your mind, sister of mine. Now go. The new Destiny awaits."* So we flew. Only stopping when the horses decided they needed a rest. I landed hard on the ground, crumbling like paper in the rain.

What the hell was all that? What was The Mother? "How did I gain yet another title when I hate them so much?"

"Did your mother create the spell Mom used to save Dad?"

"I don't know. The runes seemed more randomly placed, but that might just be Mom's untrained magic. The two daggers covered in my crystal were new. It felt so natural, I didn't even feel it happening." I looked down at my haul. "Before I grabbed the dagger, everything called to me. After only these things demanded my attention."

"We can look at them when we get into the inn. I don't trust doing this out in the open."

"The Mother."

"Yeah."

"Justin, what or who is The Mother? I can't have kids."

That left us with more silence. Warrior snorted right before Moon descended. There was an inn. The red wood, two story building surrounded by apple trees and strawberry fields could only be one place. *Princess' Peace.* This was the place the historians say Mom stayed on her route to gather her army. Any time I come this way, I try to stay here. I hope to glean something of her. The aura sight was still up. I forget to shut it off. It is an added layer of protection. Anything that is magical shows a color aura around them. Just in case Roseden or Maclow ever made a move to take me again.

With it up this time, I saw the orchard glowing with green marbled with red streaks. I have never seen a dual color like this. Mom's old magic color mixed with her red. Pulling on Moon's reins, I sat there hovering over the blossoming trees. I know this is where Knyght's Reach exports all the fruit from, but I didn't know Mom enchanted the forest.

"Lys?"

Mom was really here. Justin looked through my eyes. All her earth magic holds the orchard in growth. No winter comes to this land. That is why this is the most abundant land in the whole kingdom. Why has no one written about this? Was this just another thing Dathon had to keep from us?

"Your core magic is fire. Hers was plant life. Why? Most powerful magic families hand down the same magic type in their blood. Why are you the polar opposite to hers?"

"I wish I could ask her."

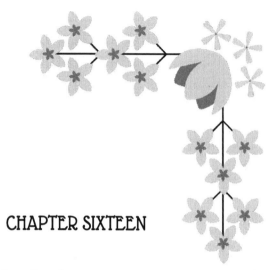

CHAPTER SIXTEEN

Justin was sleeping. Snoring.

I smiled. When had he started snoring?

Add that to the list of things I didn't know about my husband. That is something I could have learned during the five years back if Roseden hadn't made me petrified to go near him. No, the only thing I learned was when he was sleeping, I have to be awake. I have to keep him and me safe from her and her minions.

I couldn't sleep if I tried. There had been too much thrown at me. My mind spun. My mother's magical change. That my sister-in-law was a Death Knight and her soul was in me. Being called *The Mother*. Whatever it was? I paced, trying to figure it all out. Until I found a loose board. Loud enough that Justin stopped snoring and turned on to his side.

I sighed. One of us should be rested.

Out the back of the inn, was a small garden. Fae Flowers strung from tree to tree, creating a net of light over a central sitting area. From Justin's saddlebag, I pulled his journal.

Finding a second one. The second one was blank, a pencil wrapped in a leather pouch on the cover. I took that one. Someone once told me that if you write your thoughts down, they will leave your mind. Why not try it?

Dressed in a simple shift, a leather vest over it and Elven silk pants under it, I slipped out to the back garden. There I sat there until a voice made me look up. "I'm sorry. I didn't know anyone else was staying here."

Mom?

Younger than I remember her. Younger than my age now. Green dress and dyed brown hair. Her favorite velvet cloak, with the rose embroidery. "I can leave you to your thoughts."

"No. No, please sit. I would deny no one this garden. It is beautiful in the early light."

"Thank you." She sat next to me on the bench and I untucked my legs from under me and fall to the cobble path. "I am Tulora." She was using her real name.

"Lysandra."

"It is interesting to see another woman with red hair this far south. Where are you from?"

"Haven," I said, and she smiled. I don't remember Mom ever smiling. Not like this. I remember a lot about my mother, but she never smiled. My nose burned. I knew tears were trying to come. "You?"

"Crystal Keep." Oh shit, I remembered this story. Her father had forced her out when the Templars came to the tower. She went to a town, met my father, Auntie *Destiny,* and Uncle Christoph. She was married to Matix, they were attacked on their wedding night. *Destiny* was mutilated. Mom had rescued Auntie, but in doing so, lost her new husband. Christoph met them here. This is where he changed sides. "We are on our way to Haven."

"Gorgeous place. There is some clean forest area to the north of town. When I visited last, our cottage was still unused." Lys, you are playing with time magic here. Stop interacting with her. My brain screamed. "I know my mother loved our home while she was alive."

"I am sorry for your loss." I waved her off.

"She died when I was nine." I looked up at the Fae Flowers, trying to thank Daina for this gift. "I think you are going to love it."

"I hope so. Revan is not a safe place for those of our hair color." Revan? Oh, shit, that was a town not five miles from this inn. That was the town Matix was from. They got married in Revan. After her father denied her and Auntie *Destiny* at Crystal Keep, she went to Haven. I had to talk Justin into going there. I would like to see my father's hometown. I know so very little of him.

"I am sorry. I know the templars well." Almost as well as she did. She nodded. "So, what brings you out here? Shouldn't you be sleeping?"

"I can't sleep. I haven't in days. There was a templar raid. You?"

"Same. Too many dreams of death haunt me." I looked her right in the eyes. "My husband is worried I might lose my mind soon." If I hadn't lost it already, and this wasn't time magic.

"The ones we love worry about us when we really cause all the turmoil in their lives." I smirked. "Does your husband understand that until the king is gone, you will never know peace?" I pulled my legs up to my chest.

"No. That is what I am writing." My hand ran over the cover of the notebook. "I have done so much he just doesn't fully understand. How could he? I have been driving him away. I am telling him everything I can't say out loud for fear he would hate me."

"What could you have done that was so bad you had to drive him away? Is he not your *Divine Match*?" I smiled. Ah, yes, that is what we were called back then. *Divine Match*. So much clearer of a term than *Bonded*. Just another thing, the modern age changed for the worse.

"I have fought with Tabari. I have taken the head of a host. Yet he aims to take his *nephew-in-bonded* as a host. Tabari's *Bonded* lives in me. I can feel her clawing at the wards the God of Magic put up to keep her at bay, but I honestly don't know if I can fight them both."

"You're my daughter then," she said so plainly—as though it was every day you met your daughter from the future.

I smiled. "Hi Mom."

She teared up.

"I am sorry. I'm not the daughter you needed."

Her eyes went wide.

"Never think that!"

I blinked. Young Mom was quick. I hadn't even noticed her taking my hand back and placing it over her heart. "I love your father with everything in my soul. No matter what Tabari does to him, I will always love him. Your father gave me my dreams. He gave me you."

Me? "I always wanted to have a family free of the endless worry of the templars." She looked back at the building. "He is gone now. Tabari took him, for Daina knows what reason. Leaving me to heal our sweet Jean." I felt her moving my ring.

"Nothing you could ever do would make you a flaw in my eyes because you were made of that love." A soft smile in her eyes. "So you found the one Jean said you will protect?"

That I outright laugh at. Protect? Even at this point in her life, she knew about Justin. "Mom, I have been the reason Justin is in so much danger. Tabari didn't end with you. You never defeat him and I don't know how. We are on our way back to Haven to unlock your house there. My twin-"

"Twins? Mat gave me twins." Her eyes welled.

"Yeah. He says there are things that will help me figure it out. I just don't have faith I can be the protection Auntie said I would be for Justin." That is when I cried, in front of my mother. "I have caused Justin losing his mother, father, and sister. He was tortured because of the *Bond,* right along with me, when I was captured by one of Tabari's minions. Then I nearly killed Justin in my rage. I tell him I don't love him anymore, but the truth is I am so scared I will be his death. I love him so much, but I know I will fail him too. That I will not be enough to save him from Tabari. That we will both be Death Knights. If Tabari takes us, it will end your line."

"Oh, my darling." She was crying too. "I am sorry I failed you."

"Talking to you now, I think you were supposed to fail. The *Destiny,* in this time, claims I am here to cleanse Tabari. That I will be his end and he will be mine. I will die at his hands yet somehow cleanse the demon."

"If I can find it for you, my love, I will give it to your twin. I will search high and low to figure out what you need. I can't let my brother destroy you and your husband."

"I miss you so much, Mom. Jeanevera sent me so far away when Tabari attacked the house. I never thought I would get to talk to you again." She took me into her arms when I sobbed into her shoulder.

"I am sorry for everything." She pet my hair. "Do you know your father? Were you able to meet him?"

"No. He came to us when Hallon and I were nine. Tabari with him. Tabari tore out Dad's eye and caused me and Hallon to have matching burns." I let my glamor fall. She gasped, tearing up anew. "Auntie did something, and I landed five hundred years in the future. I know about your lives through history books and teachers." I smiled, knowing she would not be happy about what I said next. "I beat up a teacher for calling you a whore. We were outside the Haven house and he was saying so many horrible things about you. I couldn't take it. I threw everything I had at him. It took my *Mother-in-Bonding* to stop me from killing him."

"After I pass, he must take control of the kingdom again. The day you are taken from us, nothing will stop me from turning him to ash. He will probably use that against my memory from now on." Her hand touched my scars gingerly. "You have your father's eyes and smile. Based on what you have told me, I think he would be proud of you. I know I am. He would love you no matter what you did. You are the little girl he wanted so badly to raise." She took my left hand and placed it on her belly. "I will wait for you to be born to show you how proud I am of you. For both of us." I wrapped my arms around her neck. "My darling, Lysandra. My little warrior princess."

I giggled at that. "Mom, I'm a queen." She held me as she giggled.

I don't know how long she held me against her shoulder, but I know I heard Justin call my name from the door. I saw he knew who I was with, but before he stumbled to us, she vanished. He could catch me before I fell off the bench. "Was-" I nodded. "Her hair was brown?"

"She didn't show her red a lot until after I was gone. Tabari would hear of it and find her." The place she had sat was still warm when Justin joined me on the bench. "She was pregnant with me and Hallon." I looked up at him. "She said she was proud of me. She called me her little warrior princess." Justin just held me tighter. "We knew I have Dad's eyes, but she says I have his smile, too. That Dad would even be proud of me."

"I'm so happy you got to see her again."

"I am too." I sat back up, picking up the book. "I know I have issues telling you the things I told her tonight. I spent time writing them down." I handed him the notebook. "Justin, I love you. Just as my mother loved my father. When he came back into her life, she held him at arm's reach in case she got him killed. I know that is what I am doing with you. I know I shouldn't. Mom said my father gave Mom her dreams." I don't think Justin was breathing when I looked up at him. "You gave me mine." He was kissing me then. Pulling me to sit on his lap.

"Thank you," he said, holding me to him. "I love you "

"You are a fool."

"Yeah, I know."

The Innkeeper's wife knocked on the door to the building. Not a very tall woman. Stockier build than even me, with black-brown hair and the skin color of the earth. Her eyes shone with gold and reds. There was something odd about her, though. A wisdom only the Elven people get from living their long lives. Yet she was human. "Oh, Madam Oriana wanted to know if you and your friend wanted breakfast out here."

Friend? Would Mom and I have been friends? Would our tempers push us apart? "Do you want to go inside?"

"My mother's magic made all this. Can we sit out here for a while longer?"

"Anything you want, my love. Anything."

I pulled myself off his lap, looking up at the net of Fae Flowers. They bloomed twice as bright as anything I have ever seen. The tree above them is bright in a full rainbow of apple blossoms.

"You are beautiful." He kissed me one more time before going to the Innkeeper.

"I will find a way for you to stay proud of me, Mom. I will save Justin and cleanse Tabari and Cassandra."

I know you will. You are your father's daughter. The two of you can do anything you put your hearts to. Her voice faded.

I don't know, but I think this is the most content I have felt since I came to this damn time. My mind is not spinning out of control. Fear isn't causing my muscles to vibrate. My lungs don't hurt to breathe. I like this feeling. I hope it will last a little longer.

Justin read the book as I ate, looking at the tree. Madam Oriana said it hadn't bloomed since my mother died. That bothered me. The rest of the trees in the neighboring lands will produce fruit. Why not this one? I moved closer to it. The little rope fence was easy for me to step over. There on the trunk was the Seabrooke crest, crudely carved in a bald place. I could feel Mom's green magic dwindling there like embers. The second I touched it, I saw her again.

My father and grown brothers, standing behind her. She carved it in while crying. Her hair is full of gray. Which brings out the gray in her eyes. "Daughter, mine, Lysandra, this is the spell I bind for you. May this tree and this place be forever a place you will be safe and free. Just as we did before you were born." Princess' Peace was for me. Not Mom.

She then cut her hand, placing it on the carving. "Mother of Deities, I cleanse this tree and the surrounding area of all evil. Command delete virus." Her eyes lit blue. "Confirm yes." Her green-red marble magic exploded from her hand on the tree. The garden I saw in my time grew from the surrounding death. "I love you, Lysandra. I'm proud of you for facing the demons I could not. Forever be brave, my Little Warrior Queen." Then she pulled away from the tree.

I found I stared at my hand. Also cut, fingers laced with Justin's on the crest. Blood dripping down our wrists.

"Your mother calls you her warrior. Your uncle calls you a witch. I think I like the warrior name more."

"So you saw that?" He kissed my ear. "I think she just told us the cleansing spell."

"I need to write that down, then." His hand left mine, going back to the book. I just held mine to the crest a little longer.

"Mother of Deities!" I spun to Madam Oriana standing at the Inn door. The woman dropped to her knees, hands clasped in prayer. Justin looked at me, then back at her. Quickly, he scribbled the spell down and then went to the woman. I started that way. I don't know if I made it. I don't know at all what happened until Justin stood over me, holding my wrists. He was furious.

"What happened?"

CHAPTER SEVENTEEN

"Cassia happened." He let go of my hands. The mage metal bracelets hanging from my wrists. "She tried to kill Oriana and hurt you." My eyes widened, looking for the woman. She sat with her son on the bench as I was on the cobblestone ground. My nails were long and dripping red. "We weren't hurt badly. We healed while young Miles went to get your bracelets. I know you didn't want to wear them, but I felt it was necessary. She drew a lot of blood."

"Is Madam okay? She made me hurt you?"

"No, Oriana was not harmed. I stopped her from doing so. Cassia then turned to hurting you."

"Me?"

"Cassia was trying to tear out your eyes." Why my eyes? Like Tabari did to Matix. "What about your eyes makes both her and Tabari so angry?"

"Cuz I can see them for what they are. Dad must have had that magic. That is why they go for our eyes." Justin held me to him. I knew the good couldn't last.

"It is okay. You are okay. Oriana is fine. We saw your mother. Twice."

"You almost got to meet your hero."

"It is better that she lives in my mind as the powerful woman the books romanticize her as. I don't want my dreams smashed because she is not at all what I imagine your mother to be." Justin pulled me off the ground. He must have had to knock me down hard. My ass stung. "I will kiss it better later." I glared at him. "Go apologize. I know you want to. It wasn't you, Lys. It was the demon inside you."

"A demon I haven't killed yet, Justin." I left the tree. Miles, the younger, pulled into his mother's arms, then relaxed. Though his skin color was lighter, he was the very image of his mother. "I am sorry for anything my second soul has done to you and your son." Oriana left her son on the bench standing before me.

"Nothing much happened. It was a scare, but nothing I have not been prepared for." I frowned. "When Tulora cleansed this place, then gifted all the surrounding life with eternal life, she did for me too. She told me someday her daughter would come with a heavy heart. I loved having your mother here. She loved sitting on that bench in the early hours of the morning. Some days, she would cry. Some days, she would dance to some silent music. The older she got, the more it seemed to pain her to do what her goddess asked of her. After she was murdered, I set out to make this place a place where you may come to find peace as she did."

"Thank you, Oriana. I know all these years couldn't have been easy." She waved that thought away, hissing. "Thank you anyway. I do love this garden."

"Good to hear." She hurried her son away. "Now, I understand you don't know the prophecy about the Mother of Deities?"

"I am really, really starting to hate that term."

"I remember your mother disliked her title, too. When Christoph came, he started writing everything *Destiny* said. Neither was in the room when she told me this one. She said it was for my ears only. That someday I will meet the person to tell it to." She looked at Justin standing against the tree. His mind was in calm down mode. The breathing exercise counting out. "He cares a great deal about you."

"You could say that."

"The men who loved your mother were always great defenders of her minimal peace. Even more so after she became queen. Hadain, being the youngest, would wait on her hand and foot while she was here. The only one she would allow out here in her mornings. He would bring her tea and food. Sometimes just notebooks. He would write as she spoke. She would come here so tired then leave rejuvenated."

"I am happy about that. Growing up with her, the little I did, Mom was always in tears. Only when I started training to be her little warrior did she ever smile. Even then it was a sad smile." Miles, the older and the younger, came to us with a box showing my family crest on the green suede lid. I shouldn't be surprised there was something of my family was here.

"To tell you the story of the Mother of Deities, you need to know the history of humans arriving on this planet." Justin took the book I had written in off the table so Oriana could stack the green suede journals. Green, black and red ribbons stuck out of them. The last thing was a silver plate with a black block in the center.

"Dathon has a few of these," Justin said to me. He marveled at the silver slab. The hell?

True, I don't step foot in the library, but I have never seen Dathon walking around with something like this.

"There is a green metal one that he pulls out to look at. Normally when you are sleeping."

I sat up straight, miffed that my father didn't show me something so interesting. "Does it have a charge?"

"Yes, Majesty." Oriana handed it over to Justin. "Hallon built a charger, as he called it, for the bottom of the box. It just needs to sit in sunlight to charge." Which version of my brother? Justin placed it in front of me. On the black screen, there was now a tree. I knew that tree. That was the one outside the Haven house. The swing was there. Over it, an overlay of numbers. The old font too. Before I knew what I was doing, I typed in our birthdate.

I blinked to see Mom and Matix smiling. She was wearing the same green dress. Before a fountain. "We need to go here." Justin started chuckling. "This is where my parents met. Mom told me how they met and it was cute. You would love it."

"That is not what we are doing now, my love." Justin looked up at Oriana. "What are we looking for?"

She took the metal slab. I watched her swipe, poke and frown. Then she passed it back to me. Justin and I, wearing black, skin tight suits that looked like leather, stood in front of a metal tower surrounded by snow.

I knew that tower. That is the Goddess' Tower. That is where Daina took me after Tabari burned me. I slid the slab away from me.

"The Goddess Tower?" Justin's eyes darted from the slab up to greet mine. "The date on this, I don't understand."

"July 12, 2040?" I pulled the paper book back to me. "We are 2238, which is a year and a half for the Old Calendar. That means we have been here-" I worked out the time. Math is so easy for me. "So, this would have been taken three thousand, three hundred and fifty-seven years ago."

Justin frowned even harder.

"What's wrong?"

"There are so many pictures of us, but not us." I looked over his arm. We were not dressed the same, but we were about the same age. One was in battle, signing some paper. "I know this picture. The faces were blurry, but this was from the Time of Pain. This is the signing of the accords between Arowen and Stowera Clans."

Justin suddenly snapped to me and I backed up. He held my face. I frowned at his shock. What did he just figure out?

"You were the reason we have survived on this planet. You are the woman I see in the weird place nursing me to health. You are every hero who has ended a war since time was recorded."

"Wait what?" The hell? How can that be?

"If this is to be believed, you and I have been reborn for every major war, since Humans came here." Justin swiped back to us, standing at the Goddess tower. One more swipe and there was a design of some sort. Showing six towers attached to a central tower. Odd cones had cartoon fire drawn on the ends of each one. Three were listed as Habitat Pods. The others were listed as Terraforming, Animal Cryo, Supplies. The one in the center said Command. Above it all was Arowen 3.

"We were not supposed to come here," I said, not sounding myself. "I am not a leader."

"I think you were. I think you always were supposed to be." Pictures farther back had me standing on a beach with Numarian style domed buildings, towers of white stone. Blue sky and water. The next was a vid-e-o. I tapped the screen. My face appeared, red hair blowing in the wind. Green eyes duller than mine are now more green gray with a ring of yellow, halfway through the iris. Two small white tubes came out of her ears.

"Hey Dad. I made it to Istanbul. I have never thought it would be this pretty. Di and I are having so much fun at the Summit." She seemed to pause, smiling. *"I miss you too. Though I should be mad at you. You never told me this is where you and Mom came for your honeymoon. This place is amaze-balls. Di and I are going to head to her temple this weekend."* She playfully frowned, then rolled her eyes. *"I know Dad. There is no way my best friend is a Moon Goddess. We have been pretending for ages, though. Wouldn't it be cool? She, a Goddess, and me, a War Hero who conquered this area, naming cities after myself."* I stifled a giggle.

She sighed. *"No, Dad, we are not living in a fantasy or playing our little games. We are working. I have the design finished for Arowen 1 done. I sent it off yesterday to the engineers. You should get the report by Friday. I have changed a few things around. Made more space for humans. Even made space for a Terraforming do-dad that Mai is working on. The crew is planned. I am ready to go once it is built. I just want to see the world I am leaving."*

"The rest of my spare time is spent at this little cafe overlooking the Sea of Marmara. Normally first thing in the morning. A man plays a Ney there. He plays it so beautifully. He set up really close to me today. It is crowded here this

morning." The moving image pans over to Justin sitting on a stool. Long reeds tube off to the side. His fingers moving over the holes in the reed. The instrument that I love the most, drifting from the metal slab. *"He calls it Your Love is my Cure."*

I blinked. My favorite song. In a strange place from over three thousand years ago.

"He is not a terrorist. He is an artist. His name is Jestin Seabrooke. He is from Wales, of all places. He came here as a teen to learn the Ney. Just to learn an instrument that he could have learned anywhere." She smiled brightly. Did I look that happy? *"Really, he is very sweet."* She looked up. There was a shadow over her. *"Di says it is time to go. The summit is starting soon. Love and kisses. Bye."*

Then she was gone.

That song touches your soul and now we know why. It is how we first met. On a different planet. In a different time. I have loved you for thousands of years. It wasn't the Bond. Justin and I are storybook soul mates. That, for some reason, made me melt against him. "There is another one."

This time, she didn't look as happy. There were multi-colored vines hanging down with sparks, smoke, and flames. *"To anyone who gets this. This is not a mayday. I don't think there are any survivors. M.E.R.C. attacked. There are saboteurs here. We are crashing on the fourth planet of an unknown system. We are prepared if I can salvage enough humans. Most of the people lost have already been saved in the mainframe. Diana is trying to help me copy over the rest of the people in the pods. Cassandra is being held in the brig with her lover. Dad was right, Jestin helped them. He was one of them. I fell in love with the enemy of humankind."* She started crying. She had really loved him. Her heart was breaking. *"If any of the judges are still alive when we meet landfall, I will have them tried."* Something exploded behind her. *"Shit."* She looked back at us. *"Please don't come. Don't send anyone else to space until M.E.R.C. is dealt with. There are sixty-five hundred people going to die for their selfish nature. Yes, we destroyed our planet, but is it not human nature to learn from our mistakes? I just want to see humans thrive. If I have to kill Cassie myself, I will. I would rather not."*

"Les, you need to strap in. We are on reentry." That sounded like Daina's voice.

"Don't come look for us. I will do what my plan was. To keep something of humans alive in the universe. We have something to contribute and I will see it done." She screamed as she was tossed about. *"Alessandra Arowen out."*

"We were never supposed to be here. We had our own planet we destroyed." I snapped. "Cassia, Tabari, and you were in on killing six thousand people!" The Death Knights and Justin were working together.

"Wait for it Lysandra."

I looked back at Oriana. She had taken the slab from him and scanned for something else. He was the enemy back then. Justin was a villain.

"Day five. We are here. We are all alive and we have made planet fall. What sensors Dathon can fix for us say it is safe for humans. Maybe. There is oxygen, but something else we haven't figured out. Di went out with Mai to see what we could do. They came back sweating with a fever. Jestin wants to go out next with Uncle Alistair. They think they can stop the fire in Habitat Pod three. I don't trust Jestin as far as I can throw

him. Alistair could probably throw him farther. I don't like it. Yet we need to save whoever is left. Les out."

I didn't even have time to process what I had heard before the next started.

"Day ten. Alistair burst into flames. Cassandra has wings. Jestin talks in my mind while he is in his coma. Diana is dead. I saved her brain waves in the mainframe." She snorted. *"I spelled her name wrong, and the mainframe won't let me fix it now. She will never forgive me for the typo. In the meantime, three more people have fallen. I don't know what is going on. Bryony thinks this unknown element is changing people to help them survive. I think it is killing them. I have no faith anymore. I lost that the day Jestin and Alistair both fell. I'm heading out next. No suit this time. It doesn't seem to help. Dathon and Leila say there is life south, though Jestin says they saw nothing. I don't know if I can trust his voice in my head. Les out."*

"Day twelve. There are elves. Space elves! I have never been happier." I frowned at her cheerful voice. *"Tolkien must have known somehow. We are in Middle Earth. The crown prince of the elves has come in and fixed Alistair. He says there is nothing he can do about Cassandra. Hers is a physical transformation. Alistair's magic can be shut off. At least I think that is what he is saying. Jestin will wake up on his own. Gods, I hope. I miss him. I am angry with him, but I don't feel right. I am lonely. Les out."*

"Day - shit, I don't even know anymore. I haven't been doing a lot of these. If any. I was nursing Alistair and Jestin back to life, saving as many souls as I could, as the power started failing, plus trying to learn Elven. Prince Cael, as I call him, has been wonderful. He is fascinated by me. Well, my red

197

hair. All the Elves have gray hair and eyes. It is odd. Prince Cael claims to like the red in my hair. He is so sweet. Jestin is not happy with my close relationship with the prince. Neither are Cael's guards. I must admit, having an elf dote on you is so much better than in the books. I have lessons with him in five minutes. We are taking the prisoners to the new encampment the elves help build for us. From there, I will plan out what is next. Les out."

"Even back then, I was jealous." Justin groaned.

I laughed. "This is crazy. How is this going to help me?"

The next one started. *"I don't even know how long we have been here. I'm calling it Arowan 3. Just so people in space know it is us."* She seemed tired, defeated. *"The elves call me The Mother of Deities now. Cael found me talking to projections of Di, Bry, and Mai. Cael seems to think I gave birth to three fully formed Goddesses after sleeping with him. It was good sex, but I don't think I will have children until we are fully settled and safe here. Cael has become king overnight. I never get to see him anymore. That is okay. Jestin convinced the judge he was not a terrorist, so now his attention is back at me. I can't say I don't mind, but he isn't Cael. I don't know if I can trust the love that refuses to leave me be. Les out."*

"Ha! You pissed me off so much, I would rather sleep with an elf than with you." Justin pulled me back onto his lap.

"Well shit. Cael was using me, too. Turns out he just needed me to show his people we were safe to them. Sex was a bonus. I shake my head. I should have known I wouldn't have the storybook Elven prince. Now I have Jestin trying to win me back with music, romantic nights. Lessons in magic. Seems I am the Avatar. I can control all four elements. I refuse to shave

my hair. Jestin thinks I am more Fire Nation. I would like to be Water Tribe. My temper keeps me able to wield fire better, though. The Mother of Deities thing seems to spread to all the people in the encampment. Di says it is in some of the other pods, too." She groaned. *"I would ask for someone to take me away, but I don't know if they would. Les out."*

"It has been three earth years since we landed." This was Justin's voice with an odd accent. *"Today I added Alessandra to the Mainframe."* I died. I pulled away from Justin. I didn't want to hear the pain in Jestin's voice. *"Seems Cassandra didn't like being implanted into another mortal body. Or didn't like that she couldn't control me with sex anymore. Either way, she took my Les from me. Murdered right in broad daylight in the center of the market. Cael heard about it. He tried to heal her. Seems he really cared for her. Even kissed her as I scanned her brain. Elven ass. She was my wife. Now, I have to live in this strange new world without her. Bryony says we were more than soul mates. We were genetically perfect to have babies together. I wish she had given us a little one. It was never the right time for her to have a child. She never felt safe. Guess I know why. Bryony says she has created something called* the Bond. *To keep humanity alive, she is matching the DNA so we can make more human babies. We were only a thousand at last count. I hope this works. Les just wants people to live happily. Jestin out."*

"Lysandra out." I'm heading away from the inn. I can't handle this. We came from a planet called Earth? We crashed here? That was rather hard to believe. Yet something on the magic slab made me reconsider. The other me's annoyance with the title the Elven people gave her. We both hate titles. Was that my soul?

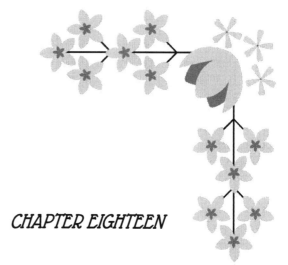

CHAPTER EIGHTEEN

Mother of Deities. She created the goddesses we know today. Mom wasn't the daughter of Daina and her *Bonded*. That would have been Dathon. My grandfather was a mage. "Dathon." I called. I was blocking out Justin, but Dathon would come to me, right?

I had found myself beside a lake half a day's ride towards Revan. Not the way I needed to go. I sat on a little pier looking over the water, watching children play with a ball in the water when Dathon finally got to me. "You know Justin is worried about you."

"Let him worry." Dathon removed his shoes and sat next to me. I smiled as he pulled up his pants. "I am guessing you saw him then."

"There is so much information to go through. Some of it I didn't remember." I snorted, shaking my head. "You expect me to know almost four thousand years of information?"

"Maybe. You are a God I created, it seems." I sighed. He pulled me into him.

"At least now we know what the Mother of Deities comes from." He laughed at my groan. "Lys, one of your past lives created our place in this world. You should be proud. That version of you created a safe place for Humans. Created ties with the local population. Protected both from evils."

"Died doing that." His arm rubbed my shoulder. "Justin loves this shit. I think it makes me worry about repeating myself. What have I done in a past life that left me unable to rest? How are my soul's failures being thrown at other people?"

"My darling daughter-" Dathon said as he smiled. "Or should I start calling you Mom?"

For the tease, I pushed him into the lake. I laughed. I laid back on the wood slats. Justin looked down at me. My father groaned, pulling himself from the water. Soaked leather and Elven silk weighing him down.

"Justin, take my daughter to Haven."

"Sure."

It was my turn to groan. My husband pulled me to my feet, a wicked smile on his face.

"You're not getting me in this water." Pulling all the water from Dathon's clothes, I used it to push Justin to my right where the bank was. He still took me with him. When we landed, it was soft. Justin was covered in mud. "Bastard." He laughed as I slid back down to him a few times before drying the dirt.

"Seriously, Lys." I laughed. He was dried into the soil, which made it harder to get out.

"Serves you right. I just wanted to think for a while." Dathon was nowhere to be seen. "I wanted to ask him about my grandfather."

"He will be with us forever. He is a God. I'm sure you can talk to him when we get home." Moon stood on the road overlooking the lake while Warrior pulled his human out of the dirt. "It's fine. You can stop being mad at me. It was your Mistress' fault I am stuck here."

Don't blame this on me. I was happily sitting here watching the kids play. You didn't need to come find me. The look the man gave me seemed hurt. Yet there was something more in his sad smile. *You have history to read. I will go to my house. I'm sure I don't need you.*

Yes, you do. You haven't slept in two or three days. We have had some very busy days. You need to sleep. It was only two days. This would be the second night I didn't get some shuteye. I was still going to be fine. *Lys, I will tie you to the bed.*

No, you won't. Before he could say anything else, I let the Mage Metal bracelet fall down my arm.

"We are closer to Revan." They caught up to us girls. Warrior wouldn't even look at me.

"We can be in Haven by morning if we fly."

"Can you do that? You need sleep." Justin sounded overly annoyed.

"Gods you nag. Yes, I will be fine. Once we get to Haven, I will sleep."

"Passing out from overuse of magic is not properly sleeping." I shrugged.

In the end, I got my way. We flew. Haven was still as small as it once was. Yet two new buildings stood. The Aldaina library and the training hall. Connecting them was the dorms. That would be where we would stay. This is when Justin got his way. I fell asleep against the wall, waiting for the dorm doors to open.

"She okay?"

"Yeah. Just haven't slept for a while." The voice said nothing as we were led to a room set for a commander. Which I still was. I did nothing for the order, yet I had my mother's rank.

"I should really take part in Aldaina missions."

"You are. You protect the king from the Death Knight. There is no higher calling." The voice said. As if I really protect him.

****

I held a sponge over Justin's forehead. Dabbing it lightly. I was concerned. He wasn't waking up. I knew I should be mad at him. Furious for betraying me, but he could be dying. He went out to stop more people from dying. He even kissed me before he left.

"Stop crushing on him, Alessandra. He could still destroy you," I said to myself.

Only in the most delightful ways, Les.

"You need to say that out loud, Jestin."

I wish I could. My body doesn't want to move. My - her hand continued to move. *I want you to stop crying. I need to feel your lips on mine again.* I could feel the heat rising in her cheeks. *I want to make love to you on this new planet. I need to make you a home so you will be safe.*

"Hush. I have a home being built. Cael says winter is only three months away, so he has ordered his people to help us build homes. I'm calling this town Haven."

Will there be room for two?

"Probably not. Stay in the Command Tube. You are, after all, too heavy for me to move. Bry didn't want me to move you into my quarters as it was."

Rather forward of you to bring me to your bed. He teased. *I would give anything right now to be holding you.* I put the sponge down, moving his arm so it laid under me. My ear to his naked chest. *I can smell your strawberry shampoo.*

"Don't get used to it. Until I can get to the supply tower, that was the last of it."

Why stay with me? Go get it.

"There are only seven of us. Cael has promised to help during the winter. Then he is taking me into Dragnu territory. They sound like dwarves. He has been teaching me that language, too. He doesn't want me to go. Well, not alone anyway."

I wish he would decide.

"Decide?"

You let him seduce you, yet he won't commit to you. He teaches you all these things but won't show you around. I don't like his indecision.

I laugh at that. *"Jes, I haven't slept with him since he took the crown. I haven't even seen him. He has asked me out to his city more times than I can count. You are the reason I don't go."* *I relaxed back on him.* *"I have always wanted to visit a Fae Realm. Meet a prince who wishes to sweep me off my feet. I would get to go to balls, learn to fight with a sword, wear a crown. Live the Disney dream."* *I sighed.* *"Instead, I fell in love with a traitorous bard."* *I kissed him. Jestin's lips were cool, dry.* *"Seduced by a sad traitorous bard. Isn't that the way of bards, though? Seducing things they shouldn't? Making all the girls fall in love with them."*

204

"You love me?" His voice cracked. I feel the smile turn to a grin as I straddle his hips. "Careful my love."

"I didn't just wake you with a kiss." He smiles with half-closed eyes.

"I think you did, my hero." I kissed him again. "I love you, Alessandra."

"Shut up."

"My hero. My knight." She smiled, all filled with joy. "My Little Warrior Queen."

I was now standing next to the bed, watching them giggle. Justin standing next to me. "Saving my life for millennia."

"You better not forget that. I gave up on my silly dreams for you." Justin pulled me into his arms. Here in this dream, there was no hum of the *bond*. It was just us, and I was thrilled. This hum in my core was not that of some medically decided *bond*. This was us. We were in love.

"I have known that my whole life. Yet I still force mine on you."

"I could have married a prince."

"You married a king. I wonder if I can unlock the knowledge of the Ney?"

"Don't you dare. How am I supposed to leave if you are the place my soul wants to be?" Justin kissed me. "I love you, Justin. Longer than I could have ever known."

The image melted around us. Another scene. *Jestin watched her in the market. Humans and Elf kind moving together. She was so pretty in Elven silk, the color of pine trees. Jestin's eyes were drawn away to watch a toddler trying to escape her mother. I could see the longing in his eyes. He wanted a child with the woman he loved. Why had Alessandra not given him one? What was her reason?*

The scream brought his eyes back to her. Alessandra was on her knees. A blonde woman was being held down. Jestin ran to Alessandra's side. Her dress was dark and wet from her right breast to her hip. This blond woman also had blood on her. An Elven dagger lay in the dirt. "I wish she hadn't pulled it out. I'm going to bleed out now." The lady with the toddler was there with her hand over Alessandra's bleeding chest.

"I am not powerful enough to help her." The woman said. Jestin was now panicking.

"At least I got my bard for three years." He tried to shush her, but a soaked hand touched his cheek. "These were the best three years of my life, Jestin."

"I love you, Aless. Please don't leave me. You have to fight. Stay alive a little bit longer."

"This trip was always a death sentence for me, Jestin. Know you made me happy in the end. I will love you for a thousand years." Then her eyes closed.

Jestin got them to their feet. With his gifts, he lifted her, starting into a run. They were in a white room with a transparent woman looking down at her. An Elf, Les knew as Cael, burst into the room.

I knew this elf. He was the one with the guards at his hip. Cael, King Cael, had been sad to see me ignore him. Oh, my Gods. He wanted me to recognise him. I failed to and hurt him.

"What are you doing, Seabrooke? Why is she not healed?" The Elf's magic poured over Alessandra's body. "No, she can't be dying."

"Well, she is." I realized then I saw Evana in that rage. *Cael's hard glass eyes glared holes into the human man. "We closed up the organs, but Cassie used some sort of poison. We don't know what it is, and I have searched her mind, but I can't*

find it. I think it was her husband who gave her the dagger, but I can't find Tabari." I gasped. Even back then, Tabari wanted me dead.

"You did this to her. Had you not come into-"

"Had I not come into her life, she would have died long ago. Cassandra would have killed her while we were in space. You never would have gotten to know her. Aless is the reason we crashed here. Cassandra would have blown us up. So do not blame this on me."

"Hey boys, no fighting," she said weakly.

"Oh Everstar, please fight for me." Everstar? The Elf king was in love with her. Everstar was a term of endearment, saying the lover was their undying guide in life. Cael had fallen for her. *"Please."*

"Everstar?" She tried to laugh, but it came out as rasps. "A few years too late for endearments, Cael."

"I have always called you Everstar. You will always be, my darling. I just knew you loved him." There was anger, jealousy but understanding in the Elf King's voice. *"My beauty from the stars."*

"I was in love with Jestin before we even left home, Cael." He kissed her forehead. *"Jestin, jack me into the matrix."*

"No. I'm trying to save you. When I find Tabari, you will get better."

"I will be gone before you can. I've read this book. I know how it ends. If you put me into the matrix at least I might be reborn to know you both again."

"I hate you when you are right." She smiled. "You need to back away a little, Cael." Jestin kissed his wife, gently. "I love you." Jestin placed a white cage over her face. Then took her hand as the Elven king had. Laying between her two men, I

watched Alessandra smile for the last time. "I swear we will get to love freely in the next life, my hero." Within five minutes, she was gone.

"Did you get her?" Jestin poked the slab in his hands.

"Yeah." He sighed. "She is saved, safe and in rotation now."

"Now give me the bitch." Cael growled. Jestin nodded. "She will die a thousand deaths for this."

"For once, we agree on something."

The image shifted again. *This time, both men lay on the beds. A female elf who was the spitting image of Evana with red hair, yet some human features stood holding Cael's hand in one of hers and Jestin's in the other. See through, Bryony hovered around. Jestin appeared to be in his eighties. Just as gray as the Elf king. Yet Cael didn't seem to have aged. Why were they both on the tables?*

"Are you sure Daddy?" The half elf girl asked.

"Since the day I met her, Evertide." I smiled. That was his daughter. Evertide was a term that meant there would always be a pull to this cherished person. Though I had never heard it in our modern time. "Your mother was special, and I wish to know her again. Another woman who looked like me but was the same age as the half elf girl took a spot next to Jestin. "Jeanne will need your strength once we are gone." Cael treasured this fully human child, too.

"Okay. We are ready." The human girl, Jeanne said. She was confident, yet sad, as she pushed a needle into Cael's arm.

"Protect each other and our peoples, Jeanne. Alessandra would expect nothing less from her daughters."

"Yes Daddy. Now go join Mom. She is probably lonely." More people joined around them. Mixed colors, ages and

races, watched as Jestin and Cael passed from this world into the Mainframe. The two sisters falling into each other's arms, crying.

"So passes the Mother of Deities, The First Elf King and The Hero's Champion." Was said.

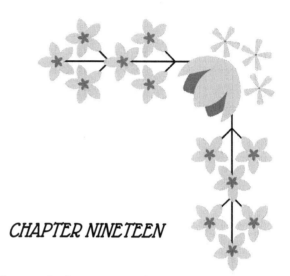

CHAPTER NINETEEN

I woke up feeling my lashes wet. Justin pulled me into him. I was warm in his embrace, but still shivered from seeing my own death. "I wonder if Cael will come back. That was one sad elf."

"Want another love rival?" I tried to joke. The words sounded strained. "He loved her for all she was worth. He might try to take me away."

"Please, you are my wife. Again. What is he going to do?" I giggled into his naked chest. "I would like to know how you had two daughters after you died. I don't remember what we did."

"I think I can answer that." We both shot up to see Calla looking exhausted. Calla looked like the human daughter. Though she wore brown hair now, her face was the same. "You should shower and get dressed. We have a lot to tell you." She simply walked to the door.

We joined my Thorns in their common area. A special place had been made for them in the library. We got to them with some difficulty. They were on the top floor. Five flights of stairs. Past three barricades and two sets of Aldaina guards. Dathon was with them. Reading over loose papers. It has been years since I have seen him enjoying himself.

"Here!" Lily exclaimed. "I found him. His line does still lead to Queen Evana, though it doesn't look like he was born this lifetime."

"Are you sure?" Calla asked, taking the metal slab. "No, that is the Welsh man again. King Cael comes up as Caelking.sol in all the registries."

"I found him. Caelking.sol installed 2153." I moved to the table. Calla had the new slab. Scowling over it.

"Oh, Lys, he was born in our village." She sounded so mournful. I blinked. That was right. Everyone in their hometown was dead. "He hasn't made it back to the system, so he is still alive." Calla took my hand and that of her sister, Rose. "Rose, I need you to sing, but only think about Cael. Nothing but the elf in those videos." Rose sang a song so soft it was hard to hear her melody without concentrating on it. It was wordless, but the siren's call beckoned me. Justin, too, seemed to be called to her side.

We were slowly moving to her.

"Who dares summon me?" He appeared. Teleporting in. It was the man from the courthouse. He was something important to me, though I wish I could remember what. "Alessandra?" Gods, he looked like someone from my dreams. Silver, strong and gentile. His hair was a braid over his shoulder. Green and black flowy mage robes of Elven Silk. Sword at his hip. I just didn't remember how much taller he was. At least a foot taller than Justin, and Justin was a half a foot taller than me,

"Lysandra now. Are you King Cael?"

"Just Cael. It seems our daughters were prolific in producing children to further our line." He glared at Justin standing next to me. "I see you got a king after all." There was some disappointment there. "You look just as you did then. So plush and supple."

"Cael-" He took two steps to me and kissed me fully on the mouth. Searching, begging me to open up to him. This differs from being with Wren or Justin. Cael smelled of pine and sea salt. Tasted like mint tea. Hands were cool but firm. I thread my hand into his baby fine silk hair. Even his body, which should have felt more breakable, was stiff against my chest. I could feel his heart racing just as fast as mine.

"She is my wife again." Growled from somewhere. Cael pushed me from his arms, smiling as if he knew something I didn't. Then he came back in to kiss my nose. The second he did, I scrunch my face, wiping my nose with my sleeve. He just laughed.

"Yes, but this is the second time we have all been born at the same time. I am greeting the woman I love. My Everstar." His hands stayed on my cheeks. His star eyes sparkling down at me. "I will forgive you this interruption, for I will never begrudge my Everstar anything." I smiled up at him. Cael made my heart flutter as if I was a teen again. The smug look told me he saw that.

"Why call me Everstar?"

"Cass-"

"The bitch is back?" Cael growled. Turning to Justin. "I thought we dealt with her eons ago."

"Somehow her soul was put inside me," I said. The elf's eyes went wider than anything I had ever seen before. He started feeling my body, looking for injuries to find the Mage

Metal bracelets. This, or perhaps the scars on my wrists, made him hiss.

What would he say if he saw the rest of my body?

One of his hands tightened on the Mage Metal. The other went to my cheek again. "Why Everstar?" He searched my eyes. Begging for understanding. "You used to delight in your powers. The smile you wore lit the whole glen. Your joy was refreshing."

"Cass-" He hissed again. "And her husband, Tabari, has gained some followers. One forced me to use my gifts to kill children." Cael sat me on the table. I looked down at his arms. He lifted me as if I weighed nothing. Maybe that was what caught my interest in him. It was as if I was a thin girl. "I have been very busy this lifetime, but I have questions. So many questions." Cael pulled up a chair, so he was at one knee and Justin could sit at the other. Justin, who never seemed to be calm when another man showed me attention, was oddly calm. "You say this is the second time we have been together?"

"I don't know if Jeanevera did something wrong with my soul or if it is the fact I am full elf, but when I am born, I remember everything from my past life. I search for you both for my lifetime. Normally I find Jestin-"

"Justin."

"Either male or female, but never you, Everstar. You are not born nearly as often as Justin is. Every time you are there is a major war or some sort of hell only you can solve, it seems. I don't like putting you in danger, but that is your lives when you are reborn." This time, it was Justin's turn to hiss.

Guess that is the proof I am cursed.

"I suspect that the bitch and her whore of a husband are up to no good."

"That is only half of it." Dathon joined us.

"Human Mage God?" Dathon kept his face neutral. "Everstar, did you birth him in this time too?" I shook my head. "Then things are indeed dire." He took the slab from Dathon. "What am I to see?"

"The prophecy of her life."

Justin held me in place as we listened to the video Cael was watching. At the same point Adriana turned on *Destiny,* Cael glared up at Justin. "Three times? You have to die three times in this lifetime?" He tossed the slab to the table behind me. "It is hard enough watching you be murdered, with a thousand years between. Three times in just this lifetime might really drive me crazy."

"Preaching to the choir." Justin pulled my head to kiss my hair.

"She said something about you missing a second soul."

"The bitch is in Lys. The bracelets are keeping her contained, so she doesn't kill Lys. However, her whore husband wants to take me over to make sweet demon babies with Lys." Cael frowned.

"How? We had to get my Mate to carry the girls after My Everstar died. She can't have babies until she is safe from these Death Dealers."

"Surrogates." I groan. "We could just use a surrogate." I closed my eyes and shook my head. "I didn't need to get your sister to make babies. We could have found someone to carry our baby. Then you would have a part of me with you."

"It's not too late, Love. You have sixteen months. I am sure we can find someone," Justin said, smiling his sad smile.

"Sixteen months!" Cael was standing again. His chair clattered behind him. "Your first death is in sixteen months?" I could tell my Thorns and Dathon had stopped talking at this point and were watching. The air smelled like lightning and ash.

I raised a hand, and the powers faded. "That is what we are thinking." Cael took me in for a hug. "This is not enough time, I realize."

"I never get enough time with you. Just once I would love to have you for myself, Everstar." His face fit snuggly where my neck met my shoulder. It's odd letting a relative stranger hold me like this without panicking. Never mind having these two men holding me. Cael caressed my scars.

"Oh Cael."

"I hate to interrupt." Calla said, inching her way to us. Only when Justin patted his back did Cael, let go of me. "I think we found the Death Palace?"

"The Temple to Hadain?" I nodded. "I can tell you where that was. Hadain put a curse on it to only show one day out of every hundred years." Calla nodded. "You take this child's word-"

"They are under her protection." Justin warned. "Calla is mine."

"For her sake, give Lysandra some children of her own already." I laughed at Cael's annoyance. "She always gives, yet we never give to her." Justin nodded. I frowned, flicking my eyes between my two men. There was some kind of understanding between them. One I was sure I would never be a part of, despite being at the core. The discomfort made me run away to follow Calla to the table they worked at.

"Tabari took that away from me in this life." Cael's chilled hand spun me back to him. "We told you about this." He searched my eyes for something. "Cael." I sighed. "My book

215

prince." I cupped his face. When I did, a tear fell onto my thumb. "It is fine."

"No, this isn't Everstar. You were meant to be a mother. Your soul is. I find it odd you never let yourself have that joy." Peaked a brow. "Let yourself have some joy. Just for one lifetime."

"I was going to, but then Roseden took it from me." And I left with Calla again. "Tell him." Venus unrolled a map of Stowera. One long older than anything we had in class. There were towns that didn't exist in this time. Wiped off the map during the time of Tabari's rule. That, for some reason, lit a fire in my mind. How many lives had I failed to protect? Sixty-five thousand souls. It was suddenly overwhelming. Why had I decided to take this on myself? I am only human.

"You are not alone, Daughter of mine. You have Ten Divine Beings, two men who love you, and your Thorns. You never have to do anything alone," Dathon said. I took a breath with my eyes closed. It helped, but I felt it was just a wall and I would break later. Either tonight or tomorrow in the training ring. "Okay ladies."

Almost in unison, the girls laid books and metal slabs on to the map. Joy filled my heart, seeing them more confident. I wasn't even really listening. They spoke of times between my lives. Some of their stories gave me memory flashes, not all of which were my own. I was gripped with one as they spoke of the Time of Pain. A hundred years of bloodshed that decimated the humans, elves, and dwarves.

Clouds darker than storm clouds spotted the sky. Somehow, we had found the one piece of green still in the central lands. His blue and silver tent was in view. Yet there were only two men standing at the flap. A table had been ordered to be placed between our two tents. Just two tents and a table in this quarter mile patch of grass.

I saw Justin and knew his name was King Austyn Rudo. With him was Cael. I felt my heart break. My men were against me. Why? What had led them to side against me? I knew I wanted a new life for women. That we should not be cattle. We have the power of life. We were the bearers of knowledge. Yet this king's father made us less than human. This boy king needed to be taught to respect women. Even if I had to kill him.

The woman at my side held my sleeve when Austyn Rudo emerged in a formal military suit of the deepest blue with silver buttons. Cael next to him was in the same uniform. The human clothing looked horrible on his Elven form. Even if they were black with green accents. Austyn's queen tried to hide around my hip as if she feared them. "Stay here. If they attack, stay in the tents. There is enough magic to protect you for a month," I said, moving towards the table.

There was nothing to fear from the men I knew without knowing them. One pulled at my mind, begging to be let in. The other at my heart. I had an irritating need to make them happy, but I didn't know how that would be. Women were not breeding stock. Women were not to be closed up in homes, never to see the light. I needed to make them see it. "King Austyn. Cael." The elf moved closer to me. Standing at the edge of the table. I could feel the tingle of him on my skin though I know he was not one of my lovers. I would remember him between my legs.

"Queen Drea." Austyn and I sat. Cael laid out the peace treaty. Two scrolls pinned the boards. The one pointed up at me said everything I agreed to in order to stop the war. Including handing myself over to him. Cael and not Austyn.

Austyn would take his wife back and she would begin the new reign with the new laws she wrote out last night while I was with a certain elf. So I signed my name. Drea Philo, Queen of Arowen. Protector of Starfall. Then Cael turned the board around to see Austyn's signature. Austyn Rudo, King of Stowera, Master of Southern Lands. There I sign my name again. Cael pours wax beside our names. His seal is pressed on the paper.

"It is done." Cael pulled me from the chair into a kiss. That was when I felt pressure in my back.

"I wish you would have slept with my husband. You both would have died." I heard. "Welcome to the new future, Alessandra."

"That is my real wife, Cassandra." Cael held me up as her last move was to tear Austyn apart.

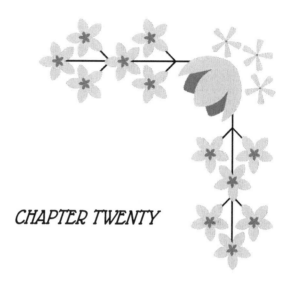

CHAPTER TWENTY

I woke up screaming. Justin is right there in front of me. Cael sitting cross-legged by our feet. Dark shadows around his eyes. Slouched shoulders. "That is not the reaction I thought I would get to being in bed with you two." He tried to reach for me. I was faster.

"Daina, screw all of you! I am seriously done." Pacing, I realized we were in Justin's bedroom. Evana held a basin of water. "Why are Tabari and Cassandra so determined to kill me? I just wanted people to survive our stupidity. Can I just be free of them?"

"You can when Dathon figures out the spells you gave them." I felt myself fall back to the bed. Cael's hand firmly on my arm. "Honestly, after two months-"

"Two months?!" I was out cold for two months? Two fewer months to spend with my family, Cael and Justin. Cael just pulled me closer into his chest, pulling Justin into some odd three-way hug.

Cael's voice deepened. "I would have expected the God of Mages to be faster, but there are six different rune sequences on the designs Justin wrote out. Plus, the spell is accessing the mainframe, which he is not even sure you can do. Once we have all that, we will get to the palace, and you can get Daxel for Justin."

"If we have the spells, why can't I just do it now?" I asked, suddenly realizing Justin was laying his head on Cael's shoulder and on my head. Wait what? The hell happened between them? Was I the only one asleep? Why did it feel so warm and cozy? Was this just residual from the memory we just shared?

"Lys, you are thinking too loud. Just enjoy it."

"Yeah, cuz once Dathon finds out you are awake, he is going to want to talk to you both alone." I know I tensed at Lizzy's words because both my men were running circles on either my back or belly. "Roseden was sentenced." We became a three-way ball of nerves at the sheer mention of Roseden. I guess it would make sense the trial was over.

As promised, before I even stood up, Dathon was through the door, kneeling at my knees. "Thank Daina." Something cold burned on my wrists. My Mage Metal bracelets glowed blue. "Just breathe."

I have many injuries over twenty-eight years, plus the memories flooding back to me of lives I never wanted to remember, yet this was worse than all combined. I could hear Justin counting. Feel Cael pressing his face into my neck. Dung, iron, and oiled wood filled my nose. My body felt every injury I had ever dealt with or was handed. I knew what this was. That bitch somehow cast her spell. Then, as fast as it started, it was over. With a decided thud.

I fell back into the arms of my men. My everything hurt. I truly hate that spell. "What the hell did I just witness?" Cael growled, pulling me away from Justin. My elf prince was being possessive, protective, and worried. I didn't blame him. My body was writhing as if I was having a seizure. I screamed in pain and my mind was blank of all things but the pain.

"Roseden." Justin whispered. "Lys, can you open your eyes?" I shook my head. "Please, Lys."

"I'm still in pain." I rasped. Cael held me tighter around my ribs, which brought forth the flashes of the black-eyed boy who I crushed with the walls of the pit. I got as far as the floor before my breathing was rushed. My head didn't feel all there. Then came the girl I pulled the eyes from. Hitting my shoulder to the stone floor brought the first one of air when I tore her wings off. My shoulders felt pulled off my ribs, causing me to gasp. The little elf boy with the moon eyes and solid tears holding my hand as he pulled me to stand before I pushed my hand through his chest to pull out his heart. I could hear all their last screams. I felt every drop of blood on my hands. Sensing the adrenaline forcing my blood faster. My mind had worked so fast at the beginning. Figuring out ways to end them quickly so they weren't tortured any longer. In the end, it worked on ways to draw out the fight to lessen my own pain. My guilt weighs on my heart.

"I have seen none of their faces before." Justin met my eyes. Even he feared me. "If I could kill her a second time, I would." His voice was unearthly, as if he too were the ghosts that haunted me. Cael was the one who pulled me from the floor.

I pushed away from him. I didn't want the love he gave me. I didn't deserve the love.

"Lys, it is over, she can't hurt you. The children she killed are not your burden."

My Elf King didn't understand. They were my burden until I made up for their loss. I was the one who ended their cursed lives. It was my fault they were dead.

"The bodies were found, identified, and returned to their families. They were cleansed of the drug she put in them. They now rest at peace because you saved them. You. Not the bitch inside you. You, My Everstar."

That brought on tears. Not just mine. Cael's, I dried away. Justin seemed to cry for me. Dathon right there with them.

"Who found them?"

"Calla." Her necromancy was coming in handy. I pulled away from Cael, stumbling a little. I caught myself, but I could get to the door. "Your Thorns are one floor down." Justin called. I waved, trying to seem confident, but I know he knew I needed to be by myself.

When the girls saw me in the hall, Calla was the first to me. As soon as she touched me, a weight came off me and I fell to the stone floor. "Leave her alone. This was no more her doing than it was yours. Your villain has joined you. Go bother her." I still felt their pain as if it was my own, but I didn't feel like they were sitting on my chest. I watched her fingers slide under the Mage Metal bracelets. "You need to use your ties to death and rebirth to send them away."

"I don't know what you are talking about."

"Repeat what I said the other day."

I knew what she wanted. How did I know, though?

She wanted me to use necromancy. Another magic that had to do with death. As if my magic wasn't normal.

"You may sleep now?"

Black, shimmering magic cuffed my wrists before snaking up my arms and across my shoulders. It wasn't cold like the little I felt of Hadain's magic. It felt electric. Alive! My red joined it.

"This is your life and death magic. As the Mother of Deities, you can tap into both."

I pulled away in shock. Calla just smiled. "I told you she would not take it well."

My men pulled me to stand. "Revealing she has more magic. Even as innocent as rebirth is a lot of responsibility."

Responsibility? That wasn't the issue. My magic brought death. My whole life. My soul's whole life.

"Thank you for helping anyway, Calla."

It wasn't Justin or Cael that held me. It was Wren.

I had an urge to get out of the castle. To get out of the city. I needed to get to Haven. I needed to be doing something. I had lost another two months. Not to mention I needed to cry. "Go back to your wife, Wren."

"No."

"Excuse me?"

"Lizzy is overseeing the execution. I was sent to watch you."

Sent to watch me? How much did Lizzy know? My mind began circling the failure I was to them all. That I had to be watched. As if I was a child. That added anger to the guilt. Honestly, what do they expect of me? I had tried to show I was capable, strong, and stubborn. Now they saw a broken, lazy, weak woman who fell apart because of the very thing they all needed from me.

Power.

"Too late. That bitch cast her spell. The kids showed up. Justin and Cael saw what it was like for me, then she was dead."

Wren's warm hands gripped my shoulders.

"Go back to your wife. I will go back to Justin after I get out for some fresh air."

"I know you better than to fall for that, Lys. You are going somewhere. Somewhere you don't think you will be found."

"I am GOING to go see Moonlight. I have had a rough day. Hell, a rough lifetime. and would like to talk to my horse if that is alright with you?"

Wren is used to these outbursts, but it still made me tear up to see him step back from me. It didn't matter that he was right. It didn't matter that they were all right to be concerned. I still didn't want to drag them down into my darkness. "You can tell their Majesties and her highness I will be in the stables for the rest of the day, if you so desire, but I will not want to see people. I just want to be alone."

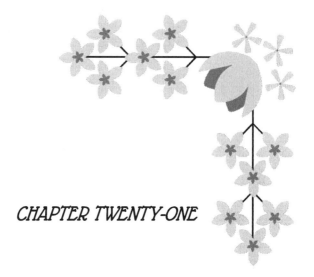

CHAPTER TWENTY-ONE

I didn't stay long in the stables. Before Wren, Justin, and Cael were done arguing, I was gone. I could hear them after I raised the mountain between me and Justin. Justin's room was on the third floor. I would like to say their voices carry but truth be told. Cael was demanding why anyone would force me to use magic. Justin responded I wouldn't let him rescue me. Wren said Justin would have died.

It got quiet for a moment.

Right before I took to the air, I heard my name called from in the castle. I couldn't make out who called. I didn't see the castle.

Forest surrounded me. Moon was still beneath me. The sun is high in the sky right where it should be at noon. Either I lost a full day or I teleported.

Teleporting is not something I was ever trained for. The other students in the royal classes claimed it could move you, just not your stomach. Though I had never felt that when

Dathon did it, this time was different. They were right. Luckily, I could get off Moon before I lost the acid. I've always hated throwing up without eating. Stomach acid was the worst.

"Are you alright?" Justin's eyes stared back at me but not in his face. It wasn't Lizzy either.

Who in my name was this?

Okay, cursing on my own name was silly. Never doing that again.

"Majesty?"

"Who are you?" She blushed. This girl wore all black, but the edges of her vest and her pants were piped with blue and green. Even her hair was black—like a shiny version of Justin's. With his eyes. Around her neck was a stone that seemed like an eye. A human eye, green and gold with a black pupil, made of stone. Ringed in silver. Yet the size of my palm. I had seen that somewhere before, too. She was around my height, although she was wearing heeled boots. Overall, she was gorgeous.

"Adriana Elizabeth Yale Sion Hy."

"That is a lot. You royal or something?" She smirked. That was Cael's smirk.

I didn't know what to make of this stranger who had just seen me puke into a bush.

"What do they call you for short?"

"Alys."

I nodded. "Haven is just down the hill. There is a feast tonight if you wish to join us."

Moon nuzzled the girl. My horse was the friendliest of the Elven steeds I had ever met, but this girl was a stranger. "Do you know who I am?"

"That is a silly question." She giggled. "Who doesn't know Lysandra Knyght, Hero of Stowera? You are queen, you know."

Okay, that was right. In my mind, that only happened days ago. Maybe a week. In reality, it was three months ago. Word would have reached the far edges of the kingdom by now.

"Princess Elizabeth has been doing a fine job while you and King Justin have been touring the kingdom. Yet I feel you need to rest. Life is just going to get harder for you."

That was an odd thing to say. What did she know?

"Come on. I am betting you want to see your father."

Father? Dathon was still in Haven. No, that wasn't right. He was there when Roseden's spell hit me. Now I was even more confused and wary. I gazed down the way she came, looking for anything out of place—a tree in the wrong place, a person hiding behind a bush or in the tree branches. "I know because my husband is talking to him now."

As if the *bond* explained anything about her.

True to her word, she was met by a burly mountain man. His hard eyes seemed to melt for her. It was clear she was the reason for any joy in the world. I could only watch. They were cutely in love.

This is what I wanted for me and Justin back in the day. The thought made my heart ache. We could never have this. At this rate, I would die alone in a palace of death to get Justin his soul.

"Lys?" Dathon was standing behind the man as big as a mountain.

Sudden laughter came over me. My God of a father was puny in comparison to Alys's husband.

"Lys."

I waved him off.

"Alys, can you leave us? It was very nice to meet you, Chasen." Dathon then took my arm heading me farther into town. "As soon as your three men started fighting, I came here. I am researching the house." He stopped. "It's not even been thirty minutes since you left us in your room. How are you here so fast?"

"Good question. I was sitting on Moon ready to take flight and the next I was here. Throwing up in some shrub. I would like to say that it was self teleport, but I have never been able to do that before."

"It could be soul powers."

"Soul powers? That crazy idea you have about the recycled souls gaining magic from the lives they have lived?"

"When you say it like that, it makes sense. Think about it. Your soul is the Mother of Deities. Would it not reason that you too would have ties to the mainframe and, therefore, magic?"

"No Dad. NO!"

He sighed.

"I don't want magic. I don't want to be my mother's daughter anymore. I most certainly don't want the responsibility of being the woman who crashed humans here. I want to be me. I want to not fear the dead. I want to live like my mother tried to. In a cottage near a stream. Like this one."

Dathon's hand ran up and down my arms. "This is all you. You are Tulora's daughter. You are a powerful mage. You are the Mother of Deities. You saved the humans by bringing them here. Sure, you fear the dead. Who isn't? Calla is, and it is her only power."

I scrunch my nose. This was not the speech I wanted right now.

"As for the cottage. You were meant to rule. Every major event in human life on this planet has been guided peacefully by you. Sure, you met your end when we were all safe. That is the sacrifice you make to keep life safe for us mortals."

At that, I raised a brow.

"You know what I mean."

"I am done being sacrificed. I want to live my life."

"You will, my darling, you will."

I couldn't remember much of that day. We didn't step foot near the house. There was a feast. I remembered Dathon taking me back to the barracks. I remembered thinking it would be nice to have a full night's sleep before having to deal with my confusing family.

From where I sat, I could see the whole court. The face of every courtier. Every guard. There had to be at least a hundred people in the throne room. Some were shocked. Some were giddy with excitement.

All were looking at me.

They made way for Dathon and two guards. Yet Dathon wasn't walking. His armor was stripped from his body with only potato sack pants. The colors on his skin told stories of torture and beatings. One bulge on his right side could even be a broken rib.

"Oh good, the mage knight. My late wife's lover."

I blinked. It sounded like Justin, but not. When I looked behind me, I saw the Seabrook green eyes that flashed red in his face before going back to Justin's ombre blue. "Now My Little Witch."

Tabari!

CHAPTER TWENTY-TWO

I tried to move, but there were chains. I tried to melt them with my fire, but nothing came to me.

Mage Metal chains attached to the stone throne Justin had gotten rid of. Cuffs on my ankles, wrists and my throat again. This time, though, there was a circlet on my forehead that also felt draining. Tabari crafted me a crown of Mage Metal.

Six! I had six bands of magic draining metal on me.

That explained why not even my fire came to me.

Justin's hands were on my hips. Moving them. Justin was deep inside me as I straddled his lap. The sheer fabric of what I wore left nothing to the imagination. Every inch of skin exposed. Every burn for the world to see. Tabari was using me, in public, in front of Dathon while in Justin's body. How had I failed so horribly? We were nowhere close to taking him on. Yet, overnight, he had gotten Justin, beaten Dathon, and was raping me.

The two guards on Dathon turned into blobs of tar like black goo that held him up as if on a rack. Dathon was acutely conscious as a whip of black ooze scored his back. He did not scream or howl in pain.

Justin—no, Tabari—kept my movements in time with the whip, which seemed in time with the music of my favorite song. No matter what I did, my hands were locked to the stone throne. My knees tucked into Justin's thighs. My movements were only what Tabari deemed necessary. "Justin." I called, hoping that my Bonded *was in there.*

Somewhere trying to get control.

"Look at your dear father, Little Witch. He is so full of life. His eyes still reflect defiance although I killed his lover, took her son and have made you my slave."

I was suddenly reminded of the Mage Metal collar with a chain around my neck just as he yanked it.

"What would your darling mother say if she saw this? How, you failed, even worse than she did?"

My body was suddenly falling into a world of pleasure I had not felt before. I was disgusted with the betrayal of biology.

"My Little Witch is peeking already? Oh, if only your Soulless Prince could see you releasing your juices on me. Would he be as excited as you are for the pain you are witnessing?"

I screamed then. Screamed bloody murder. My body was betraying me. The Bond failed me. I had failed Justin, Dathon, the whole kingdom and as punishment, I was Tabari's whore for him to father as many children as he could eat. Save one. The one who would be his heir.

So I screamed.

I heard laughing from the crowd. Yet I screamed over them.

"Lys." I heard Dathon call me. "Lys, fight him." I heard in such a weak and tired voice. "You can do it. You are stronger than him."

This was not the man being torn to pieces in front of me.

"Lys, I can see it. Fight Tabari. This isn't real."

I heard Justin, my Justin was in my mind.

"The Mage Metal cannot hurt you. Burn his minions to free Dathon."

I shook my head.

"Please, my love. We need to save Dathon," *he said as Dathon's left arm was torn from his body.*

"He will die if you don't break free of Tabari."

In that second, Dathon's head was cleaved on his shoulder, rolling to the foot of the throne.

I screamed.

My power burst from me in a firestorm. Dathon's death broke every ward on my magic like shattering glass with a stone. Daina made Dathon's death the key to my full gifts. Melted Mage Metal rolled down the fire that was my skin.

"Oh, shit." *Justin said.* "Lysandra, you need to wake up. You are going to hurt more people!"

I could smell burning wood and feathers. And heard the fire roaring and glass shattering. The taste of ash covered my mouth as I continued to scream.

Then I felt the pain in my left hand.

My eyes fell on the matching ring. Justin's ring. Tabari had not been wearing it in the vision. A dagger through our hands pulled me back to reality.

ALEX O. KNYGHT

"I'm here, my love. You broke free of Tabari's illusion magic. You are safe now." Justin pulled me into his arms. Our *bond* hummed. The lattice work of blue, green, and red swirled around the raging red flames. Through it I could see Dathon. My Dathon. His face was not contorted with agony. There was just fear. His head and arm were still attached.

"Shut down the magic, my love. You will kill him. I can't hold the barrier much longer."

As if a switch went off inside me, my magic fell dormant.

We were crashing. Not far. but enough that my ass hurt as we hit the floor.

"Okay. It's over." Justin groaned. His eyes were full to the point of overflowing with tears. "You are safe now. He can't hurt you here."

I broke.

Justin, my real Soulless King, holding me in the remains of my bed as all the fear of Tabari washed over me.

When I was done crying, I found myself in Justin's arms, on his lap in Dathon's rooms in the barracks. Justin quietly rubbed my arms. Our clothes smelled of smoke. The hem of my pajama bottoms and shirt singed black. We may have been in Dathon's dorm rooms, but my father was not here with us.

"He is beefing up the wards of the complex with his Knights."

I looked up at Justin.

"Do you need to see him? I know you must not be able to trust me right now."

The ache in our hearts, across the *bond*, told me this was real. That this was the man so hopelessly in love with me, he would brave my flames. "What was that?"

"A nightmare? An attack? I don't know. I do know I was at home when it started and here when you screamed. I was so scared of us. Who would not be afraid of the overpowered, petrified redhead who screamed so loud she shattered glass?"

I shattered glass. I melted Mage Metal with magic.

"Thank you." His smile tugged at my heart.

He tightened softly around me.

"I'm a mess."

"No, you just create them." He laughed.

I leaned back in his chest. This was home. He was home. The darkness in my mind made me wonder if I felt that way because of the *Bond* or if this was real.

"I love you, Lys. I will fight him tooth and nail to keep you safe."

"I know," was all I could say. I knew he would die in doing so. That nightmare could have been real.

He kissed my head. He was far too good to me. I felt him stifle a laugh at that.

"Forever."

I nodded. His heart skipped under my ear. His breath caught in his throat. Tears threatened as he looked down at me.

"Well, that is done. Lys' room will be unusable for a while." Justin released me when I saw my father waltz into the room. Singed as we were, soot covered his cheek and forehead.

"Adriana's-"

I slammed into him—my arms wrapped around his waist as I had done as a child.

"Good morning to you, too."

I wanted to cry all over again. Dathon was safe. Normal even. There were no broken ribs. No bruising, save one blossoming on his shoulder.

Justin gently pulled me back to the couch.

"Do you want to tell me what that nightmare was about?"

No. I never want Dathon to know anything of what I saw.

"You should. It wasn't a real nightmare, was it?"

I didn't have to look to know Dathon was shaking his head at Justin's question. I sighed. Dathon fell to his knees, taking my hands in his.

"You know I love you. You are my father, my best friend, one of the few constants since I came here." My voice broke. I can never have him die. I would fall apart.

"Lys-"

"Tabari was torturing you to torment me." It came out so fast. We both knew that if this was not a dream, then Tabari would kill Dathon too.

"Justin said something about Mage Metal."

"I was chained to the throne. There were five different cuffs on me this time. Plus, a crown. I was powerless and weak, though it wasn't draining my life yet." My hand went to my neck. It wasn't there, but I could still feel its weight cutting my skin. Just like with Roseden. "Tabari won. I failed to stop Justin from being taken. You were being torn apart. All the while, he was using Justin's body to use mine."

My father sat back on his heels.

"Until you were dead."

I was sick then. Dathon, ever the prepared father, placed a bucket before me. When I finished, he handed me water as I leaned back into Justin.

"How did you know it was happening?" Dathon asked.

Justin sighed. "I was there. Lys was deadly beautiful until I realized what he was doing to you. I clawed, beat, raged against the glass barrier placed before me. I was forced to feel him take you as you watched his minions whip Dathon. The second you started screaming, I was out of the dream. Running here." He kissed my hand. Dagger wound was almost fully healed. "It got your attention."

"Technically, he attacked you both." Dathon groaned. "Well, hopefully, our wards will be enough to keep him out. Just in case, I'm moving what is left of Lys's room into Adriana's. When she was alive, I placed so many wards on the room that not even a mouse could enter." He then took our locked hands. "I know you don't want to hear this part, but you two are going to have to share a bed. Your *bond* is the best protection. Had Justin-"

"Okay," I said.

They both were in shock.

"I saw our *Bonded* barrier. I'm not foolish to think my control over my flames kept you safe, Dad." His jaw dropped and his eyes teared up at the word Dad. It was as if this was the first time I had called him Dad? By the look he gave me, I think it was.

He was hugging me then.

"I'm sorry I'm a horrible, horrible mage. A horrible wife. I even suck as a daughter," I whispered. Justin just held my hand tighter.

We stayed like that until there was a knock at the door. A mage knight popped her head in. Black hair in a braided bun, blue eyes as bright as Justin's, and a smile that melted my heart.

"Yes, Alys."

She said nothing, not taking her eyes off Justin and me. She just stood in the doorway.

"Alys?"

"Sorry, they are so much in love. I never thought I would see it." She admitted. Dathon moved her from the room.

"What was that about?" I frowned. Did we know her? I mean, I've met her once. Why was she so shocked to see Justin holding me?

"Don't know." Justin put me on my feet. "Time to get you dressed. As much as I love to see you in your jammies, I think I am burning these."

My jammies were simple shorts and tank top. Not really all that sexy.

"It is the fact I can see so much of your skin, love. You are free of the glamor when you are sleeping." He kissed my burned shoulder. "But we have a job to do."

Tabari made me forget Mom's cottage. Nightmares threw me normally. This was more than that. I could still smell the blood. Dathon came back into the room just as Justin's hands wandered.

"Who was that girl?" Dathon paled. "Dad?"

"Go get changed," was all he said.

CHAPTER TWENTY-THREE

I went into the bathroom. Justin followed me. He was right. I really didn't want to see him right now, but I knew I was going to need him. He is the other half of my soul. What I didn't think that I would see is Cael, naked as the day he was born, leaning on the stalls. "There is my Everstar." Justin made no move as my Elf King picked me up to kiss me. Picked me up, like Wren did. Why was this relationship different from with Wren? Justin was jealous all the time with Wren. With Cael, he just let the elf have his way with me. "Now my darling, we need to get you showered, dressed and ready to face Tulora, The Red's magic. Is that correct?"

"Seriously, I had planned on doing this alone." I groaned, putting my arms around my elf's neck. "Who said you boys could come?" Cael's hands left phantom brushes on my shoulder blades. It was oddly comforting for a man I knew for like a day.

Cael put me down. "You lost any alone time you were ever going to have the moment that girl sang me to you."

I laughed at that.

He flicked my nose. "I never got to have you the way I wanted to. I couldn't convince the Elders that you would be a great queen for me. So now you are stuck with me. Forever the betrothed of the Undying King." Undying King. Really? Shouldn't that make them not want me more?

"Great." Justin didn't sound so pleased.

I just laughed.

"Remember that she is my wife, Cael. I'm right there when she needs me."

"That is only because your Bleen didn't know me when she made these silly *bonding* pairs. I will forever be the proper man for my Champions." I laughed even harder.

Justin sighed, smiling. At least he wasn't being possessive. "Now, what will our queen wear to challenge the queen of old?"

"The same thing I always wear when I am here." A breath later, the leathers replaced my singed sleep wear. The armor clung tight to my skin, pulling my shoulders back because of the weight of the skirt. Lips were on mine again. Chilled.

This was Cael again. He really loves to kiss me.

"By Leila. You really learned something from the lessons that I did with you."

"Leila?"

"Elven Goddess of the night. Twin sister to Sulien. God of the day."

That gave the templars a new spin. Were they started by an elf to kill Tulora and me?

"Oh no. You just realized something. I know that face."

"Lys?"

"The templars. Followers of Leila. Goddess of the stars. Hunter of all that is wrong in the world. The group that hunted Tulora down to kill her because Tabari told them red hair was evil."

"Evil? How can you be evil?" Cael frowned, holding some of my hair. "Tell me more."

"Not now. Lys needs a bath."

"I need to burn my soul to ash to be reborn. Just to get their touch off me."

Justin spun me to face him. "Well, I'm not letting that happen. I have seen you die too many times and if you burn your soul to ash, what will become of me?"

I shook my head.

"He has a point. What would become of us without you to keep us sane?"

I was pretty sure Cael just didn't want me to leave him alone. He really thought he loved me, so let him think it.

"Can we please just take showers? I smell like smoke," Justin said, passing my Elf King. In doing so, Cael slapped his ass.

I bit my lips to keep from laughing.

"I am not in the mood, Evertree."

Evertree? The tree that is always home. I was the star that guided Cael's path in life. What was Justin then?

"Wouldn't you like to know?"

"Everstone." I smirked.

"Cause he is stubborn as a mule?" Cael asked me with a wink. "Well, come my Everstar, I will wash you down."

Justin groaned. I knew he was following us. Had the nightmare not been fresh in my mind, I have a feeling I would have had both my men kissing me back into bed. Not something I remember us doing before. But still a fun thought.

Carefully and lovingly, Cael and Justin helped me back into the Aldaina armor. Justin called his armor. "I feel very underdressed for this outing."

"Maybe because you are not dressed at all, Darling," I said teasing.

"You may be right. I don't have magic that will get me dressed like you two."

"Justin, can you go check on Dad? I know he is going to want to come with us." I started to the door. "I don't know what we are going to need.

"What are you going to do?"

"Catch up our Elf King on twenty-eight years of Tulora, the Red, Matix Seabrooke and my siblings. He needs to know what the hell we may be walking into." Justin kissed my forehead. "I don't know what version of my brother we are going to get, so I don't know what to prepare for."

"We will have Dathon. Just remember that." I nodded. We will have Hallon. That had been the farthest thing from my mind but the most volatile being in my past life. "I love you."

Then he was gone.

Cael and I walked back to his room. "You still can't say you love him?"

My eyes drew to my Elf King. This serious, quiet side unnerved me.

"I read the transcripts. Had to beg the Mage God to get my hands on them. Know that I will never let that happen again, Lys."

"You are far too good for me, Cael."

His arms wrapped around my waist, grinning like crazy.

"Both of you are."

"No, I am just the horny one."

I stifled a laugh.

"One day you are going to share. Just like you did when you had feelings for my first soul."

"Only if you keep me around." As if I would send either Justin or Cael away.

CHAPTER TWENTY-FOUR

Heavens knew what the people thought when I walked towards Tulora's cottage, three men following me. What I did know was that the house was just as we had left it when we were in school. The empty field around it, where I used to play. The tree had grown massive since the day that Mom and Christoph planted it. A swing hanging from it. Justin came to my side as I touched the tree. This is where I had been standing before I attacked our teacher.

"I know that we have to do this, but do we really?"

"We need to know what your brother hid."

"I don't think that we do. Your mother showed me the runes. My mother gave me the spell words. What more can my brother give us?"

"We won't know until you unlock the cottage."

I really hated when he's right.

"You are adorable when you know that I'm right." He kissed the bridge of my nose. "Come, darling."

I took his hand. This might have been the first time I noticed the temperature difference between Cael and Justin. Justin was more my warmth, yet Cael cooled and calmed me.

Lys?

I shook my head, dropping his hand.

"As from the notes the girls wrote out, it looks like we just need your blood and this locket," Dathon said. The locket lay in his hand. "Have you looked in this yet?"

"Not in three hundred plus years." I shrugged. I didn't even remember looking at it when I was a kid.

Dathon opened it. A woman holding a pair of children, only two by the old calendar, was projected from the gold. The woman had red hair, blue-green eyes, and wore a brief summer flowered dress. Though the children looked lively, the woman's eyes were sunken in.

The part of me that remembered my first life knew who she was. "Cordelia Arowen." My eyes dropped to the twins on her hips. "Core?" My first Mom. My Earth mother died of cancer.

I ripped my eyes away, trying with all my might to avoid the confusing memories tearing my mind asunder. When I heard the locket close, I fell back into cool arms.

"You are not in that life. She is long past gone. The sorrow you are feeling is misplaced, Everstar."

I nodded. Of course, the only ones I trust are elves. Justin has hurt my heart so many times over our lives together. Cael just seemed so pure and young. Safe.

"We are here for another mother who left you alone. Once we are done here, too, your sorrow can fade to a distant memory."

I realized my eyes were closed when Cael kissed them.

"Are you ready?"

"Do I have a choice?"

"Breathe deep, then do what you know you must." His hands slowly left me as if he didn't want to stop touching me.

I didn't want his hands to leave me, either. We must have been truly deeply in love. Justin's hands don't even feel this safe.

"Later, my love. I will hold you while you cry later." Cael was a warm, safe place where I could hide.

I wondered if he would be a better *Bonding* than Justin. It was based on DNA. Could Cael's DNA make a better match for me? It was possible. Jestin changed sides for Alessandra. Cael chose his people over her. But damn if I didn't feel a void now that we were not touching.

So, there I was standing before the magicked house, demanding the magic to allow me into my childhood home. Justin on my left. Cael my right. Dathon held Tulora's dagger.

"Prove you are of the blood." My father cut open my palms in one motion with a hiss. "Go, daughter of Tulora, place your hands on the door."

As I was told, I walked up to where the door had been, had Tabari not blown it off the hinges in the attack. Though I couldn't see inside because of the swirling magics, I knew where the door should be. I heard Auntie singing. Heard my mother instructing me. It was more than just blood magic I needed. I needed my crystal sword. I needed my Aldaina magics. With each summons I felt the magic seep into me. Worming their way to my heart where they now swirled.

"Mother, I'm home."

Come Lysandra, we have lots to speak of. The house was as it was when I was a child. Green and turquoise paper streamers wrapped the banister towards the sapling where a group of

245

tables were set up, decorated in similar colors. Mom sat on a bench with my brothers standing on either side of her.

Before you go in, I need to know that you are okay. She looked so tired, sad, and lonely. Where my brothers were in full mage armor, as if they expected the worst.

Seeing them and knowing the truth flicked a switch in my mind.

I had to let them go.

This was not their fault, it was mine. A mistake from eons ago.

"No, Mom I'm not. I am going to die soon. I am going to leave behind so many people I love. My found family and three men I love dearly."

So, it is getting close to the time you told me about at the inn. She deflated. *Your brothers have worked hard to gain what you need to know. Most of it is at the Temple of Death at Uhtred. I also left you something that will help defeat Tabari, hopefully so you don't leave your loved ones.*

"That would be nice. I have barely even gotten to know my Evertree and my Soulless King. I had hoped after my last birthday I would get to introduce you to them." I glared at Hallon as he moved closer to me. Mom was confused. Hadain just blocked him with an arm. "You do not get to touch me, brother." I glared. Mom stood confused at our aggression.

I sense Cassia in you. Hallon said. Mom gasped, moving her eyes to my bracelets. *Mage Metal is holding her at bay for now, but the second you are in the domain of death, she will be free to do what she does best. Kill you.*

"Well then, dear brother, you kill her. Cleanse her yourself. Rid me of the knowledge I will become this family's curse. She is your wife, after all."

You know I cannot. If I change things, your life will not happen as it has.

"As if I care about magical paradoxes." The angry, spiteful laugh I felt leave my chest was strangely relaxing. "You don't know what I have been through, Hallon. You never will. I have seen hell firsthand. Would you like to visit it?"

Mom rose to hold me back but was blocked by an invisible screen that shimmered Auntie's blue.

"I realize you were just a stepping stone to defeat Tabari. That is why I wasn't allowed to stay with you. As much as I am attached to you, all I owe you for is giving birth to this body. Though I am pretty sure that even if you didn't, I still could have been born."

Hadain frowned at me.

"Little brother, you have ten months to come up with a plan to send me back here to the people I love. I will take no other solution. I am here to keep the Soulless Prince alive, and I intend to do that."

You love them more than you love us?

"I don't know you."

Mom's eyes fell to the ground.

"Cael, helps me reach the calm that you so desperately tried to force on me. He has loved me since we came to this planet. He will always own my heart." I felt Cael's hand enter my right hand. "Justin has loved me for longer than that. I have failed to tell him I love him more times than I can count. He is the other half of my soul. That is why I will not leave him this time." Justin's warmth took my left. Our rings vibrated as they hit.

"I don't want to leave them. I never do. I know no one can stop what is coming. So this I guess is good bye. The first of many."

Goodbye Lysandra. They were gone in a blink. *May the Mother of Deities bless you.*

"I can't bless myself." The dark magic spinning around my heart began to and mix with Justin's and Cael's, encompassing the three of us.

"Dathon!" Justin called a second before the magic blasted out of my body.

There I was floating in blackness. I pushed the boys away.

Finally, fully powered, I see.

I called my sword. I knew that voice.

Now my son will also be as close as fully powered as he could be while missing a soul. Wait for me, Cassia. I will come back to you.

CHAPTER TWENTY-FIVE

The world was drowning in water, cold and quickly flowing. The black was gone. Just sunlight shifting from beneath the water. I didn't feel the ground beneath me—instead; I hovered in two sets of arms. I could see the shifting faces of Cael and Justin holding me steady.

Please Lys, breathe.

I knew I wasn't. When I did, water rushed towards my lungs.

My men swung me out of the water, bent over one of each of their arms. Air and water fought in my chest. My hands dug into their arms as red streaks flowed with the water.

"I was sure that he was going to get you this time." Justin pulled me into his chest. "He is so close to us."

"He needs me to be in a new body if he wants to have a child while he is in you," I said, reminding him of the thing we never spoke about: my death.

What would come after?

"He takes you now, his bloodline ends with you."

Cael swung me back to pick me up.

"I feel like shit," I said.

"You used new powers we didn't know you had," Dathon said. He was looking over me for injuries. "I have never seen you tie yourself to the souls of the past. Calla summoned you, but this was different."

"Mother of Deities?"

"Maybe. More something from a myth from the old world."

This line piqued my interest. Earth story. From what I saw of my past, I had never seen her use magic.

"There is a myth of the Queen of the Underworld."

At that, I laughed. No way I was queen of the dead. Not even close.

"She has control over souls."

"Shouldn't that be Calla? I am the Mother of Deities."

"Your first life gave birth to gods by taking the souls and making them Deities."

That metal tablet, moving the names to the mainframe and giving them control over the program. Shit. Shit. Shit. No, no, this is not something I wanted. I may have wanted it then, but not now.

Cael set me down but didn't let me leave his arms.

Justin took my hands. "Breathe Lys."

I blinked over and over. I didn't need another title. Everstar. Tulora the Red's Missing Princess. True High Queen of Queensland. Queen of Stowera. Champion of Arocana. Mother of Deities. Death Knight. Queen of the Underworld?

"Stop it."

I looked into Justin's glaring blue eyes.

"Most of them don't carry any meaning."

I snorted.

"You are the Queen of Stowera and our Everstar. Those are the only ones that you should care about. The rest of them are just names. They are not who you are."

"Then who am I, if not an all-powerful goddess?"

"You are not a goddess. You are my wife. The woman we love." Cael's arms tightened around my waist. "You are no longer your mother's missing princess. You said goodbye to them. The High Queen can go take her test and shove it up her ass. You won't take that throne. I don't even know what that entails. I just know I am not allowing it."

I stifled a laugh. Allow me. As if he could stop me if I wanted it.

"You stopped being Colin and Evana's champion when you took my mother's ring. You are my wife. That is the only reason that you are queen. Nothing more than that."

"That doesn't stop me from being a Death Knight."

"No, these do." Justin held up my hands. The bracelets clinked together. "These and your powerful stubbornness."

I raised a brow at that.

"You heard me. You are the stubbornest person who I have ever met."

I pointed to Cael.

"Yes, even more than Cael. You protect everyone, but you won't let us do that for you."

"You know the demons I'm fighting. I'm not willing to put you in their path."

Cael laughed into my hair.

"If I didn't love you so much, I would have locked you in the dungeon ages ago." Justin groaned.

Cael just laughed more.

"You two never change."

"Don't fight me on this, Justin. I was raised to do one thing. To protect you. That is what I have been trying to do. You make it so damn hard by not doing what I need you to do. Years, Justin. With one thought in my head. Keep you out of the hands of anything that wants to do you harm. I did it when Tabari attacked your sister. When he killed your mother. When Roseden took me. Then when I was sure that I was going to die to get your soul back. This is part of the reason that I was born again in this age. This is the only reason I exist."

"I don't need you to protect me, Lysandra! I need you to live for yourself. We have always been better working together. The moment we separate is when I have to watch you be murdered." Justin was yelling now. People were gathering. "I love everything about you, but you have to let me help you. Let us help you."

"It was hell watching you lie in that coma. Only hearing your voice in my head. I never want to feel like that again. Just stay where I tell you and you will be safe." I started back to the husk of my former home. The waterlogged leathers were so heavy.

There better be something in here, more than therapy. I didn't want to deal with any more emotions.

Dathon had moved the broken kitchen table to see the blood marking, long turned black. "This is some ancient magic. She put you in status, then called Daina to you." Dathon's magic relit the runes. "I see. That is what took Daina so long to find you. Your aunt didn't let Daina know which tower you were in."

"She was in a rush. Tabari was trying to kill us," I said, lifting the bookshelf that had once pinned me. It wasn't nearly as heavy as it was before. Charred books still lie around where I had fallen, creating an outline of my body on the floor. I lifted the other bookshelf where Hallon had been laying. There, too, was a clear spot. His face held scars, but was he not as burned as me? Jealousy ate at my inside. He got it so much better than I did.

"There is so much magic in this house. I thought you said magic was banned?"

"It was. The only safe place for Hallon to learn his magic was in our bedroom. Last door to the right." Dathon called light to his hand.

I smiled as he stepped on the squeaky board in front of Mom's room. If you didn't know it was loud, it could wake the whole house.

Justin dropped to the spot I had fallen, gingerly touching the clear polished floor. I moved back to Mom's room, avoiding the loose board. The walls were cedar logs painted white, which had been cleared out to make our home. Mom made sure there was never a spot of dirt on them. Her door was the same white paint. I remember painting my doll sitting on his stump throne. Mom never painted over it. On Christoph and Auntie Jean's door, I drew a cloaked woman with fire for hair holding a glowing green hourglass.

Before I could open Mom's door, Justin spun me around and kissed me. Tenderly. Then moved his lips to my burns. "I'm sorry."

I relaxed.

"I have seen your nightmares. Yet it didn't seem real until now."

I placed my arms around his waist.

"I love them even more."

"You're crazy."

"Then we both are." Cael's cool fingers ran down my face to my collar before he, too, kissed my scars. "I haven't seen your nightmares. I wasn't here for you. I regret not having Justin's *bond* with you. I want so much to help calm your mind."

We looked up at him.

"My Everstar."

He kissed my lips. Justin's arms tighten around me, but it wasn't jealousy. He was aroused. I smiled into Cael's kiss.

"You calm me fine, my Elf King."

"Can you three keep on target, please?" Dathon sounded annoyed. I didn't stop smiling.

"We are ending the turmoil in her mind, Mage God. Do you want her powers to get out of control again?"

Again?

Justin showed me engulfed in black flames, smoke and ashes.

What the hell am I?

"Whatever you are saying to her, stop it." Cael ran a thumb under my eyes. "We won't let any harm come to you, Lysandra."

I jumped to wrap my arms around the neck of my Elf King.

"Can I please have my daughter now?"

I sighed. I didn't want to go into our room.

"I doubt that this is the norm."

I frowned. In our room was a toy box in the middle with my name on it. But in my memory, this toy box should still be under my bed. So, what the hell was this?

"This I don't remember. The only toys I had were my dolls and my training sword." I moved to the box under my bed.

When I opened the lid, I frowned. I don't know why I expected my dolls and sword. I knew where they were.

Dathon motioned me towards the chest.

Gingerly, I knelt there. I didn't know the magic that came off the chest. Protective. This was not a magic that was in this house growing up. Warm, sure, but it smelled like flowers. A flower I couldn't remember the name of.

"Where is Christoph when I need him? It would be so much easier for him to just dispel this." I closed my eyes and concentrated on the power. A barrier that called to me shimmered a green silver. "Daina?" I sat on my heels as I slid my hands up the sides. "No."

This time, there were no magic sucking tentacles that surrounded my hands. No cold. No wind. This was more like Adriana's and Justin's magic. Warm as dying embers. My fingers brushed the polished black metal. That is when I felt the magic leach from me.

"Mage Metal?" My name was also in Mage Metal across the front. "Why would someone make me a chest with Mage Metal?"

"Is it too much to be around?" Dathon asked.

I shook my head. If anything, it was comforting. Dathon's hand rubbed my back as he had done when I was a child. "This is unlike anything I felt. There are parts of Daina, Adriana and you in this magic. There is a smell to it too. I don't know anyone that has a smell to their magic." I flicked the latches. Why I was expecting something to happen was beyond me. They just simply opened.

"I hate to jinx this but-" I opened the lid, only an inch, to no trap. No magic backlash. No, instead Dathon and I looked up to see my father standing over us smiling. "Matix?" He was older than the coronation painting.

Why do you think she will come back to the house? Hadain's voice but he was not in the scene.

If what your mother said is true, then your sister will want anything she can get to get an edge on that bastard. Tabari has taken so much from her already. Just like he took from Tulora. This is something I have been gathering for her since I felt she and Hallon were born. Something, I hope, will bring her joy. Then he was gone.

I threw caution to the wind, swinging the lid wide open.

I gasped: two ring boxes laying on a sheer iridescent fabric. "It's a hope chest. I remember Auntie Jean tried to convince Mom I needed one. Mom said if they had to leave in a hurry, it would be lost."

I reached my mind out to Justin. My father had meant this for our wedding. I bit my lips. My nose burned. "They had hoped I would have a better wedding than Mom and Dad had."

Justin took the rings.

I took out the dress. Holding it up to my body, I realized it was my perfect size, and it shimmered in reds, greens, and blues. The skirt was full, but not nearly as bad as Chantara's. It swished as I spun around the room. *I won't have a chance to wear this. Justin and I were married.* That is when it hit me that the father who wished this for me would never see me in it.

"Lys." Justin hugged me with the dress between us. "We can keep this safe, my love. Our next life you can use it." *That wouldn't fix the issue.* "Or we can have a second wedding since our first one was a bust."

"Matix wished for us to be happy. This is his hope for me."

"You are happy, aren't you?"

Could I really be?

"Lys?"

My magic flared, unbidden. With it, something I had never felt. A hunger. A hunger that thought my loved ones were delicious.

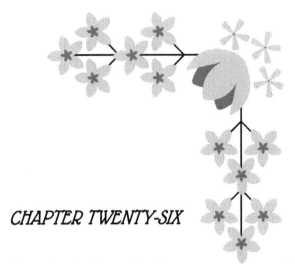

CHAPTER TWENTY-SIX

Tar glopped off my hands. I saw the blue-green, green and silver souls of my loved ones. I hungered for the soul of the man who refused to follow orders. He betrayed me for the love of a woman. Love? Sex with him was great. He was just what I wanted when I couldn't have Tabari.

I don't want sex with Tabari. Why the hell would I?

Because he is my husband. Cassandra. *I have control now and Tabari is almost here.*

I could see myself in that dark room, yet it wasn't from my eyes. Red and silver lines of code bound me to a chair. I wore the black leather suit from my first life.

Your little spells won't work this time, darling. Tarbari is going to feast on the soul of your prince.

"Justin is a king." I groaned, struggling with the binding. They didn't want to let me go. "He is going to know you have taken me."

I'm counting on it. She laughed. *Your Undying King has never looked more tempting. I know you don't remember, but know that once I finally end my mission, your boys will be gone forever. Your first father wanted you out of the way. Your first father paid me to kill you. I was going to use Jestin, but he fell in love with you. It was so cliche.*

"Cassandra, you're monologuing." I smirked. "Nothing more cliche than my villain monologuing." The look on that blonde's face was precious. "Bring on all your cliche shit. Justin is right. With the two of us together, I will never fail."

"You know nothing, Lysandra." The old fear returned. *"My son may be a romantic, but love doesn't solve everything."*

"Tabari." I sneered. I can't let him taste my fear. I can't let them have Justin or Cael.

"My darling, you know I love my food ready for me."

I watched Cassandra toss the daggers out the window of the house. She gave me a look that said she won.

"That is better."

Justin slammed my body to the wall.

"I will enjoy torturing my sister's daughter." Tabari's gray eyes were clear as day. He really did look like my first mother with a little of Alistair.

Where was Alistair? Shouldn't he be here to take on Tabari? Didn't he promise to protect me? Who is Alistair?

"Did you just remember something? Whatever it is won't help you." No tar. Just a man sneering as if he too had won.

"You two forget I'm the reason you are even still here." The binding on me finally gave way. "We will never let you stay as you are in Our New World. This is the time of humans. This is not the time for your petty revenge plans." I reached for my body.

"Lysandra?" Justin held me to the wall of my childhood bedroom. Hands above my head. Knee between my legs.

"Justin, get everyone out. Tabari is coming."

He pulled back a little.

"Lys-"

I kissed him.

"I will fight Cassandra as long as I can. Just get safe." Cael pulled on Justin's shoulder.

Cassandra pulled on mine.

"Don't let her hurt my husband, Cael."

Then I was bound again. This time there were no other souls in the darkness as I was hanging from a hook on an invisible wall.

"That was foolish. I will have Justin's body. He will see me tear you down, Alessandra. There will be nothing left of you."

CHAPTER TWENTY-SEVEN

"LYSANDRA!"

Blood poured from a gash in Justin's chest. His eyes were bloodshot. Cael's face was swollen. So much so he only had the use of one of his eyes. Justin held one of my hands, Cael the other. Between them, Dathon looked unsure. Though he was less wounded than my men.

"She is back."

Back? Where did I go? Where was Tulora's house? Why were we near the ocean?

"Thank Leila." Cael dropped to his knees. Justin, right with him. There was still weight on my arms and one around my neck. "Was it the Crown?"

"I think it was a combination. She won't be able to use any of her magic. If Tabari wants to attack her, she may not survive," Dathon said. His hands cupped my cheeks. "Lys, Darling can you talk to us?"

"What happened?"

Dathon took me in his arms.

I felt the all too familiar collar. Air filled my lungs. Eyes wide. "Why?"

My family thought I needed to be chained. I gave a whimper.

"Lys, no." Dathon seemed to sag. "No, honey, it was not to hurt you. It was Cassia. She took over. She broke the binding."

I screamed. Cassia won power over my body. I became a monster.

"No, please Love, we stopped her at every turn. You didn't kill many people."

Through the tears, I gave them my defeated voice. "Sure, not MANY people. She made me kill just like Roseden did." My body crumpled.

"We tried to fully stop her. She could only kill a dozen Aldaina."

I felt the Metal at my ankles, my wrists, neck and on my head like in the nightmare with Tabari. There was another over my heart. I saw the Seabrook crest tattoo ringed in Mage Metal, in the scar that Roseden gave me. That is when I realized I was naked.

"How long? Will she do it again?"

Cael placed a cloak around me.

I pulled away from them. The last thing I remembered was wanting to taste their souls. "Will this really hold her back?"

"I talked to as many of the others as I could while these two hunted you. We decided we needed all of these to stop all your powers. There were ones that no one knew you had."

"How long?" I asked, even angrier. I knew they didn't want to tell me, but why? "Dathon?"

"Ten months," Justin said.

"TEN MONTHS! I have been killing people for ten months?" Ten months. That meant that next month I would have to face the Palace of Death.

Justin gripped my shoulders. "Lys stop."

My shoulder blades hurt suddenly. Heavy for some reason. Rib cage aching as if it was broken in certain places.

"The only reason you killed Aldaina Priestesses was because we - I didn't know what was going on. You were there thinking about Matix, the next everything was silent in your mind. You were laughing. Cassia looked up at me with her red eyes."

"How much did she hurt you two? How bad am I?"

"She didn't consider that every time she hurt me, she hurt you."

I reached Justin's ribs to get a hiss.

"Evana, Lizzy and Alys are waiting in town for us."

I shook my head.

"You don't have a choice, Lys. You are just as banged up as we are. Maybe more. I am not sure how much she took out on you."

I frowned.

"I couldn't feel you, but in some fights, it was like part of you was fighting her. Every scream of frustration she gave us gave me hope we could get you back, and that you were not lost to us."

"I don't care how much of this crap is on me. You are in danger. All of you. Cassia broke through it last time. She could do it again."

I tried to call my armor. Nothing. My sword. Nothing. "Dad, give me something to wear."

My travel pack appeared in his hands. Cael growled. Justin glared.

"Thanks Dad." And with that, I walked away.

Dathon, being the doting father, also packed me with money and credit slips. I had never had to use credit slips before, but I was sure there wouldn't be much to it. Hopefully useful. The problem I found was that I was on a naked beach. No towns, homes or even roads. I had no idea where I was. How was I going to get home? How was I going to get to the Palace?

"Dathon wasn't going to leave you completely alone."

I spun to the voice. That dark-haired girl again stood next to my pack as I stood waist deep in the ocean.

"Alys Hy. I am sure you remember me." She didn't wear the Aldaina armor this time. Just black leggings, knee-high boots and a baby blue shirt. One I have seen a million times before and hated. It was far too large on her.

"Why would my father send you?" I groaned, walking up to the shore. I had laid Cael's cloak out so the minute my feet were not in the water, they would be in the satin.

"Dath thinks you are going to do something foolish. I can't say I will ever know why he can't let you be?" She sat next to my pack. "You have survived plenty by this time. Why won't they just leave you alone?"

I dressed next to the girl. "So, are you going to tell me who you really are?"

She laughed, leaning back. "Jean would age me up to a hundred if I tell you. Frankly, I just had my daughter. I am not letting that go."

"So, I have to guess. Just like I made my mother?"

She smiled. I know that smile, too. "You are too much like your father."

I sat down next to her. "I am guessing Justin raised you, not me."

"Yeah, well. You tried, but life will not be kind to you and Dad." She sighed. "I understand why I was sent back. You didn't get to raise me. You didn't know much about me until I was past saving."

"Saving?"

"Nothing truly bad. It's not like I was becoming a demon. I was trapped with the men of our family, so not the girliest of girls."

"You seemed to turn out alright. Although I still hate that shirt."

"Yeah, I know." She winked. "Dad sent it with me. It's comfy. He tells me he wore it to remind you that you are mortal and can't do everything."

I groaned.

She laughed. Even laughed like Justin.

"You are his daughter. Though I don't understand. I am going to die in a few weeks." Her eyes went to her hands. On her finger was a ring that was a curved arrow. She fiddled with it as a tear rolled down her face. "Somehow I come back to him."

She said nothing.

"Or I don't really die."

"Call it a curse on our family." Alys offered.

"Who thinks you are dead?"

"Chasen Hy. After he had to deal with me. I nearly died four times on him. Each time was worse than the last time. Now our daughter is born, I am in a coma while Jean sends me here to protect you." She bit her lip like I do to keep from full tears. "I never thought I had a *Bonded*. I am a soul created from parts of both of you. I'm not in the system. There was never going to be a match for me."

A new soul? Is there such a thing?

"Yet he was, in those blasted mountains, surrounded by all that damn snow. We fell in love almost the second his keep was attacked the first time. Then my fiancé, Tavin, tried to kill me. Once mine and Chasen's *bond* tried to kill me and almost won. Then Tavin came back to finish the job. Dad was none too keen on me being killed in front of him." She hid her face into her knees. "I don't know when I will get to go home to Chasen and our daughter. I have been here for almost a year. I am so scared that I won't be the same woman that he married."

"You were here when your father was almost killed by Roseden. You were the one who pulled me off her," I said.

She nodded.

"I thought that was the same moment I would not be the woman Justin loved. I have never allowed myself to feel that fire before. I have not used my magic to harm anyone since The Pit. There I was using Roseden's own spell against her."

This girl looked at me. The shining blue eyes filled with an empathic hurt. There was so much of Justin in her.

I needed to tell her the truth we learned. If that is the only thing I gave her, it had to be a truth. "The thing with the *Bond* is that it is a farce."

She frowned. That was Justin's too. Alys was Justin's daughter. How? I don't know.

"If you fell in love with Chasen separate from the *bond* being consummated, then your love is genuine. Justin and I have been *Soul Bonded* for so long, I don't know what is real

266

anymore. I know your fool of a father is beyond saving. He loves far deeper than I can imagine. I can't save him from the world of pain he is going to feel when I am gone. Hell, I am surprised he isn't waiting over by that tree." We both looked back to see him leaning there. "Never mind."

She laughed. I smiled back. This was our daughter. My heart ached knowing how I had failed to raise her. Justin had though. That was something.

"I don't bite, Dad," Alys said as Justin strolled toward us. "He figured it out the second I pulled you off, Roseden. He said we have the same angry face."

I laughed. Justin sat next to me on Cael's cloak. I leaned on him, which got me a kiss on my temple.

"Alys, Dathon is going to be very cross with you."

"Let him be. I don't get time to talk to Mom anymore. As if I ever got a chance before the war."

The way she said it made me realize I had passed.

"I named our daughter after you two. Lysandra Justine Hy."

I had a granddaughter. I didn't think I would ever give Justin a child, never mind a grandchild.

"I'm dead then?" I asked to confirm.

"Not the first time, either. This time you took Dad with you. Now Chasen is there alone, and I can do nothing about it." She rubbed her arm. The shirt fell to show a scar over her heart.

I reached to see more.

"Saving me was the last thing you did, even though you didn't know me, you still protected me like a mom would. You died in my arms with Dad on the other side of the field with Chasen." Her eyes filled. "You were gone so much of my life keeping the magics from dying, it was no wonder you didn't know me."

"It took me a minute, but you are so like your father. Whatever your father did to raise you would have been the way I wanted you raised."

"You never seemed proud of me." Her shock was deep.

"I have been a horrible mother. Just like my own."

Justin pulled me farther into his chest.

"Your mother doesn't like to show emotions well. Unless it is anger and fear." I elbowed him. "See?" She laughed. "If I was proud of you, it was from both of us," Justin clarified. "We are of one mind. Most of the time."

"Hard not to love a stalker." I teased.

Alys played with her ring. "Or a kidnapper."

I bumped shoulders with her. "There is a story there and I can't wait to hear how this man took you to the one place I hate the most."

She smirked.

That. That was me.

"That is the one thing I know I got from you." She glared at her ring. "The freaking mountains. During the fall. When Winter hit, I was trapped in that drafty castle. I hate the cold and the snow. He had the nerve to throw me into a snowbank, too. I am still pissed off about that. Even if it was to save my life."

I laughed.

"It was four feet deep!"

"She does have your angry face," Justin said.

We both glared at him.

"Just saying—she may look like me, but she has your expressions and a temper like yours."

"You better leave before you have your wife and daughter pissed at you."

Justin kissed my hand, then stood. "Town is two hours east. Take the time to bond."

We watched him get to the tree and vanish. Dathon probably teleported him back.

"He loved you even when you weren't home. The few times I saw you growing up, I knew I wanted to love my *Bonded* as much as Dad loved you." She smirked. "Chasen knew he loved me before I knew I loved him. We were under constant attack back then."

"I'm sure your father told you about our lives."

She stifled a laugh.

"He has always wanted a daughter. Before I found out that this body couldn't have kids." I fingered Adriana's ring. "However you came into our lives, I will forever think I am blessed. You are the child I wanted to give the man I loved, even when I wouldn't allow myself to love him."

"Dad used to tell me the same thing," she said as she stood. "We should get going. It is going to be night when we get to town."

I stood, too. I didn't really want to walk. I had grown spoiled with my Moonlight always at my side.

"If they ask, we are sisters."

"Are you expecting trouble?"

"Call it a hazard of being *bonded* to an outlaw." Alys smirked at the inside joke.

"Well, tell me how you met this Chasen Hy. We have time. I want to hear everything I will never get to experience."

So we walked and talked. I have never met a person who thought the same way Justin did with a tinge of paranoia. I guess that was expected from a person with no magic.

I got the distinct feeling she was the youngest of a lot of children, but the only one who was wholly ours. Though she never gave their names, she spoke as if her oldest brother was her favorite. As we approached an inn, she was telling me about the day she was kidnapped.

I was shocked.

Two separate groups came for her at the same time.

Chasen got Alys though.

Morning came with her cuddled up to me. "My darling, you are a joy. I am proud of everything you have done. Justin raised you perfectly."

At that, she disappeared from my arms.

That was when the guilt hit me. No matter how much I didn't want to be like my own mother, it sounded like I turned into her.

"Thank you."

I left the inn and took the first teleportation circle I could find to get me to Haven. From there, I met with Calla. She looked disappointed when she saw me. Calla was silent as she took me to Hadestown. The closest town to the Palace of Death. Justin, Cael, Dathon, and Christoph were waiting for me. I strode up to Justin and pulled him into a kiss.

"I love you," I said.

I have known Justin almost my whole life, and this was the first time I had ever seen him fall to his knees. Our *Bond* was freaking out as much as his mind was. There were far too many conflicted thoughts and his body shut down.

I couldn't help but smile as I dropped to my knees with him.

"Are you sure? Lys, please don't be playing."

A small chuckle escaped my hold. "You raised a beautiful, brave, brilliant daughter. I'm just sorry I never got to see it."

"Daughter?"

We both raised a hand to stop my father.

"I see more of you in her than me."

"Yeah no. She is all you. I have never been so proud of something in my life. We created a great queen. I may have given birth to her, but you gave her life."

Justin started kissing me then.

I have and will always love you most in this world.

"Mine," he whispered into my lips.

I knew that night, I was going to try to let him claim me. One last week of memories before I go into my next life.

CHAPTER TWENTY-EIGHT

The palace was only a day away riding. But first, I needed Justin to sleep. To stop being at my hip. To get him to trust, I won't do anything foolish.

Right before I did something foolish.

In the week since I got here, Justin and Cael made sure one of them was always by my side. Calla tried to be a sounding board for me, but I had a feeling it was something more.

"Daina's blood, Lys, you're going to have a sore neck if you don't get that towel off your head." Justin motioned to a chair in my room.

Calla gave a questioning look to Justin.

He just kissed her head. "Go sweetie, it will be fine."

I know he knew I was planning something. He wanted to prevent me by not leaving my side. Or he could just want to brush my hair. So, I sat.

Having long hair has always annoyed me. Hard to maintain mostly. Having to style it every day bugged me, so I shaved it all off for the tournaments. Ten years of no styling, washing or worry.

My three wigs were all I needed to be presentable.

Now that a year had passed, my hair was back down to my waist. Red as my mother's had been. Thick like my father's. In the mirror, I watched Justin smile, holding my brush. Bleen save me, if he wasn't adorable. This could be the only good thing to come of me losing control to Cassia.

"So will Cael be back by morning?" I asked Justin.

"No. He decided to scout ahead. He said he would meet us at dawn." Justin hummed.

Cael had joined us a few times this week, but he knew when he wasn't needed. Cael knew my plan. Tomorrow the Palace will appear.

Justin wasn't included in my plan.

These last few days felt like hell not having any memories. Sure, I was scared that Cassia would take control, but letting Justin have more joy of being my husband trumped that. We never even got to finish our two weeks of dates. I could feel that roll around in his head over the last few days.

Also, a countdown.

Every morning, waking up in his arms, he would count the days until the Palace took me from him before he took me to a meadow for training. After that, he would bring food up to our rooms, where he wouldn't let me do anything but lay next to him or between him and Cael. Before bed, Justin would put me in the shower, wash my hair, then brush and braid it. Justin enjoyed that. It was an us thing.

He told Cael it was a husband's duty.

Cael would be grumpy, but watched Justin have the ritual.

"Were you going to sleep with it on? Are you that worried about Cael?"

"As much as we both enjoy our nightly routine, tonight may be my last night in this realm. Tomorrow night I will be with my family." Anger, disappointment, sorrow filled our *bond* as the passive king stared at my hair.

"So, you are leaving in the morning without a goodbye?"

I looked anywhere but his eyes. Justin's hand tightened on the brush.

"So, I'm the last to know. How is it that my soul mate, *Soul Bound,* could keep such a secret from me, for so long? Shouldn't that be against the divine laws?" Our eyes met in the mirror. He was crying.

"For this very reason, Justin. You weren't supposed to be here. You and Dathon were supposed to stay at home."

"Fuck that." My chair spun around.

I had only seen his face this emotional when he was drunk. I wouldn't blame him if he was. Though swearing in the old tongue?

"You know you're my every thought. Every decision I make is based on you. You have always been my moral compass. Yet for ten years, you have been lying. Not just to me, but yourself. I will never be okay with your death. It will haunt me for the rest of my days."

"Justin-"

"Don't you fucking use your sweet voice on me."

I blinked.

"We both know I will melt to your whim if you do, and I am far too angry at you right now."

Sweet voice? That was what Justin called Chantara's soft voice. The one she used when she wanted something from Justin.

"Excuse me?" I stood up, facing him. "I don't have a fucking *sweet voice*. I'm not one of your palace girls wrapped in sugar. I'm me. Champion of Arocana. Mother of Deities. A Death Knight."

"And MY *Soul Bound* wife." He pulled me into his arms. His hand cupped my scarred face. "I'm weak against you. You may not think you have a soft voice—you are a skilled warrior in name and blood—but you will always be my weakness. The woman I love with my whole heart."

I said nothing. I thought nothing. My heart shattered onto the floor.

"Lysandra, you are my whole world and now you are going to destroy that."

"Fate is doing that, not me." I tried to pull away, but he held firm. "Had I not known, I would have joined the Aldaina, been trained, then returned to you with Lizzy so I could be your mistress. You know I have never wanted to be your queen. I could, however, give you heirs through Lizzy and protect you. Protecting you is why I was sent to this time."

He kissed me. For the third time in our short lives, he kissed me out of frustration and anger. He laced his fingers through my hair. My hand clenched on his shirt. Our *Bond* surged forward. Years of repressed power overcame us. And before either of us could think, we were on the bed. Justin pulled off his baby blue silk shirt with the mismatched buttons before pulling the tie to my robe.

My flame-licked scars were bare for him to see.

"My warrior goddess, born of flame and snow." He continued kissing me. We only stopped to breathe when Justin found me shaking.

"We have been married for seventeen horrible months."

"Yes." Justin groaned.

"You won't hurt me, Justin. I haven't seen their faces this week. Whatever Calla did sent my ghosts away."

"I wanted us as equals. I want us to be of one mind. I want us to be happy. Even if my soul is missing, I know it will die with you."

I kissed him this time.

"From this life into the next, I will love you, Lysandra Seabrook Knyght."

A gasp left my lips. He looked back into my eyes.

"Show me how it would have been to be your *Soul Bond* wife, my love." That was enough. There were no words as we made love.

When he was finally asleep, I dressed.

Our horses nuzzled each other out in the pasture as I came to the stables. "Sorry, miss. The stud would have torn down the stables to get to your beauty," the stable boy said.

Honestly, I had forgotten this inn even had a stable hand. "Don't worry about it. We knew it would happen one of these days." I pulled my wallet from my pocket. I wouldn't need money where I was going. "Take this. It should be enough to cover any damages Warrior caused."

"Do you want me to saddle the horses?"

"No. I will do it if Moonlight wants to wear it." Warrior pulled the gate open to me.

"Well, thank you, kind sir," I said with a smile and a bow. "I appreciate you waited for us, but it is time to go, Moon. Cael is waiting for us, and we need to get there before the sun is fully on the Palace."

She nodded.

I kissed Warrior. "Take care of him. He is going to need you both."

Warrior nuzzled my right side.

"I know I don't want to go either."

And we were off. Flying tonight seemed lonely. I couldn't ease the hurt in my chest. One man I loved slept after my goodbye. The other stood against one tree on the path to the palace.

"So, is it done?" Cael asked as I landed.

"Yes." That was when the *Bond* woke. Dammit, he's on his way. "Justin is a mile away."

"Damn, he caught up fast. Everstream is as stubborn as his namesake."

I laughed. "I guess that's why we love him. He knows what he loves. Nothing will stop him from keeping it."

Gazing behind me, Dathon, Christoph, and Justin landed next to Moon and Little Keister, Cael's horse. Dathon and Christoph probably knew I would pull something like this. Justin pretended he didn't.

"Get the door open. I will hold them off." Cael sighed again.

Before I could turn, he took me into his arms. "If I can't get in there, know I have and will always love you, Lys. My Everstar." Then he kissed me. "I will wait for your rebirth."

"I'll come back, Evertree." I moved towards the door.

A bizarre pad lay next to the locked door. The letters on the keys were ancient. I should not have been able to read them, yet the ability lay in my memories. As the Palace powered up in the morning sun, instructions scrolled across the screen with six stars.

Taking Zaidon's book and my Aunt's locket, I reread the passage about the door.

I needed a code that would have been important to Tulora. I tried her birthday. Her wedding. Her coronation. All the dates in her history except two: the day we were born and the day I *died*.

The next page of the book was one of the images of our past lives. With her was a stuffed toy before I got him from my aunt.

My Soulless Prince?

The first one. Jestin had given this to me. The day we came to this planet. July 8, 2035.

Alessandra's birthday.

I heard Justin and Cael fighting. Dathon trying to calm them. Looking back, I saw they were still at the tree line. Christoph smiled at me. Cael positioned Justin back to me as he gave me a nod.

I gave Cael a thumbs up just as Justin spun around to see me. Since coming home from the Pit, I had never seen him so defeated. This was the last chance he would get to see me. I wasn't allowing him to die right next to me.

He punched Cael before running toward me. I smirked, knowing he wasn't going to make it here before the door closed again. I said goodbye to my old life.

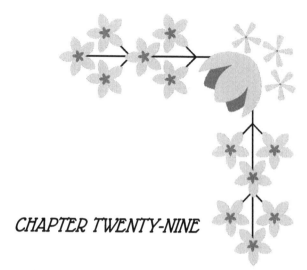

CHAPTER TWENTY-NINE

The inside smelled of old bones, like a crypt. The walls were covered in pictographs of a man with black, bat-winged figures pulling souls from bodies that lay on the ground. Justin was still bellowing my name from outside. It was no use, if these things were in here, there was no way I was letting Justin anywhere near them. My crystal extended daggers into my hands.

No more distractions. I had a job to do.

I was at the base of some long since crumbled altar when I heard something slide across the floor. My men calling my name became silenced.

"I refuse to have you die without me being there."

I spun around to see Christoph and Cael both brushing dust from their knees as they stood up. The dust on the floor had been swept aside where they had slid under the door. Fresh green leaves clung to both elves, as well as the skeleton by the door. Cael brushed off the dirt from his coat.

Justin was going to be pissed if he got in here.

"I was there for your birth. I will record your death again," Christoph said.

"Elven speed is a wonder." Cael winked at me. It was something I had said to him just this week. Now was not the time to be flirting with me, but it felt wonderful to know he would be there this death.

"The plan was to keep out the distractions." I pointed at Cael.

He faked being appalled, but I saw sparkling mirth in his eyes.

"You suck." My Elven lover waggled his eyes.

That got me laughing. "Everfool." I sighed.

Cael's hands landed on my hips.

"Well, the two who would stop you are outside. Probably still arguing on whose fault it was."

Of course they were. Justin should have seen this coming. Dathon should know some sort of spell to get the door opened.

"The last time I was here was the plague," Christoph said, touching the altar. He seemed so far away.

"Templar Crowley, welcome back." A male voice said.

I turned. There stood Hadain. Slightly grayer than what I saw in Haven.

"Who is your guest?"

"Hadain?" I reached for my lost little brother. This could very well be the first time I have seen him without Hallon. Would Hadain want to see me? Was he ever the least bit curious of the daughter Mom mourned?

"Lysandra?"

Had he not been transparent, I would have hugged him.

"What a treat?"

He sounded cold. Maybe he didn't care to know me at all. I smirked to myself. Again, the want of a blood family was all on my side.

"This might hurt." Cold tentacles squirmed up my foot, slowing when it hit the Mage Metal cuff on my ankle. They didn't go past the knee. The cold bite of Hadain's magic gripped me, pulling me to the ground. My hands hit stone as more tentacles snaked up my arms. Between the death magic and the Mage Metal, I felt as if I would throw up. The tentacles squeezed, and the cuffs pulled the magic they squeezed out of me, until I felt like a husk.

"Please take her to block S, corridor M. Our mother has left her a gift."

I heard Christoph gasp. "Knowing them, it would be."

The Mage Metal no longer pulled from me. Falling on the stone floor. I was finally magic-less. Yet my brother made no move. A statue of Death incarnate. I can see why people fear him.

"Cry over it later, Lys. You are going to love this."

Cry? Only in joy.

We were suddenly running. Downstairs.

The Palace now seemed to glow, allowing us to dodge the bodies on the stairs. Only when we stopped did I notice there were people in the glass coffins. As we passed, screens lit up red—but the one we stood in front of now was blue.

CURED.

Inside, I saw Matix. My father. Every cell wanted him to talk to me. To tell me he loved me. Yet I turned away.

My goal was the beast at the core of the Palace. The monster that held Justin's soul.

No more distractions.

"Lys?" Christoph looked saddened.

"I guess you didn't know he was here," Cael asked for me.

"Matix vanished three months before Hallon and Hadain were murdered. A few months after, Tulora fell to your sister-in-law. I never could find him."

"So that is what they hid from me. The cure and Tulora's faith," a voice said.

I stumbled, feeling off center. Something pulled at my soul.

"Cassandra." Cael snarled. This was the woman in a painting holding the little girl I had seen when Justin was catching me up on the Death Palace. She was my sister-in-law. The woman Christoph thought killed my family. The mother of the High Queen's family line.

The very Death Knight we thought we locked inside me with all the Mage Metal.

"Better believe it." She ran a finger down Cael's chest.

A heart beat against my chest.

This was Roseden and Justin all over again. I had to stay calm, though.

"What better way to hide than in the one woman who could destroy me. It wasn't all bad. Having you in bed was amazing compared to that of Jestin." The transparent woman glared down at me. "Though Lys does not meet my expectations of a child of Cordelia."

Her grip on my chin felt like static shock. "A family of overachieving bastards. Except you, Lysandra. Mind you, you over-excel as a whore."

"You were my second soul," I said. "I'm sure that makes you one, too."

"I'm the reason you don't remember your own wedding." She sneered. "Most of those dates that Soulless Brat took you on after our time in that wonderful place you call The Pit."

My eyes widened. She was the one who took my time, but Justin had never said anything about dates we did while I was recovering.

"That is enough, Cassia." This time, Hallon didn't look impassive. Dathon had to be in the Palace now. With Justin.

"Oh, look now. My rock of a husband is in the Mage Matrix. Should have known that you would have a backup plan for your backup plan."

"My sister is not here for you to torment."

She came down to my side.

"His last words were about you. His last thoughts were to help you but that was because I killed his *Soul Bond* mate."

Somehow, my hand could clench around her throat. She coughed and sputtered. My hand itself glowed with my red magic.

Hadain just drained me.

How was I doing this? I didn't have time to figure it out.

"You killed them. Tabari helped you. How long had my uncle bed you before you were corrupted?"

My head was forced into the stone wall.

"It was the other way around. When I was ten, I sought him out. Seduced him until I was the only one in his bed. It was harder on Earth with me being a child. Then I stayed hidden in his quarters sleeping with him to remind him his sister, Cordelia, your real mother, was evil. That she and her family, you and Mr. Arowen, were a threat to him. In this life, Queen Adriana was no match for him. She died holding your hand and making you promise to be with Justin forever. You could have saved her if it weren't for that goddess suppressing your godlike pow-"

Adriana's dagger ran through her belly. "I have lived through worse speeches than that."

My magic worked its way through the dagger. "You missed the days when shit like this was my norm. Now be gone."

The red light engulfed the transparent blue form. Adriana's runes wrapped around her. Tulora's dagger joined Adriana's. Mom's magic engulfed Cassia. *"As Mother of Deities, I cleanse this soul of all evil. Command line delete virus."*

She screamed.

Confirm: Yes? No? A broken voice asked.

"Confirm yes."

Glass shattered within the bubble as Cassia exploded into fine, shiny slivers.

Someone caught me.

"That is some powerful magic. Are you okay?" Justin brushed my now loose hair from my eyes. I hadn't felt him come anywhere near me.

Was that what Hadain took from me? Did he take the *Bond* from me?

"Red?" An unfamiliar voice questioned.

Justin turned to Christoph, holding my father.

"Lysandra!" Matix lunged for me. Probably for a hug, but my brain said to attack me. Everyone else from that time has wanted to do me harm. Except Evana.

I suddenly missed my best friend.

"Don't touch me." I snapped.

He backed away.

The magic in this place shifted to ice cold air. Justin's normally warm hands turned to ice. I felt two of him in that second. As if part of my magic had been looking for him.

How?

"Found you." Willing myself to his location, I teleported through the building. Puke was the worst kind of bread crumb. I have never liked self-teleportation.

But I found a door near the top of the palace.

"Patient 0," the door read.

Justin's protection magic filled the other side.

Stepping through was a nightmare. There was nothing there. No second soul. No answer to my questions. No death waiting. Just a yellow wall.

Everything was yellow. The walls. The floor. The ceiling. There was light, with no source, in here where the rest of the place was barely candle lit. Before me, another password panel. This one with the outline of a hand on it as well. There was something beyond the wall. From the layout of the other floors, there was indeed something here.

There was nothing in the book for this room, so I did the obvious. I placed my hand on the print. A screen came up with words I could only read half of with a yes or no.

"Yes."

Enter code.

Code? What code? The wall blinked a countdown timer.

I entered my death date.

Nothing.

My birth date.

Red words flashed: *One more attempt.*

I took a deep breath and tried one more: the day my mother died.

The wall before me lowered down. In its place a shimmering yellow magic wall. Stepping closer to the soul I felt on the other side, I reached for the wall.

It crystalized when my skin touched it.

That was when I saw it: the mutations the book spoke about.

The thing was maybe twenty feet tall and half that wide with rolls of fat folding over themselves. Black tar seeping between the folds. Mage Metal cuffs on his ankles, wrists and neck. Just like the ones I left downstairs. They were holding him like this for three and a half centuries. I could see his foot was the same height I was. Human skeletons lay scattered around the room. Right near the transparent wall, one that wore Aldaina commander armor and a ring similar to the one I had seen in the hope chest.

"Mom?" I said, looking for any sign that this was Tulora. This can't be where she died.

"Lys, if you are hearing this, I know I failed. By Daina I failed. I am fully aware you told me I was going to, but that didn't stop me from trying to save you from this. It was bound to happen. I am still sorry. We found your Soulless Prince's soul a year ago. That younger you would have laughed at the argument I had with your aunt. We could have kept you, too. You could have saved him before he became what you see. He was Cassia's incubator for the Death Knight Virus."

I should have tortured her longer.

"Hadain placed Matix in one capsule to keep him safe from Cassia. I honestly don't know what I plan to do with him. We don't have a cure yet. Both my sons are working on it."

"Which they will fail." I heard Cassia over the speaker. *"Well, Tulora, daughter of Daina, tell me what it feels like when he eats you."*

A scream, then silence. Cassia fed my mother to Justin's second soul.

The scream woke the behemoth. I saw then he had blue eyes—Justin's eyes.

Who was he? Who had he been? Was I about to kill him? To cure him? There were no notes. No path but the one I make now.

I was afraid. I was overwhelmed.

The Destiny had seen me die three different ways and now I was in this room. My mother's tomb.

Assault had me kicked to the ceiling, then a heel dug into my body during the fall. This monster got a hold of me before I could gain back air into my lungs. He was faster than I imagined. This monster brought me so close, his breath smelled of rotting flesh.

"You look like Tulora, but I killed her. Who are you?"

I didn't know how I knew, but I knew he felt guilty for killing Tulora.

We weren't *Bonded,* so I wasn't feeling his emotions. His face was too distorted for me to see them. Yet two of his three eyes sagged at the mention of my mother and I knew.

He tossed me into the electric wall, which released a shock through my body as I fell beside my mother's corpse.

"Lys!" Justin was there as the monster rose.

The field held fast.

"Daxel." My father stood with Justin.

"General?" Justin knelt to my side on his side of the field. "How long until your sons cure me?"

"That is why my daughter is here. We had to wait for her time."

No pressure. Except, of course, for the heavy pressure in my chest. It hurt to breathe in too deep.

Can you hear me?

I looked towards Justin, nodding.

I can't feel your emotions or pain. Seems that this is the only way I can get into your mind.

"Wonderful." If I died here, which was likely, Justin wouldn't.

Don't be a smart ass. Come on out, Lys. We need to make a plan.

I shoved Mom's skeleton towards the field. With no effort, it slid through to him.

"It only blocks living objects." I sighed. Figures. Even if I wanted to be out there with him, I couldn't.

"So you can hear me through this?"

I rolled my eyes before looking back at Matix having a conversation with Justin's salvation. "What is the password?"

"There is no password to this cage. You need my hand." I pointed to where Cael, Christoph, and Dathon stood.

"How long have I been asleep?" Daxel whispered.

"Five hundred-ish. By the old calendar," I said, walking the length of the electric wall. "Forgive me, father. I am about to die where Mom did. Take care of your *Son-in-Bond*."

"Lys," Justin hissed when he touched the wall. "Don't do this, Lys. We can think of a way to deal with this."

"Your soul needs to be cleansed, Justin. Just like what I did for Cassia. That means getting close." I let tears fall. "I do not leave you lightly. I have only a hint of how to protect you."

"I don't need protection if it costs your life. Come out, my love. My magic doesn't work here. Please."

I have only ever seen Justin beg like this twice. I closed my eyes with my back turned to him.

"Please Lys. I can't live without you."

"I would have lived my life with you, Justin. I would be-" Suddenly I was in the air, unable to breathe. Two massive arms are tight around my chest. I couldn't summon my sword. I could barely see.

"Matix, come to see your failure?"

Everything was slipping away.

"Your daughter is less of a challenge than your wife? I'm pretty sure Cassia made me kill Tulora." He laughed.

Goddesses his breath smelled like literal shit and rotting meat. I threw up.

"Put my daughter down, Daxel." It was an order. Which the monster followed. Only so he could clean the sick off his arm.

I was on my knees. Breathe in, one, two, three, four. Out one, two, three, four. I had the daggers in my hands. All his attention was on my father, so I ran awkwardly up his leg to his chest.

"As Mother of Deities, I cleanse this soul of all evil. Command line delete virus."

The magics flared through me as it had with Cassia, but it wasn't nearly as fast to encompass his body. I locked eyes with the monster as his meaty fingers wrapped around my shoulders. And squeezed. Two pops and some cracks later, I was screaming. It was nothing I had ever heard from myself.

High pitched and raw.

Yet the monster kept squeezing. Last moments of my life were wet gasping.

When the magics finally did their job, I was expelled from his grasp. *"Move Daxel.sol into JestinSea file folder."* This time, there was no shattering glass. The room dimmed.

A panicked Justin and Cael were suddenly over me. Cael telling Justin not to move me. Both my fathers knelt beside them. Christoph at my feet, praying to Leila.

I couldn't feel Justin's mind.

I only felt liquid drooling out the side of my mouth.

His were the last eyes I saw with my own. My first death.

ABOUT THE AUTHOR

Alex was born in a small town in Saskatchewan, Canada, moved to a slightly smaller town before she was one. All the time and nothing to do left her to imagine worlds beyond this one. Worlds of far off futures, dark pasts and even darker nights. At 14, she finished her first full novel, which was rejected. At 16, well-meaning friends introduced her to gaming. They still regret it. She started writing again after a car accident. She enjoys Sci-fi, Fantasy, and Paranormal books, so that is what she writes. Coffee addict, forever DM, author, GEEEEEEK, cute and evil stuff, these all describe her personality. More hobbies than she has time for. More ideas for novels than there are hours in the day. Currently, she lives in a big town, Alberta, with her husband. Sadly, they are currently cat-less.

You can visit me at alexsknyghts.wordpress.com   for other releases and dates.

Now here is the sneak peek of the next book in The Arowan   Chronicles

SOULLESS PRINCE: SECOND LIFE

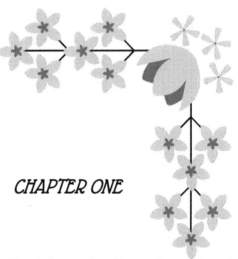

CHAPTER ONE

I woke in the snow as I had done when I was five and again in pain. Freezing added to the pain. I could use my arms. No blood pooled in my mouth. I wore a skintight suit but not made of leather. Black and green with my last name written in the old script. The suit first me wore when she landed on this planet.

"Ah good, Lysandra. How nice to finally meet you?"

My eyes shot to the male voice.

"I have no time. The window is very short for you to go back." He wore the face of my brother but the same skintight suit as me. His suit, said Hades. This was Hadain. I was standing before the God of Death. Not Alistair, Dathon or Daina.

"You'll heal me?"

"Heavens no." He basically laughed at me. "Your old body is gone. This is just your soul. No, if you agree to the terms, I will send you back to the body you were meant to have before Jeanevera interfered in your life."

I chuckled. Even the God of Death didn't like that I was pulled from my own time with Tulora. It made sense. If I was the great equalizer of all human problems, that would mean I was needed during this time and that would have just been so I knew what the problem was. Even then, I still felt as though I was missing a piece to this puzzle that was my soul.

"Terms?"

He stepped closer to me. The snow didn't move as he walked through it. I didn't feel the cold either.

"Did hell freeze over cuz I died?"

He stopped and looked me over, and then laughed. Outright laughed at me.

The God of Death was laughing at me.

My little brother, who I never got to meet except recordings, who now presides over the dead, was laughing at me. As if I was the funniest thing he'd ever seen.

"It's not that funny."

"Sorry, it was something Hallon said to me when I brought him here to talk to Tulora."

Nice to know we still thought the same. Even if it was a bad joke.

"I am supposed to call witnesses to your life and weigh your soul. However, I will make you a deal. Become the Mother of Deities again. With all your gifts and memories.

This time literally, and I will give you back to Justin in your proper body."

"Which Deities would Justin and I be giving birth to?"

"This cycle would be Jeanevera and I."

Two? That wasn't so bad. Twins run deep in my family. It could easily be one pregnancy. I wish I could ask Justin if he was okay with that.

"No, let go of me! That is my son's *Bonded.* My Life Mate's daughter." I heard a woman shout to my left. Adriana was breaking free of two feather winged women. "Lys!"

Now this is when I broke. I was dead.

"My Lys." She was with me in the snow. "Hush, my darling."

"*Destiny* was right. I died. I tried to make it so Justin wouldn't see, but he was holding me as I died." My eyes saw nothing through the tears pooling in them. "I finally told him I loved him."

"I know I saw."

I cried into her shoulder.

"What are you waiting for, Hades? Send her back."

"Adriana, you of all people know there are rules."

She glared down at the God of Death. Ever our Adriana. Never scared of things that she should be.

"She has to agree to the terms."

She pushed me away from her to look me in the eye. She was just as torn as I was. "Do it, Lysandra. Don't worry about what will happen. The Deities gave you a short thread. Shorter than your soul deserves." She smiled. God dammit, even Adriana knew. "Jestin will just be happy to have you back. You have weathered worse than whatever this asshole is asking of you."

Asshole. My *Mother-in-Bonding* called the God of Death an asshole.

That shouldn't have been funny, but it was.

"Our children would not be our own," she snapped back to the God of Death.

"Swear to her, she will give Jestin one mortal child. One child completely free of the trappings of the gods. They need this. They deserve this. They have waited three thousand years for this chance. Don't screw it up for them."

Hades took a step back for every step she took towards him. I couldn't wait to tell Justin about this. His Mom yelled at the God of Death and made him cower from her.

"Hades, she is saving the damn world every time you fools send her back to the planet. She and Jestin deserve some happiness for once. Just let them be happy. They can't fix everything. They are just human, after all."

"Fine, but the window to send her back is closing."

"Lys, honey, I know you love my son. I have never been unsure of his love for you in all these thousands of years. Make the deal, go back to him. He needs you as much as you need him."

"Okay."

Her smile turned to a toothy grin. Justin's real smile.

I turned my gaze from her back to Hades. "Send me back."

"That's my girl. Tell Dathon I miss him."

She knew Justin as Jestin.

All these thousands of years. That was when I remembered Adriana, older, full gray, living with me and Jestin in a cottage near a stream.

It was home.

Our home.

Other books!!!

Coming Feb 14, 2023

Adam never thought he would find the woman of his dreams at Virtual Reality Entertainment Expo-VREX. She was brilliant, beautiful and a gamer. Golden Apple of Forest for the Games was there to review his game, Silent Souls Online. She was his everything. Then the worst happened. Adam faced the unbeaten Blue Dragon King. He saw the glitch. He can't log out. He and the dragon are now one person. Adam's only thought was he would never see his Golden Apple again.

Five years later, I'm thrown to his feet. He is everything I remember of him. Does he even remember me? His little sister tells me I have to kill the man that I was in love with to save him and his Rainbow Legion. Am I strong enough? Can I level up to be?

Coming July 7, 2023

Space was where I belonged. Mom kept me rooted in our small town, but the first chance I got to go to space I was hooked. There were so many different people out here. I found an alien that adores me. A family I would die for. A future spoken to me in visions by a female Axalairian, Aracne.

Her people were 25 000 years extinct, with no mention in the history books as to why. Their religion is strangely similar to Earth. Aracne, haunts me, shows me the ignorance of people afraid of life and the joys. I just wish I knew how? I'm a Xeno-archaeology student. I guess I am going to have to put my skills to use and find the Axalairian's Oracle.

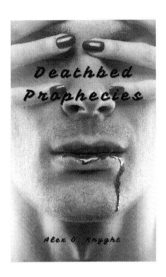

Coming Oct, 2023

The supernatural has always dogged me. I have the soul of a priestess from before Hammurabi came to power. Her soul mate, Theodōros, is the most annoyingly endearing general of the Akkadian period. I remember all our lives together. We have a son. I remember I am the reason that he is a vampire. I remember he is the reason I am murdered in every lifetime.

This time, This time is different. This time, I have the power to heal through blood magic. We also have warnings. Prophecies of dying witches telling me that there is a monster looking for me. A goddess that doesn't want that to happen. The monster has taken Theodōros best friend, Adam, through the soulmate bond. Theodōros is sure they will do the same this time to us. I can't see the hurt in his eyes as he is forced to watch me die again. I love my vampire.

Coming Nov, 2023

One down, Two to go.

I did it! I got Justin's soul back and deleted the virus that was Cassia.

Now I just have to find Tyson, my uncle, and delete him.

Problem: I'm now trapped in the body of my soul sister. Dathon's biological daughter. Xandy has been in a coma since I came to this time. I didn't know she existed until I woke up the night of my funeral in her body. She's got a lot to learn if we are to take on Tyson.

On top of all this, I made a deal with the God of Death to give him and his twin sister a mortal birth.

Fun fun fun.